UPENDRANATH ASHK, 1910–1996, was one of Hindi literature's best-known and most controversial authors. Ashk was born in Jalandhar and spent the early part of his writing career as an Urdu author in Lahore. Encouraged by Premchand, he switched to Hindi, and a few years before Partition, moved to Bombay, Delhi and finally Allahabad in 1948, where he spent the rest of his life. By the time of his death, Ashk's phenomenally large oeuvre spanned over a hundred volumes of fiction, poetry, memoir, criticism and translation. Ashk is perhaps best known for his six-volume novel cycle, *Girti Divarein*, or 'Falling walls'—an intensely detailed chronicle of the travails of a young Punjabi man attempting to become a writer—which has earned the author comparisons to Marcel Proust. Ashk was the recipient of numerous prizes and awards during his lifetime for his masterful portrayal, by turns humorous and remarkably profound, of the everyday lives of ordinary people.

DAISY ROCKWELL is an artist and writer living in northern New England. She paints under the takhallus, or alias, Lapata (Urdu for 'missing'), and has shown her artwork widely.

Rockwell holds a PhD in Hindi literature and has taught Hindi–Urdu and South Asian literature at a number of US universities. Apart from her essays on literature and art, she has written *Upendranath Ashk: A Critical Biography* and *The Little Book of Terror*, a new book of paintings and essays on the global war on terror. She is currently working on a translation of Ashk's 1947 novel *Girti Divarein*.

UPENDRANATH ASHK

Hats and Doctors

Translated from the Hindi
With an Introduction by Daisy Rockwell

PENGUIN BOOKS

PENGUIN BOOKS
Published by the Penguin Group
Penguin Books India Pvt Ltd, 11 Community Centre, Panchsheel Park,
New Delhi 110 017, India
Penguin Group (USA) Inc., 375 Hudson Street, New York, New York 10014, USA
Penguin Group (Canada), 90 Eglinton Avenue East, Suite 700, Toronto,
Ontario, M4P 2Y3, Canada (a division of Pearson Penguin Canada Inc.)
Penguin Books Ltd, 80 Strand, London WC2R 0RL, England
Penguin Ireland, 25 St Stephen's Green, Dublin 2, Ireland (a division of Penguin Books Ltd)
Penguin Group (Australia), 707 Collins Street, Melbourne, Victoria 3008, Australia
(a division of Pearson Australia Group Pty Ltd)
Penguin Group (NZ), 67 Apollo Drive, Rosedale, Auckland 0632,
New Zealand (a division of Pearson New Zealand Ltd)
Penguin Books (South Africa) (Pty) Ltd, Block D, Rosebank Office Park, 181 Jan Smuts
Avenue, Parktown North, Johannesburg 2193, South Africa

Penguin Books Ltd, Registered Offices: 80 Strand, London WC2R 0RL, England

First published by Penguin Books India 2013

Copyright © Neelabh Ashk, Anurag Ashk and Shwetabh Ashk 2013
Translation copyright © Daisy Rockwell 2013

Pages 219-220 are an extension of the copyright page

10 9 8 7 6 5 4 3 2 1

ISBN 9780143417187

Typeset in Sabon Roman by SÜRYA, New Delhi
Printed at Sanat Printers, Kundli, Haryana

ALWAYS LEARNING   **PEARSON**

Contents

CONTENTS

Introduction

On sunny days in his last autumn, the Hindi writer Upendranath Ashk used to be brought out to the courtyard of his Allahabad bungalow, where he would lie on a charpoy with a black umbrella fixed to a nearby chair to shade his eyes. He had broken a hip, and had contracted bedsores during his recovery. His eyes, milky with cataracts, could no longer see well enough to read, and his hands were too arthritic to type or hold a pen. Despite his deteriorating condition, his mind was sharp and his entire household revolved around him. He continued to write, dictating in Hindi to a daughter-in-law and in Urdu to a man who had been hired from the neighbourhood. In the fall of 1995, he was kind enough to receive me—an American Ph.D. student in Allahabad conducting research on Ashk and on progressivism in Hindi literature—despite the fact that he found my research methods inadequate, my preparation woefully lacking and my preoccupation with the Progressive Writers' Association annoying.

Ashk was moody, irascible, imperious and always very interesting. During those days when I visited him daily against the wishes of his family, who felt, quite rightly, that he needed to rest, I lived in terror of him. Though I was always received, I was never sure if I would continue to be in favour from one day to the next. Some days he would be full of interesting anecdotes and, on others, he would ask me roughly how many questions I had, expecting that there was a numbered list we would plough through. Later, I learnt that he used to charge Indian graduate students a certain price per question. I was fortunate, my source told me, that I had been allowed to chat with him for free.

It was during this time that I was presented one day with a large sheaf of papers, translations of his short stories, he explained to me—some by himself, others by various people—which he feared were not good enough. He asked me to edit them and send them on to a publisher. Up until that point, I had been trying to convince him to give me permission to translate his six-volume novel cycle, *Girti Divarein* ('Falling walls', 1947), but in the world of Hindi letters, especially during the Independence era, the short story was the premier genre and, for Ashk, getting his short stories translated was a more pressing task than working on the novel. This, despite the fact that he felt that his novel was his most important work.

Embarrassingly, though I had read thousands of pages of his writing, I had never read any of his short stories. Authors of Ashk's generation, who began writing during the Independence movement, were hugely productive, writing assiduously in every genre as they sought to forge a body of literature in a wide variety of Indian languages. To measure the output of Ashk or Yashpal one would find a yardstick more useful than a simple ruler and, if truth be told, I had been concentrating on his novels and autobiographical writings. To this day, I have not done more than skim the surface of his plays, for which he is also very well known.

And so it was that when Ashk presented me with the collection of short stories and requested that I do something with them, I was wholly unfamiliar with the works in question. Murmuring that I would look at them and hoping that the stories would not need that much help from me, I took home several volumes of short-story collections on my one-speed Hero bicycle and began to comb through the package. Unfortunately, he had been correct in his assessment that the stories had not been well translated. On top of this, I came to realize that a number of them had already been translated and published in literary journals over the years. This made the project more complicated. Was I to edit the translations published by other people? I brought this question back to him and delicately broached the issue of copyright.

'None of them asked my permission to do these translations! So we don't need to ask their permission either.' He was irate at the thought that anyone needed to be consulted. Further investigation revealed that stories which had appeared to be translated by Ashk had in fact been translated by other people; Ashk had edited and retyped them himself. In cases where he himself had translated the stories, he would more often than not partially rewrite the actual story. As a young scholar, I was petrified at the thought of wading through those muddied waters of altered texts. Which would be the originals? Whose permission would need to be sought? Some of the translators were well known and I was not convinced that all his translators had brazenly published his stories without his permission.

In all likelihood, I might have ended the matter there, and refused, renewing at a later date my request to translate Ashk's novels. But, as fate would have it, this request would prove to be Ashk's last to me, as he passed away in January of 1996. Deeply saddened by Ashk's death and at a loss as to where to take my research without my subject, I felt obligated to honour his final request of me. Thus, I began to work on the project in earnest, often in consultation with Ashk's son, the poet and translator Neelabh, who finally suggested that I do my own translations if I was so unhappy with the state of the manuscript I had been given. With Neelabh's permission to carry out the spirit—but not the letter—of Ashk's request, I began to explore Ashk's short-story oeuvre on my own.

The resulting volume should be viewed not as a scholarly compendium of representative works, nor as anything close to a complete collection. Instead, it is a selection of stories that I personally enjoyed and wanted to share with others. One story—'Brown Sahibs'—is in fact an edited version of a translation by Edith Irwin, from the original manuscript Ashk gave to me. 'Mr Ghatpande' is adapted from Ashk's own translation of his story and, with Neelabh's permission, I have reverted to the original text and not used Ashk's additional English passages, though I have kept his glossary of terms related to the treatment of tuberculosis, updated from the footnotes that had appeared in the original text. Ashk himself had suffered from the disease and was concerned that a newer generation of readers would not know as much about TB and its earlier forms of treatment. For the rest of the selections, I was faced with some difficult choices. For instance, I have not included some stories from the original collection of which Ashk was very proud and for which he had received much acclaim at the time of their publication. On the other hand, I have included some excellent stories that are less known. I can't say if Ashk would have talked me out of my choices, but in compiling this collection, I have tried to select those tales that, to my mind, epitomize Ashk's wicked sense of humour and sharp eye for human frailty.

In fact, my decisions to exclude or include stories have mainly revolved around an organizing principle of humour. Ashk was an immensely funny author and even some of his most pathos-inflected passages in *Girti Divarein* are tinged with a sense of irony and dotted with acute observations of absurd human behaviour. Two stories in this collection— 'Furlough' and 'In the Insane Asylum'—in fact later made it into volumes in the *Girti Divarein* series; in each of these, one sees Ashk's skill in showing that humour and despair can go hand in hand. There are also many stories in this volume that are just plain side-splitting, such as 'Formalities', in which a film writer ruins his household by being overly hospitable towards a director he wishes to impress (who, in turn, has recently ruined his own household by behaving with excessive hospitality towards a starlet); or 'The Dal Eaters,' a story about cheapskates on holiday in Kashmir.

Many of the stories also include a bit of biting social commentary—a reflection, one might surmise, on the dominant aesthetic of progressivism in mid-twentieth-century Hindi literature. 'The Aubergine Plant', for example, is a progressivist story that clearly contrasts the resources of the rich and the poor, and even 'The Dal Eaters', for all its comedic effect, offers a sly critique of the ill effects of stingy tourists on the lives of poor Kashmiris. Though Ashk liked to protest vehemently that he had no part in the progressivist movement and never belonged to the PWA—the Progressive Writers' Association—the historical record suggests otherwise. Indeed, the PWA was an important part of the movement for Indian Independence; and, after 1947, it gained steam, becoming a national body with local-language branches that were engaged in creating a new idiom for the new nation. It would be difficult to find a writer in any Indian language during the forties, fifties and sixties who was untouched by the organization and its aesthetic, whether or not he or she wanted anything to do with it. The PWA in those days could be harshly prescriptivist, and authors, such as Ashk, who did not wish to be told which themes they could and could not address, certainly bridled at progressivist criticism.

Since Kaushalya, Ashk's wife, started a publishing company, Neelabh Prakashan, in Allahabad, after they moved there in 1948, Ashk did not, in fact, have to kowtow to anyone's rules and, as a result, his work is highly idiosyncratic and wonderfully original. One outcome of self-publishing was Ashk's unedited introductions to his work, in which he took on all comers and answered even minute bits of criticism in increasingly lengthy and personal essays. He was known to complain about the behaviour of particular people, even going so far as to describe at length his disappointment with the revered Allahabadi poetess

Mahadevi Varma for her unwillingness to help his family find a good home to rent when they first arrived in Allahabad. And it was perhaps because of this public criticism of his colleagues that Ashk, by the time of his death, was decidedly not the most popular author in the world of Hindi letters, though he himself always attributed the hostility towards his work to be wide-spread anti-Punjabi prejudice in the literary community centred in Uttar Pradesh.

Ashk's unpopularity within his milieu was a state of affairs that he was keenly aware of and there is ample evidence that his disgruntlement with his colleagues only drove him to further fan the flames. In his five-volume memoir, *Chehere: Anek* ('Faces: Many', 1975–85), Ashk wrote painfully funny satires on virtually every contemporary he had, skewering just about everyone but Urdu short-story writer Rajinder Singh Bedi (1915–1984), whose friendship he treasured to the last. In his most blanket condemnation of his literary world, Ashk dubs his adopted city of Allahabad 'the city of sadists':

> . . . Ashk thinks—and he has been involved with life in Allahabad for the last thirty years—that Allahabad should be called 'The City of Sadists'. Actually, the kind of literary people who live in Allahabad are incapable of getting any work done. They do not even write much. But since there has to be some dirt to chat about if they are not writing, they enjoy making their friends prey to sadistic pranks and then they can talk about it for days and weeks afterwards to entertain others. They have often wasted time in this hobby, as well as money, and sometimes they even go to a good deal of trouble too. By making fun of other people, they spread joy—albeit, a somewhat cruel joy—in the slow life of this city. What Ashk is trying to say is that sadism is Allahabad's specialty.[1]

---

[1] *Chehere: Anek*, vol. 3, p. 22.

It was because of Ashk's antagonism towards the world of writers and critics that he felt quite sure that I would have trouble publishing translations of his work in India, warning me that even in the English publishing world, everyone was against him. He may have been correct. Readers will notice that I began the project in 1995 and that the volume is being published only now in 2013.

~

To be perfectly truthful, Ashk's request that I edit his volume of short stories was actually his penultimate request to me. He also made a final request—that I attend his grandson Anurag's wedding in December of that year. This, I told him I could not do, as I had to fetch my mother from the airport on approximately the same date. He was enraged.

'You Americans!' he hissed. 'You're all the same—all business! Go, go, leave me alone. I won't speak with you again,' he added, waving his hand for me to leave.

Devastated, I mounted my Hero bicycle and rode home to contemplate my state of banishment, and to wonder if I would need to change my dissertation topic. A few days later, Ashk sent another grandson, Sukant, to fetch me on a motorcycle. When I entered the courtyard, I saw that Ashk was seated in the sun, his umbrella attached to his chair.

'He wants to talk to you,' said his grandson as he wandered away, showing no inclination to protect me from any possible choleric outbursts. I approached Ashk fearfully. A chair had been set next to him. He greeted me and then he said he had a special request to make. I asked him what that was.

'My grandson is getting married in December,' he began, thoughtfully. 'You and your husband are invited.'

I blanched.

'That is very kind,' I said, 'but I have to pick up my mother from the airport at that time . . . '

'Go! Go!' he cried. 'Leave me,' he waved me away again. Aghast and now without my bicycle, I walked across the courtyard in search of a ride. It was arranged that the grandson would take me back again, when Ashk called him over and spoke to him. Sukant returned to me and said that his grandfather wished to speak to me again. I approached him, worrying that the conversation would be a repeat of the previous two times.

'You may send a telegram,' he said distantly, looking away from me. 'If you send a telegram, that will be fine.'

'I will,' I said, 'I will send a telegram. I promise to send one.'

When I returned to Allahabad shortly after his grandson's wedding, Ashk had been hospitalized with acute protein deficiency, from which he never recovered. Though he was largely incoherent on his deathbed, I was sure I heard him cry out accusingly in English as I stood by his bedside, 'You are a very difficult woman to work with!' No one else seemed to have heard it. Was it my imagination?

～

Seventeen years have passed since I first met Ashk. When I returned to Allahabad a few years ago, Ashk's sprawling bungalow had been split into smaller homes and the wide-open yard where he used to receive me under his black umbrella is no more. In the past weeks, while preparing the manuscript for this collection, I decided to add one final story, 'Dying and Dying', a tale about a middle-aged man's proud memories of his own virility on his honeymoon twenty-five years ago. By the time I reached the story's ending, the slim volume in which it had been published nearly disintegrated in my hands.

The most financially fruitful effort to build a national literature since Independence in 1947 has been that of Indian writing in English and, in the simple terms of such economic indicators as paper quality and bindings, that fact is painfully apparent. There are many readers in India today who will read Ashk for the first time in this collection. Though they could easily read his work in the original Hindi, they would never think of doing so. This could be for many reasons, not the least of which is the much poorer distribution of non-English books. Hindi bookstores, for example, tend to arrange their books alphabetically by title (works by a single author could be all over the store), as such stores are not built for browsers and casual customers; they function primarily as shipping warehouses that fill orders for textbooks and school curricula.

Perhaps a translator should hope that her readers will develop a taste for the author in English, so that she can bring out more of the author's works in translation in the future. My hope, however, is the opposite: that some of these stories will induce a few readers—even just one or two will do—to turn their feet towards a Hindi bookshop one day. Out shopping in Old Delhi, they might stroll into Hindi Book Centre on Asaf Ali Road, and say to one of the booksellers, 'Yaar, do you have anything zabardast in stock by that amazing author, Upendranath Ashk?' They will be handed a few thick volumes which they will weigh in their hands, wondering if they dare attempt one of his long novels or if they should just go with some short stories instead. They will, no doubt, notice that the paper is already curling at the edges of the dust jacket, but they will decide to buy one of those books, long or short, and take it home.

That evening, perhaps after some trepidation, they will dive into the world of Ashk. They will return to Ashk the next night and the next, and, if the paper begins to crumble, they will lovingly tape it together and read on, avidly now. Later, they might tell certain select friends about this experiment and maybe one of them will attempt it as well, even if the rest of them laugh at their friend's idiosyncrasy. And so, if all goes well, by the time I have completed my translation of Ashk's novel *Girti Divarein*, those few particular readers will see a fresh copy of *Falling Walls* lying in an English bookshop somewhere and, turning to a companion, or even a stranger, they will say, 'Ah, Upendranath Ashk! But of course, kya kehna hai bhai, he's so much better in the original.'

Who Can Trust a Man?

Professor Gupta looked hopelessly depressed when he paid us a visit, a month after the death of his wife Shanta.

In the course of conversation that day, my aunt remarked that, with Shanta gone, he must be feeling very lonely; she then went on to discuss the difficulty of looking after two children; and finally she suggested, in all good faith, a second marriage for the professor.

He, however, reacted to the idea with passionate disfavour.

'Can I ever get a wife as pretty, as affectionate, as accomplished, as sweet, as intelligent and as considerate as Shanta?' Professor Gupta protested. 'Never ... Sometimes I don't know how to mourn my loss. I have lost a treasure—an irreplaceable treasure.'

Throughout the rest of his visit that day, the professor related several happy anecdotes of his conjugal bliss with a view to impressing upon us the beauty, the sweetness, the intelligence and the many accomplishments of his wife Shanta.

My aunt repeated most of these anecdotes later on, in envious admiration of the professor's great love for his deceased wife and his remarkably successful married life. She pitied the poor man for his incalculable loss. And almost every day, once or twice, she made some reference or the other to him or to his beloved Shanta.

∽

About fifteen days later, the professor came again. I noticed that the pall of depression that day was not as heavy as on the previous visit. My aunt, for lack of any other subject, once again began to emphasize his loneliness and the difficulty of bringing up two children without feminine help.

I was sitting beside my aunt, knitting. On scanning our visitor's face, I noticed that the clouds, though still quite heavy, were suffused with the warmth of pale sunshine. He smiled as he said, 'I agree with you; I have already decided to do what you are suggesting. In fact, a date has been fixed . . .'

'But to whom? You should have at least told us!' My aunt was heartily pleased to hear about his engagement.

'With a colleague's younger sister, Shakuntala. She graduated this year. Of course, she isn't much compared to Shanta. Shanta was Shanta. But I couldn't resist the persistent persuasion of this friend of mine. Besides, I thought that, being educated, she would be immune to stepmotherly meanness.'

'A graduate wife will be perfect, I think,' my aunt happily agreed.

'How can it be perfect?' Gupta protested. 'No one could ever fill the vacuum left by Shanta's death. That is a wound which will never heal. In fact, I have agreed to this proposal to hide this precious wound from the vulgar gaze of others. I consider it my own private treasure . . .'

The professor then sighed and recited a couplet from Kabir, in which the poet enjoins the unhappy sufferer to keep the anguish of his soul to himself, for who can ever share another person's pain?

The professor left after some time, but my aunt couldn't sleep properly that night. I should perhaps say that she was rather romantic in her inclinations. So, she began to compare my uncle's cold indifference with the passionate attachment of Professor Gupta to Shanta and said, 'No one will even remember me after I die.'

'No one' meant, of course, my uncle.

Her sighs that night were very long and very deep.

∾

After his marriage, however, when Professor Gupta called on us, it was difficult to detect any trace of Shanta in his consciousness. As long as he was with us, Shakuntala was the sole topic of his conversation and praise. Her education, her culture, her sharpness and many other qualities of her personality were enumerated and dwelt upon at length.

My aunt was so charmed by Professor Gupta's enthusiasm for Shakuntala that she invited them to dinner the next day.

As soon as the Professor left, she began to issue elaborate instructions to the servant about the next day's dinner. She was obviously feeling jealous of Shakuntala's good luck in having landed such an affectionate husband. My uncle, it seemed, was well versed only in the art of making money; he just didn't know a thing about the art of making love. Or at least, he could not hold the proverbial candle to Professor Gupta in this latter respect.

In the evening, my uncle came home and, as usual, got busy with the kids—he played with them, danced to the music on the radio and told them stories of ancient kings and queens. My aunt, meanwhile, kept heaving sighs as my uncle, it seemed, had no time to spare for her.

The next day, Professor Gupta came for dinner with his newly wedded wife Shakuntala. I saw that his visage looked like a mirror reflecting a brilliant sun. He seemed to be drenched with the light emanating from Shakuntala. Her smiles and words and expressions evoked corresponding smiles, words and expressions from him with an immediacy that indicated a remarkable harmony between the two of them.

Occasional flashes of envy could be detected on my aunt's face beneath her veneer of enthusiastic hospitality. Once or twice she even sighed quite audibly. As the guests departed, my aunt looked at Shakuntala with unmistakable envy in her eyes.

Shakuntala's position was indeed enviable. On his next visit, Professor Gupta referred for the first time to quite a few defects in his deceased wife Shanta. Shakuntala's excellent qualities had apparently opened his eyes to these defects. A man riding a camel naturally regards the camel to be the best and most useful animal. But if, by some stroke of luck, he happens to enjoy a ride on an elephant, he comes to recognize his mistake; he cannot help but realize the enormous difference between the awkward seat on the hump of a camel and the comfort of sitting on the vast back of a mountainous elephant. Professor Gupta had had the advantage of both these experiences and was the wiser for them.

He told us at considerable length of Shakuntala's solicitude for the education and health of her stepchildren. The older child had been admitted to a hostel and the younger had been sent to a residential nursery school. She paid them visits twice a week and took particular care of all their needs.

'I am afraid your children are too young to be left by themselves in hostels,' my aunt remarked with genuine surprise.

This inspired the professor to deliver a homily, a fairly long one, on the advantages of keeping small children away from home right from the beginning. He pointed out that this encouraged the children to cultivate independence and self-confidence; moreover, their latent faculties would get the opportunity to develop freely, uninhibited by the thoughtless excesses of affection from doting parents.

~

Unfortunately, however, Shakuntala failed to survive her first confinement, thus depriving Professor Gupta of her self, and his children of the encouragement she was to give to the uninhibited development of their latent faculties.

The profundity of Professor Gupta's grief, on his first visit to us after Shakuntala's death, moved my aunt to copious tears. His face had darkened so completely that I was reminded of a mirror blotted out by black ink. He kept praising Shakuntala for the care she had taken of his children that was so surpassingly maternal. He told us that she had gone to every single residential school before sending the children to the schools where they were at present. He was of the opinion that Shanta herself couldn't have been more solicitous about their well-being.

My aunt, at this stage, happened to refer to the future of the poor motherless children now that Shakuntala was no more. Professor Gupta met her implicit suggestion with so desperate a nod of his unhappy head that it was clear to my aunt that Shakuntala would have no substitute, that such a thing was impossible.

∾

But hardly one month after the departure of Shakuntala, we heard that Professor Gupta was preparing for the arrival of one Miss Sita. Miss Sita was a schoolmistress; she had convinced Professor Gupta that infinite harm could be done to sensitive children by hostel life. She was of the definite opinion that the teachers and other functionaries at a hostel were inherently incapable of bestowing on children the kind of affection that they always demand, and generally get, from their parents. For a few days, we listened to Professor Gupta's detailed accounts of the foresight and sagacity of Miss Sita. I was, therefore, not surprised, when, two months later, I heard that Miss Sita had been transformed into Mrs Sita Gupta.

My aunt had been preparing herself and the household to give a warm reception to the new Mrs Gupta. All these preparations were unfortunately cut short by a sudden collapse of my aunt's feeble heart. The attack proved fatal, and my uncle couldn't save her no matter how much he tried.

∾

My uncle did not marry again. He got numerous offers, of course. His friends also tried to persuade him to marry in view of the children and the other usual considerations. But my uncle just would not countenance any offer. 'After having lived with Santosh, the question of living with any other woman just doesn't arise,' he said with a definitiveness that put a stop to all further arguments.

~

Professor Gupta calls on us every now and then. Shakuntala faded into oblivion before Sita, just as Shanta had before Shakuntala. I am sometimes reminded of the sighs of my deceased aunt; the reminder is always accompanied by a sigh of my own that I cannot suppress.

Brown Sahibs

Shrivastava came out of the District Magistrate's office and glanced at his watch. It was eight o'clock and the office boy had told him that the District Magistrate would return at nine, which meant he had a whole hour to kill. So, why shouldn't he go find Gajanan and deliver the good news of his arrival in Allahabad in person? 'Two jobs on the same street'—that was his motto, and if those two jobs happened to turn into four, he'd be sure to finish them all off along the way. It was because of this attitude that, in just six or seven years, he had moved up from a sixty-rupee-a-month journalist to the post of Deputy Collector. Not only that; he was also such a sharp operator that, once appointed to the post of Deputy Collector, he had managed to bypass assignment to some godforsaken rural district and land this posh appointment in Allahabad. This was his first day in Allahabad and he had immediately gone to his superior officer's place to pay his respects. But the District Magistrate happened to be out paying his respects to some minister on tour from Lucknow. Shrivastava's boyhood friend, Gajanan, lived in Allenganj, a nearby locality, and was a lecturer at the university. Since he was sure his friend would be at home, Shrivastava decided to use his free hour for a visit.

Passing by the court, he stopped in the middle of the street. *Someday I'll be the top man in this court!* As the thought struck him, his pride lifted him a little off his heels. He fidgeted over his stiff collar and then straightened his bush shirt, tugging it back and forth by the hem a couple of times. Then, in front of the pillared offices of the court, he noticed two rickshaw-wallahs who seemed to be arguing as they headed his way.

'Rickishiyaw!' he called, pronouncing the word in a lordly tone, twisting it a little for effect.

'Yes, sir!' both rickshaw-wallahs shouted as they raced over and stood before him.

'Say, fellows, will you charge by the hour?'

'Where d'you want to go?' The first rickshaw-wallah asked.

'Wherever I may like,' Shrivastava snapped.

'So how much would I get for an hour?'

'The usual rate, whatever it is.'

'Sixteen annas.'

'Ten annas.'

'Very well, sir, please come right this way, sir,' interjected the second rickshaw-wallah, speaking and gesturing with the exaggerated politeness common in Lucknow.

'Okay, okay, bring your rickshaw over.'

When the second rickshaw pulled up, Shrivastava hopped in and sat down. He fixed his shirt again and lifted his trouser legs a little so as not to mess up the crease. He didn't dare sit back comfortably for fear of rumpling his bush shirt. After all, he wanted to keep himself looking sharp until he met the District Magistrate. There he sat in the rickshaw, looking alert and upright as if he were sitting on a chair in the presence of his boss.

This rickshaw-wallah was wearing a relatively clean khaki outfit. By appearance alone he wouldn't have been mistaken for any common rickshaw puller. Village types predominate among the rickshaw pullers of Allahabad. During the slack season of the agricultural year, the men of the neighbouring villages would dress their lanky bodies in homespun jackets with a length of cloth tied at the waist. Then they'd set out for Allahabad with enough food for one meal tied up in a bundle. They'd arrive in the evening and rent a rickshaw for the night.

After collecting fares from passengers, they'd be able to buy fried barley flour for the next meal. In addition to the usual paan preparations, crude bidis and Western-style cigarettes, many paan sellers would cater to these village rickshaw pullers by keeping trays of barley flour decoratively arranged in pyramids with green chilli peppers stuck in for a curiously festive effect. When these rickshaw-wallahs got a little time off from driving, they would buy a handful of the grain mash, knead it into a ball and then swallow the stuff with the help of some chillis, washing it down with a few gulps of water from a nearby faucet.

They say that when a jackal is about to die, he heads for the city. There is no significant difference between the proverbial jackal and these villagers. They drive their rickshaws all day long, every day, and sometimes all night too. Although they might earn enough to pay the year's rent, they blow their lungs out in the process.

There are other rickshaw pullers—Allahabadis—who used to work as labourers in the city, but were laid off after the Second World War. They go on driving their rickshaws, their ribs sticking out and signs of tuberculosis peering from their eyes. In these expensive times they must go on driving just to fill the bellies of their offspring.

Being a native of Allahabad, Shrivastava was quite familiar with these two types of rickshaw-wallahs, but this driver of his didn't fit into either category. It seemed that a third type was beginning to pop up here. Sporting thin, sword-like moustaches cut in the style of Ronald Colman and wearing military shorts, or a bush shirt, or only an army cap, these men who had been discharged from the army after the war were now beginning to drive rickshaws. The tilt of their heads, their rigid posture and their way of pedalling with knees and toes turned out, made them immediately identifiable as ex-soldiers driving rickshaws. Clamping a bidi in the right or left corner of their mouths and dreaming of the Third World War, they drove their rickshaws

jauntily, entertained by visions of Egypt, Iran, Italy and
Germany, and of the free atmosphere and the beautiful fair
women they would have there. Independence had made them
forget their ingratiating manners and had taught them to hold
their heads high with self-esteem. However, the majority,
being only half-educated, were ignorant of the thin line that
divides self-respect from arrogance. Why should they bargain
for fares when they considered every passenger a hostage
seized from enemy territory?

In spite of the fact that this rickshaw puller wore military
garb, he lacked the rigid posture of a soldier. What was more,
his face had the elastic quality of kneaded dough and was
decidedly different from the standard military mug, which was
about as pliable as coarse, dried flour.

Shrivastava had grown tired of sitting straight, so he relaxed
a little and asked, 'Tell me, fellow, were you in the army?'

The rickshaw-wallah went right on driving as he glanced
back to answer, 'No, Sahib, what would I do in the army?' His
words were accompanied by an ironic and slightly
contemptuous smile, beneath which Shrivastava detected a
twinge of pain. It was a smile which seemed to ask, 'Do you
think I would sink so low as to do the menial work of an army
lackey?'

'So you have your own small fleet of rickshaws?' Shrivastava
asked.

'Why, certainly, Sahib!' laughed the rickshaw-wallah with a
hint of irony. Then he continued, 'This rickshaw isn't even
mine. I pay rent to drive it.'

Sensing a certain degree of civility in the fellow's tone,
Shrivastava felt sympathetic towards him. 'So what makes you
do such backbreaking work? Driving a rickshaw puts a terrible
strain on the lungs, you know. Villagers who are used to
driving a plough and swinging a mattock may be able to drive
all day and all night, but such work is beyond the strength of
city people like you.'

'Listen, Sahib, you think I drive this thing for fun? There's my wife, several kids, my mother and two widowed sisters—and it's up to me to support them all.'

'Then why don't you find yourself another job?'

'Because I don't know how to do anything else, Sahib.'

'You mean you've driven a rickshaw all your life?'

'Oh, no, Sahib, just since Independence.' Still steering with his left hand, he thumped his forehead with his right. 'It's only since the English left and the brown sahibs took over that my fortune has exploded in my face. The native officers don't understand my work, so of course they don't know its value. I had no use for their business, nor they for mine. I didn't know how to do anything else, so I asked if I could be sent to England with them. Naturally my request was ignored.'

'What was it, anyway—the work you used to do?'

'I worked at Commissioner Duck's place. I got fifty rupees a month, two rooms to live in, and the clothes the Sahib gave me. If you'll pardon my saying so . . .' Then out of embarrassment he cut his words short.

'No, no, go ahead and say it,' Shrivastava urged, sitting up straight again.

'Take this bush shirt you're wearing,' the rickshaw-wallah said, turning around and speaking very respectfully, 'I used to wear one just like it when I worked at the Sahib's place.'

Shrivastava slumped back in the seat again, not even noticing that his shirt was getting rumpled.

'Nowadays, where's the good life we knew under the British? On holidays there would be a bonus; and not just for me either. There would be clothes made up for my wife and kids. Now tell me, these days where could I find all that? How am I supposed to keep up with the money my family spends? All I can do is drive a rickshaw, even though the blood's drying up in my veins, until one of these days I'll just vanish into nothing.'

'But really now, what's the problem? Why couldn't you work for some native sahib? We still have commissioners and collectors, just as in the British days.'

'What native sahib could afford my services?' And the same derisive smile spread across the rickshaw-wallah's lips.

'What were you at Commissioner Duck's place?' Shrivastava asked with a mixture of annoyance and curiosity. 'A cook?'

'No, I wouldn't do cooking.'

'Well, were you a bearer, or what?'

'Yes, I was a bearer.'

Shrivastava sat up again. 'So what's the problem? You could find another servant's position. I have a bearer at my place.'

'Oh, no, I wasn't that kind of bearer. I never did any of that food-carrying business. I looked after the Sahib's clothes.'

'Yes, of course. You took care of his clothes and cleaned his boots.'

'No, Sahib, the sweeper did the boots. I only had to see to his clothes.'

'You mean all day long all you ever did was look after his clothes?'

'What can I tell you, Sahib? You wouldn't understand,' he said with a grin. 'Those English had class. They'd wear a special suit for each occasion. A different one for the night, for the office, for daytime lounging, for outings. Then there were dinner suits, golf suits, polo suits, dance suits and hunting suits. It was my job to keep them all in order, give them to the washerman and get them back, and to dress the Sahib. Now, how could any native sahib understand or appreciate my work? Day and night, month in and month out, year after year, they go on wearing the same one suit right down to threads. See that red house we just passed? The sahib who lives there is an important man, but sometimes he wears a suit which must have been salvaged from his college days. Where you find an office today, the English used to have a bathroom. And Saturday nights were so splendid. And that garden—you saw how they've let it go to pot. Well, did you ever get to see how beautiful it was under the British? It's not just that garden either; the very mention of the British sahibs sends the whole of

Civil Lines into tears. It's like having to look at the shaved head of a widow.'

Shrivastava found this rickshaw-wallah's contempt and disdain for the Indian way of life disturbing. He had a predilection for the good life himself, but at this point, each and every manifestation of the British culture angered him. Thinking he might help this blind fellow see the light, he said, 'There's a big difference between their habits of dining, dressing and high living compared to ours. They don't see anything wrong with eating meat and fish or drinking alcohol. They eat the meat of the cow and the pig, while in our houses it's a sin even to touch either one. Their women dance, but in our houses—'

'Not at all, sahib,' the rickshaw-wallah interrupted, pedalling harder to emphasize his point. 'Our country is a country of slaves. We've closed ourselves up like snails and talked about poverty as though it were heaven. Even when we're rich, it's our habit to live as though we're poor. We put our money in banks and subsist on humble chapatis and dal. My Sahib told me that in ancient times when India was free and the Aryans had just arrived, they too used to eat and drink well, dance and sing and live gaily. They never used to veil their women or put restrictions on what people could eat and drink. The Sahib used to say that money was only good for spending, not for putting in banks. When rupees are spent, they bring money to craftsmen, labourers and shopkeepers; and when they're not, unemployment rises. Every year my Sahib would have the furniture, doors and window refinished; and every six months he'd have the whitewashing done. There were two gardeners, two bearers, a cook and a sweeper, all kept as servants in his house. Because of him, the bread man, the egg man, the cabinetmaker and God knows how many others, all had regular wages.'

A spark caught fire in Shrivastava's heart. He wanted to get up and give this foreigner's dog a good punch in the neck, but the rickshaw was going too fast. Instead, he vented his anger on his former white officers.

'Who cares about those bastards? They had a hell of a good time while they robbed the people blind.'

'You mean to say our current masters rob people any less?' the rickshaw-wallah asked with a humble yet sarcastic grin. 'All public servants, from the lowest to the highest, steal from the people, but in those days, a distinguished officer was capable of feeling some shame—now it's just one big free-for-all. These officers know well enough how to take, but not how to give. Where you found an Englishman taking, you would find that at the same time he was supporting ten men. These people here hoard the money they steal. There's no need to speak of elegant living, it's not their style. They wear the same dhoti and kurta all the time, indoors and out. Every two or three weeks—no, more like every month or two—they'll get themselves shaved. Now, what do the barber, the washerman, the bearer, or the cook get out of these people?'

Shrivastava had begun to squirm inwardly, but he kept quiet so as not to be drawn into a row with such a lowly person.

'Why go so far afield?' The rickshaw-wallah asked, continuing his stream of conversation. 'Take the rickshaw- and the tonga-wallahs. When a wealthy man hires a rickshaw, you can be sure he'll haggle over the fare. There's an honorary magistrate here in Allenganj, an important man who also runs a printing press in Chowk. He's always waiting here at the stand, looking out for a chance to split the fare. If another passenger doesn't come along, he might go on standing for half an hour. Even an ordinary English soldier wouldn't haggle over the fare. If he had a rupee in his pocket, he'd give a rupee. If he had two rupees, he'd give two. One day, my Sahib's car broke down, so he gave a rickshaw-wallah a five-rupee note to go from Allenganj to the court.'

They arrived at Gajanan's house and Shrivastava hopped out, only to find that his friend wasn't there. So he left his card, returned to the rickshaw and told the driver to get going quickly. Just as they arrived in front of the court and Shrivastava was getting out, he glanced at his watch and saw that an hour and ten minutes had passed.

If it had been any other occasion, and the agreed rate had been ten annas an hour, he would not have given more than twelve annas. But he was hesitant to give this rickshaw-wallah just twelve annas. Giving the graves of the British sahibs a mental kick, he said, 'It's been a few minutes more than an hour. Even if it had been two hours the fare would only have come to one rupee four annas. But here, take two rupees. The fourteen annas extra you can keep as a tip from me.'

The rickshaw-wallah salaamed in his modified military fashion. Shrivastava rose on his toes and headed for the District Magistrate's office.

∽

'So, how much did you get?' The first rickshaw-wallah called loudly from the stand where he was waiting.

'Two rupees!'

'Phew—two rupees!'

'Yup, two rupees. Have I ever got less from a native officer? Only I know how to handle these miserable brown sahibs.'

∽

Shrivastava overheard this last sentence. He sagged down on his heels and even his strut was gone, as he entered the District Magistrate's office walking as though he were just an ordinary man.

Translated by Edith Irwin

Hats and Doctors

Mr Goyal was the local representative of the *Bharat Times* (Delhi/Calcutta) in Lucknow. His friends generally considered him a dapper man. In their schooldays, they had seen him attired in a turban decorated with a plume. In college, he had dressed the dandy, wandering about bareheaded, a light splash of water on his long curly hair. During the Congress movement, he had preferred milky-white homespun kurtas and dhotis, topped with a Gandhi cap at a rakish angle. In later years, he had appeared decked out in a black achkan coat and a black cap, or, on occasion, resplendent in an English suit and hat. A number of years ago he had gone to Russia with a delegation of journalists. He brought back a large beautiful velvet cap. For a couple of years, the dignity of that expensive Russian cap—worth one hundred and fifty roubles—reigned triumphant, but in 1954, he went to Kabul, and from Kabul he had returned with a Qaraqul hat. For almost a year, his costly Afghani hat had been the subject of constant praise among his friends. But two years later, he went to Kashmir and returned with three or four boat-shaped caps—which, at some point, were called 'Jinnah caps' and nowadays are called 'bakshi caps' . . . It was because of his hats, a new one every day, that he was famous for his dapperness, and also because he was constantly changing hat styles. But no one knew the secret weakness that lay at the root of his penchant for hats.

~

The secret was that his head was extremely sensitive to cold. If he could have found any way around it, he wouldn't have worn hats: his hair was so beautiful, black and curly; wearing any hat on top of it was singularly unpleasant to him; but his sensitivity to cold gave him no other option. If there was just the slightest chill in the air and he left his head bare, he would catch a cold. He had hidden his weakness behind a veil of dapperness; maybe he had gone about bareheaded for a few years in college, but as the years went by he had made hats his constant guardians. He liked the hat he had brought back from Russia so much that if it had been in his power, he would have worn it every day for the rest of his life. The only problem with that hat was that he could not wear it to meetings or social gatherings.

Whenever he sat around bareheaded he ended up battling a cold for weeks. The Qaraqul hat was useful in the extreme cold, but it became uncomfortable when there was only a slight chill in the air. It was a very warm hat. His head always became drenched with sweat even when it was cold outside, but if he took the hat off he started sneezing. The trip to Kashmir had eased that problem. The boat-shaped hats there cost between five and fifty rupees. They were the kind of hats that could be worn in the middle of the summer, not only when it was a bit chilly, and he had bought all kinds of hats in this style: less warm, medium, very warm; white, black, brown, speckled.

He always wore a hat that matched his suit; if his friends praised his suit or his hat, Mr Goyal always smiled and accepted their praise with thanks: but sometimes, deep down inside, he felt terribly sad. The realization that he couldn't live without a hat dampened his enthusiasm. Whenever he went for a walk in the evening in Hazratganj and noticed people walking around with their heads bare, even when it was very cold, or tearing around on bicycles and motorcycles bareheaded, he wished he could take off his hat and fling it into the street. He would not let anyone pick it up; he would just watch it get crushed and torn to ribbons beneath the wheels of cars and bicycles and tongas, and so become a happier man. And now that he had passed his fortieth year, he was beginning to have to wrap a scarf around his neck as well, just below his hat. If he felt a cold breeze on his ears when he was driving his motorcycle, his nose started dripping. He had to stop the motorcycle, wrap the scarf that was around his neck over his head and ears, tie it under his chin, put his hat back on and continue on his way.

And now a new factor had come into being which made his problem even more upsetting. Since last year, in Lucknow's annual exhibition, a Kashmiri shopkeeper had started stocking piles and piles of boat-shaped hats. And so, right before Mr Goyal's very eyes, practically all his friends started wearing exactly the same boat-shaped hats he wore—maybe not quite as expensive; maybe they were actually less expensive, but still, his feeling of originality had been completely done in. No one praised his hats anymore.

Then the Basant holiday came. Mr Goyal was Punjabi and, although everyone else in his household had already said the last rites for the turban and turned their backs on it forever, his father still wore one. Though he was seventy now, he always had it dyed yellow for the day of Basant. This year, when he saw his father dyeing his turban, something got into Mr Goyal. He ordered a terrific-looking muslin turban, had it dyed yellow, wrapped it around his head with the greatest of care and, on the day of Basant, he roamed around all day long on his motorcycle, his turban flapping about in the cool breeze.

When his friends praised his turban to the skies and said that, in comparison to all other hats, a turban looked the very best on him, and when they asked him with curiosity why he had never worn one before, all Mr Goyal's listlessness turned to dust, and he decided that from now on he would always wear a turban. He went to see a friend of his in the market, and on the way he dropped in to speak with a hand-dyer. He told the dyer he would bring him three or four turbans if he could dye them for him in one day. In his boundless enthusiasm he even chose the colours: fawn, dark gray, pearl and light ochre.

But right around four o'clock he started to get a terrible headache. He hadn't worn a turban in a long time. His long hair had gotten badly squeezed from being tied up in that suffocating knot. He was sitting in the coffee house with his friends, when suddenly he felt he wouldn't be able to bear sitting there any longer if he didn't take some medicine. So he called for an Irgapyrene tablet and took it with his coffee. But instead of getting better, his headache got worse, and, to top it all, he started feeling nauseous. So he left his friends and went home.

From outside his house he could tell that his wife had gone to the Gomati River to celebrate Basant with the neighbouring ladies. He rushed noisily into the bedroom. He took off the turban and flung it on to the bed as hard as he could. When he looked at his face in the mirror, he saw that the coils of his constricted hair had formed a sort of a bun on the top of his head because of the twists of the turban; his eyes were squinty, the veins of his forehead were taut and he looked extremely exhausted. He went to the bathroom; he splashed his face with water; he smoothed his wet hand over his hair and combed it; he folded his handkerchief and tied it like a bandage around his temples; he pushed the bedclothes and the turban on to his wife's bed, next to his. Without changing out of his trousers, he crept under the quilt.

Even though he had tied the handkerchief tightly over his temples, he did not feel any better. Bang-bang, bang-bang— someone was ceaselessly hitting his temples with a hammer. He felt incredibly suffocated. He got up and drank a glass of water and then stretched out across the bed again.

After a little while he began to feel extremely hot. Still lying in bed, he took off his pants and threw them on top of the Basant turban and the bedding on the bed next to his. He felt like putting on his pajamas, but instead he just lay there in his underwear.

He still did not feel any better. The rays of the setting sun fell on his eyes through a gap in the curtain that hung in the door across from his bed. He felt as if the sun's rays were operating the hammer banging against his temples. He no longer had the strength to get up and fix the curtain. He turned over and began to moan softly with his face to the wall.

~

'Oh my goodness! What's wrong?' shrieked his wife from the doorway when she saw him lying there, moaning.

Mr Goyal didn't turn over. He moaned.

Mrs Goyal was wearing a gorgeous spring-yellow silk sari and a silk blouse of the same colour. She had wrapped a beautifully embroidered yellow Aurangabadi shawl around her shoulders. There was a garland of yellow marigold flowers wound around her bun. Her face, which always looked yellow because she was sick all the time, was pink and glowing from holiday cheer—or else from walking outside in the sun. This was so even though she was wearing a spring-yellow sari, the colour of which usually reflected on to her yellow face, making it look even yellower. She threw her shawl to one side and sat down at the head of his bed. Smoothing her hand over her husband's head, she asked him again:

'What's wrong?'

Mr Goyal turned over. 'I have a terrible headache, my temples are bursting.'

'You should take four Belladonna 30 tablets.'

Mr Goyal wished he could guffaw loudly, but because of his headache, all he could do was smile. He said, 'What's your Belladonna going to do? I have already taken some Irgapyrene.'

'Now how can I explain this to you?' Mrs Goyal said,

rubbing his forehead with her right hand. 'I've seen Dr Avasthi cure the most extreme headaches with those pills.'

'Oh my God, what does your Avasthi know about anything?' asked Mr Goyal, pushing his wife's hand away and pressing both his temples at once with his thumb and middle finger. 'That clerk, who treats patients by examining their astrological charts . . .'

'But I've been feeling better . . .'

'But you start feeling better every time you change to a new doctor.'

'Why do you always have to make fun of everything? Dr Avasthi is famous all over the city; are all his patients fools?'

Mr Goyal fell silent. He considered it pointless to argue with her.

His wife had an old intestinal complaint. She had already tried out almost all the doctors in the city and she had put her faith in every single one of them. Nowadays, she sang the praises of Dr Avasthi.

Dr Avasthi was certainly not a degree-holding doctor. He was a senior clerk in the education department of the Secretariat, but he had started practising homeopathy along with working as a clerk, and slowly he had become more of a doctor and less of a clerk. He was cheerful, friendly—a lover of literature and art, and he had earned quite a name for himself. The other clerks handled his work and, when he wasn't being called before very important officers to listen to their complaints and dole out pills, Dr Avasthi spent his time at the office studying large thick books on homeopathy. Everyone was his patient, from the ministers right down to the errand boys. His practice had done so well that he really didn't have any need for a job. But when it came right down to it, he was a clerk at heart. He was about to retire in three or four years and the lure of his pension had kept him stuck to the office. There was a popular story in the Secretariat about a particularly strict superintendent who had scolded him once and told him that if he came to the office late, or did any other non-office work on the job, he would be dismissed. But only one month later, the superintendent's son had fallen very ill. When all the other doctors in the city had forsaken him, he took refuge with Dr Avasthi. He fell at his feet, pleading, 'Do whatever it takes, just save my son, please.' Dr Avasthi had made him fit as a fiddle again with just four packets of powder.

Mrs Goyal praised this story rapturously. 'That day, same as today,' she would say when she was telling the story, 'not just the superintendent—not even the Secretary or the Minister—has had the courage to say a single word of complaint against him.'

These days, she advised her acquaintances to consult Dr Avasthi for every sickness imaginable and was constantly praising the virtues of homeopathy as compared to allopathy. 'Sister (or brother), homeopathy hits the mark like an arrow,' she'd say, 'illnesses that even important surgeons can't fix can be cured by these teeny-tiny homeopathic tablets in just days.' And she would tell them how Dr Avasthi had fixed a tumour in the uterus of a girlfriend of hers with just one round of medicine: after the birth of her child, her friend had started to feel a heaviness below her navel and, when she started feeling pain even when she was sitting in a jolting rickshaw, her husband had taken her to the hospital. The doctor had said, 'It's a tumour; we'll have to operate. Come during the cold season!' She had practically died right then and there just hearing the word 'operate'. In the midst of this, someone gave her Dr Avasthi's address. He gave her four doses of medicine. But she lived in Chowk and Dr Avasthi lived on Park Road. She took the medicine but she didn't go again. Her husband was a little eccentric. Right in the beginning of December he took her to the hospital, thinking that if she had to have an operation, they should book her a room in time. When the doctor examined her he was astonished and said in English, 'It is not there. It has completely vanished!'

And reversing the sentences, Mrs Goyal would repeat that part of the story in her thin voice with its convent-English accent, 'It's true! The doctor said, '"It has completely vanished. It is not there!"'

~

Everything his wife had said about Dr Avasthi passed through Mr Goyal's mind as he lay there on his bed. Despite his headache a smile spread across his lips. A few moments later he said, 'Give me two Aspro tablets.'

'But there's no Aspro in the house,' said his wife. 'I'll call Dr Avasthi and ask him what he thinks.'

And before he could stop her, Mrs Goyal had gone into the office and called Dr Avasthi. When she came back, she said, 'That's what I said, didn't I, why don't you just take four Belladonna 30 tablets? That's exactly what Dr Avasthi said too.'

'Could you just call Dr Chatterji, please,' Mr Goyal said, mentioning his favourite allopath, of whom his wife had taken leave long ago.

'Did he ever tell you what medicine to take over the phone,' Mrs Goyal said with irritation, 'that he'll tell you this time? If you want I'll call him, he'll come and take a look, but if I call now he won't come until nine-thirty. He leaves his Care Centre at nine o'clock. Just do what I say, I'm going to give you four tablets of Belladonna. If you don't feel better, I'll call whatever doctor you want.'

Before he could object, his wife picked up a small bottle lying on the portable coal heater and tore off a scrap from the newspaper. She dropped four pills into it and said, 'Open your mouth!'

Mr Goyal opened his mouth reluctantly. He tasted a light pungency on his tongue along with sweetness. The pills must have been soaked in the medicine, because one or two marks were left on the paper.

Half an hour later, Mr Goyal's headache had disappeared.

∾

The next day, Mr Goyal, wearing one of his old boat-shaped hats, went with his wife to Dr Avasthi to get some more medicine. While he was preparing the medicine, Dr Avasthi asked him how the pain in his head felt now. Mr Goyal told him that he had taken Belladonna and that it had made him feel much better. Dr Avasthi then began to enumerate the merits of Belladonna.

He was praising the miracles of homeopathy and telling him which deadly illnesses he had cured for whom, when Mr Goyal revealed to him the real reason behind his headache and said, 'All the world wanders about bareheaded: I'm the only one who has to walk around wearing a hat, not just in winter but even in the middle of summer. Let's see if you can cure me of that.'

They say that even a rock will get worn down if a rope moves back and forth across it often enough. His wife's chatter had finally made an impression on Mr Goyal.

'Hmm,' said Dr Avasthi, as he prepared the powders. When he was done, he placed a large book in front of him and began turning the pages. After a few moments, he said, 'Here we go, found it.'

And he read aloud in English: '*A Person Who Wears a Headdress Even in Summer*.' He closed the book, took some pills out of a bottle, shook another bottle, dropped one or two drops of medicine on to the pills and said, 'Open your mouth.'

Mr Goyal opened his mouth. Dr Avasthi poured the powder into his mouth and told him, 'There. God willing, your hat will come off in three days.'

∾

In three days Mr Goyal's hat did come off, but he started feeling so jumpy he had to go back to Dr Avasthi. Dr Avasthi made him up another powder, told him to open his mouth and poured it all in.

After three days he didn't feel any better: the jumpiness had increased, his appetite had completely died, his urine had turned yellow. Mr Goyal moved back to Dr Chatterji's Care Centre.

There was always a large crowd there. The round table and the round bench around it in the middle of the big hall outside was for the middle-class, cultured, educated patients: it was packed to the gills. There wasn't an inch of free space on the benches which were set aside on either side of the door for the lower-class patients; in fact, some women were even sitting on the floor next to the benches. Mr Goyal parked his scooter near the door and went inside. He took an old edition of a weekly paper from the round table and, propping his elbows on the right side along the counter, he stood and waited. He had opened the newspaper, but he couldn't get himself to read it. All his attention was focused on his turn coming up.

Mr Goyal liked the cleanliness and order of Dr Chatterji's clinic quite a lot. What he didn't like was this crowd. Whether you came first or last, you would definitely have to sit and wait for your turn for an hour and a half to two hours. Dr Chatterji was on duty from eight in the morning until noon, and then in the evening, from six to nine o'clock. He never saw anyone out of turn, no matter how important they were. He never went on visits during clinic hours. If someone got there early to take the first turn, he would most definitely have to sit and wait just as long for the doctor to get there and, if he got there late, he would have to wait for him to take care of the other patients.

After an hour and a half, Mr Goyal's turn came. Dr Chatterji was sitting all neat and tidy behind his little table in his little room. The books on his little table were arranged in order, and he wrote out his prescriptions—which only his compounder could read—very quickly on small slips of paper. Under the piece of glass that covered his table he had pasted three typed directives for his patients:

—Please do not rest your elbows on the table!
—Please do not touch anything lying on the table!
—Please keep your children away from the table!

Behind him there was a partition, on each side of which were two doors that led to the two examination rooms—one for the middle-class patients, the other for the lower-class patients. Mr Goyal was always amazed at the speed with which Dr Chatterji took care of his patients. When he came out of the examination room after looking at a patient he always hit the bell before writing out the prescription, and then motioned to the next patient to go into the other examination room. He would write out the prescription and give it to the previous patient and then go in to look at the next one. As soon as he heard the sound of the bell, the compounder would send in two more patients.

Sometimes, Mr Goyal felt truly amazed by Dr Chatterji's speediness and he wondered how many miles the doctor must cover in one day, walking back and forth between his table and the examination rooms.

As soon as he entered Dr Chatterji's room, he greeted him; the doctor acknowledged his greetings without looking up from writing out the previous patient's prescription.

A fake cockroach had been pinned to the partition behind the doctor. Under the cockroach hung a lizard with its tail crooked. The first time Mr Goyal had come to Dr Chatterji's clinic, both these creatures had looked completely real to him, and for quite some time he had waited for the lizard to leap up and seize the cockroach in its jaws. Even though he had since learnt that both were fake, he always found himself riveted by the cockroach and the lizard when he went to Dr Chatterji's clinic.

As he sat gazing up at them now, Mr Goyal nearly rested his elbows on the table without thinking about it, when his eyes fell upon the directives under the glass. Quickly he sat up straight. Just then the doctor addressed him, 'Tell me, how can I help you today?'

Mr Goyal told him his problems: his heart felt all heavy, his appetite was gone and his urine had turned yellow.

The doctor motioned to him to go inside. Mr Goyal went in and lay down. After a few moments the doctor came inside. He checked his pulse, looked at his tongue, felt his stomach a little and then said, 'You work night and day, you travel around on a scooter. You need to do a little walking.' He left the room. When Mr Goyal came back outside, Dr Chatterji put the prescription in his hand and said to him, 'I've prescribed medicine for three days. You'll have to get injections of calcium and vitamin B. Take your medicine, take the injections, do some walking, everything will get better.'

And he got up and went into the other room, where a lower-class patient was lying on the brown oilskin spread over the rough table. He stepped inside and pulled the curtain shut.

Mr Goyal went outside and gave the prescription to the compounder, for which the compounder took five rupees and sixty paise. It was ready after half an hour. When he was walking down the stairs of the Care Centre, Mr Goyal cast a glance at the sweepers and labourers sitting on the benches, those lower-class patients for whom Dr Chatterji made no concessions. And he laughed involuntarily at the name of that clinic which announced its so-called concern.

It had recently snowed in Kashmir, Shimla, Nainital and Mussoorie. A cold wave came through the town so that even though the days had been getting hotter and the sunlight was unbearable, it was suddenly so cold that people had to dig out their overcoats. Mr Goyal seldom went out when it was cold, but recently, according to the doctor's orders, he had been going out walking every day. Sometimes, he felt so overheated

that he would walk without an overcoat, muffler or hat all the
way to Gautam Palli, and sometimes even as far as Shivaji
Street. But despite all the walking he didn't feel the slightest bit
better. His heart felt even heavier than before, and his appetite
was almost gone.

He had already been given three rounds of injections, when
one day his wife exclaimed, 'Your eyes look all yellow!'

Mr Goyal made it to Dr Chatterji's that evening and told
him he had jaundice. The doctor pushed down the skin beneath
his eyes a little and looked carefully. There was no way he
would be able to see that pale yellow in the electric light. He
said, 'You people have very active imaginations. There's no
jaundice here at all. Come in the morning, we'll see.'

The next day Mr Goyal came again. Looking at his eyes this
time, Dr Chatterji remarked carelessly, 'Yes, it seems like a
little bit of jaundice; this medicine won't work! You'll have to
take another injection.'

Mr Goyal was going to tell him—as he had already told him
several times before—that his urine was also looking yellowish.
Dr Chatterji never listened to what he said. He wrote out the
prescription on a slip of paper and gave it to him, instructing
him not to have any milk or ghee or bread for a few days and
to eat plenty of fruit and boiled vegetables. Then he went into
the examination room to examine the next patient waiting for
him.

By this time, Mr Goyal had already thrown away twenty-
five or thirty rupees. He felt extremely angry with the doctor. 'I
told him, the colour of my urine is yellow now, I feel jumpy,
I'm overheated . . . and he gave me vitamin B injections!' And
for the first time Mr Goyal felt irritated by the speed with
which Dr Chatterji managed to take care of three patients at
once, that speed which he used to admire so much.

≈

When he came home he cursed the doctor up and down, picked up all his medicines and dashed them to the ground and told his wife that from today onward he would drink only sugar cane juice and eat only fruit and boiled vegetables. His younger brother had once had jaundice and he had found some relief from drinking only sugar cane juice. He was going to take the same cure and he would never let his head be turned by another doctor.

Mrs Goyal remarked once in a subdued voice that perhaps Dr Avasthi had given him some high-potency medicine, maybe he should just ask him for an antidote.

But that suggestion prompted such an enraged glance from Mr Goyal that she did not have the courage to say anything more on the subject. She quietly sent the servant out to get some mosambis and oranges, and some vegetables.

Mr Goyal's health had become particularly terrible by now. His entire body had turned yellow along with his eyes, but he would take refuge with no doctor. His wife sat in the chair next to his bed all day, constantly embroidering or knitting something and talking about this and that; but she never ever mentioned Dr Avasthi or the word homeopathy even by accident. Slowly Mr Goyal's health started getting a little better, he started getting hungry; the yellow in his eyes began to fade. Then one day, his wife mentioned Hakim Mehboob Alam Chishti.

Mrs Goyal was knitting a woollen beret for her nephew. Every year her nephew went to the mountains and she wanted to knit him warm clothing and send it to him in time. Suddenly she said, 'Pandey's wife is really taken with Hakim Chishti. Her sister got typhoid, then somehow lots of heat went to her head and she went crazy. All the doctors tried to cure her and failed, even Dr Avasthi was treating her for a few days'—she said this just to make Mr Goyal happy—'but nobody could do anything. In the end he suggested they send her to Agra, Bareilly or Kanki. Everyone recommended Kanki. Her sister was so young and so beautiful—they were planning a huge wedding for her. That summer was the most auspicious time for the marriage to take place. Mr Pandey was not prepared to send her to Bareilly or Kanki, but there was no way she could be looked after in the house. Just then someone told them about Hakim Chishti. He is seventy years old and he is a very famous doctor. He travels all over; from here to as far as Calcutta and Amritsar. He made her better in six months. If you want, I'll call for him.'

Mr Goyal wasn't listening to a word she was saying. He was watching her hands knitting the almost-finished red beret. All of a sudden he asked, 'Can't you knit one or two hats like that for me?'

'Hats!' His wife looked at him with surprise.

'That colour is too flashy, it would be best if you could knit me two hats, dark blue or dark gray, to match my suits.'

'I'll get some wool and start today.' Then she again suggested calling for Hakim Chishti. She said, 'You've grown weak. I'll have Hakim Chishti called here, he'll give you such strong medicine you won't feel hot any more and your body will get strong again.'

'I'm better now,' chuckled Mr Goyal, 'because my head just started to feel cold again. You didn't notice, today I sneezed two or three times. Why don't you just get some wool the colour of my suits and knit me a couple of hats.'

≈

One week later, when Mr Goyal, now healthy, emerged from his home wearing a blue suit, there was a woollen beret on his head which drooped a little to the left and matched his suit. His friends were sorry he had grown so thin, but their admiration for the new hat he sported made Mr Goyal forget all his abuse at the hands of doctors.

The Ambassador

The stranger's beard was scraggly, his salt-and-pepper hair brittle and unkempt; he wore a dirty shirt with no buttons, a loose coat full of holes, baggy trousers patched and torn, and boots that seemed worn down by centuries of use. The houseboy thought he was crazy and was chasing him out of the bungalow, when the stranger saw me. He advanced towards me, brushing the houseboy aside.

'Hello, Bakhshi!'

He held out his hand to me warmly and, in perfect English, told me that my houseboy was impolite—a complete fool— and should be turned out at once.

His English pronunciation was perfect; there was such confidence in his tone. Inadvertently I reached for his filthy hand as I tried to recognize his face. In the whole face there were only eyes: sharp, stubborn, careless, but deep, nonetheless; they looked quite familiar. But I had lost the rest of his features in a haze of forgetfulness.

'You don't recognize me,' he said. 'I'm Bhola. We lived together in a room on Mall Road in Lahore in 1938.'

'Bhola! Hargopal! What's happened to you?' I led him by the hand into the drawing room.

He began to reminisce about those days in Lahore. As I listened to what he said I came to believe that he was not crazy; he perfectly recollected those days in their every detail.

He sat down on a costly cushion in the drawing room with that same familiar and authoritative air of his.

31

'What happened to you?' I asked, hesitantly. 'You were supposed to become an ambassador.'

Bhola seemed not to hear what I was saying. In his perfect English, he remarked, 'If it's possible, could you please give me something to eat? I haven't eaten in two days!'

I called the houseboy and told him, 'Dakkhilal, bring some food for this gentleman.'

'Gentleman'—a gleam lit up in Bhola's eyes and then a faint, barely noticeable, but grotesque, smile played on his face.

The houseboy was about to turn away when I stopped him. 'Listen, tell Rani Ma an old friend of mine has come, and to send some food here . . .'

As he turned away again, I added, 'Pick up this centre table and move it over there, bring that teapoy over here and take the gentleman over to the washbasin, so he can wash his hands.'

'My hands are always clean,' Bhola told the houseboy. 'You bring the food.'

The houseboy went away.

I tried to learn something of Bhola's life. But besides those days in Lahore, which bore a connection to me, he remembered nothing at all. He and I had once taken the Indian Civil Service exam together. We had lived together in one room for three months. Of the people who qualified in the exam, I had actually scored very low and Bhola had scored among the highest—he only had to retake the oral section. He remembered everything that had happened in those days as well as the year and the dates. About the rest of his life, he had nothing to say, save to dismiss it with a wave of the hand. It seemed as though the outline of Lahore was sketched in the upper portion of the blackboard of his mind, but the lower portion was completely empty.

After I had entered the I.C.S. competition for the first time and had qualified, but was not selected, a friend of mine, Sudarshan, who had been admitted into the I.C.S., gave me some advice: 'Listen, Bakhshi, I'll tell you the secret of success: try to make friends with Bhola. He broke the record in English in the B.A. exam, he came first in English in the I.C.S. exam, he's the second rank in the Aggregate; he wasn't selected only because he has to take the oral again. But he will definitely be made an I.C.S. officer. It's only thanks to him that I succeeded. If you can make friends with him somehow and move into his room, you can live with him and prepare for the exam there.'

I was a student at D.A.V. College and Bhola was from Government College. The Government College students looked on the D.A.V. College students with a good deal of contempt. That made me feel nervous about meeting him. And then, I also lived with my uncle in Sutra Mandi and Bhola lived in a room in a three-storey building on Mall Road, near the Coffee House. His room was on the second storey. Outside the room there was a beautiful porch, with a small balcony jutting out from it that overlooked Mall Road. I asked Sudarshan to introduce me to Bhola. He took me to his place and said lots of nice things about me. From that day on I regularly visited Bhola at his flat and managed to make such good friends with him that three months before the exam I had moved into his room.

Bhola's store of knowledge was unparalleled. He told me dozens of secret recipes for success in the exam, and when, after three years, I was finally made an I.C.S. officer, those three months spent with Bhola had a good deal to do with it.

～

The houseboy brought in the food and Bhola attacked it. It was hard for me to sit and watch the way he gobbled it down. 'Why don't you eat? In the meantime, I'll take care of some important paperwork,' I said and stood up.

Bhola did not even look in my direction. He waved his right hand in the air as if to say, 'Go ahead and do your work.'

I went into the office and called for Dakkhilal. 'Look, feed him until he's full,' I said. 'Make sure there's plenty of everything.'

'Sir, that crazy ... gentleman—' he said, most certainly adding the word 'gentleman' to 'crazy' for my benefit—'wanders around Chowk and Civil Lines all day every day, that's why I didn't let him come in here!'

'When did you see him?'

'Sir, I see him every day. When I go to take letters and paperwork to the Deputy Sahib I see him. He wanders around all day long. He never sits down. He never gets tired. He's completely insane.'

'Well go on and feed him anyway. Stand near him. If he asks for anything bring it to him.'

When the houseboy had gone away, I pulled some files in front of me, trying to push Bhola from my mind. But I must have taken care of only three or four files when my mind returned to that room, that verandah and that balcony on Mall Road.

≈

One day, we had grown bored from sitting in the room since morning. A little before evening we went out and sat on the balcony with our books. But perhaps we were tired of reading. We started chatting. Nowadays, people are selected for the I.C.S. in the very first competition, but it was nothing like that then. There was no shortage of competitors who sat for the competition three times and ruined their eyes with studying, but never met with success. Bhola told me that he had two more chances—his father had had the foresight to enter his age as two years less than it actually was—and because of his previous ranking he had got an offer for a job as an Executive Officer. He thought he would accept it after taking the exam. If he got into the I.C.S. he would quit the job; if he did not get in, he would continue to enter the competition until he turned thirty. He would definitely be made an I.C.S. officer at some point while working there.

I was astonished by his self-confidence. I secretly decided I would do the same thing. If Bhola had not told me that secret of success I would have grown discouraged. In the end, I got in only after taking the exam five times. But at that moment, when he shared his secret with me, I laughed and said, 'If the government knows what's good for them, they'll just keep quiet and take you this time.'

'But the government isn't that smart,' he replied.

And we both chuckled.

'If I get into the I.C.S. just once,' he said, 'no one can stop me from going into the Executive Council. And if India ever gets Independence, I'll live to see the day I am made an ambassador. You wait and see.'

I sat and gazed at him, astonished. I felt sure he would be made an ambassador.

I had been living there for a month or a month and a half. During that time I noticed that, after working tirelessly for several days, Bhola would sometimes disappear in the evening without telling me where he was going, and then return home rather late at night, and get back to his work with renewed zeal. I asked him where he went, but he tried to put me off. When I insisted he tell me and assured him that I knew how to hide my friends' secrets in a deep well where the outside air would never reach them, he said abruptly, 'I went to a whorehouse.'

For an instant I was struck speechless. I felt I must have heard something wrong. 'Do you mean a brothel?' I asked.

'Yes, yes!'

'What have you gotten yourself into?' I asked. 'If you get the clap, my friend, you can kiss both your P.C.S. and I.C.S. goodbye.'

'I've taken care of that.' And he proceeded to enhance my

knowledge on the subject, explaining that science had made great advances in that area.

'But have you abandoned your vow of being made an I.C.S. officer one day?' I asked.

'That's the reason I'm doing all this.'

'What do you mean?'

'What I mean is: I was unable to concentrate continuously for a number of days; my eyes would be on a book but my mind would run off and wander all around. I couldn't sleep at night. Then I decided to get at the root of my restlessness. One should always have some kind of a safety valve. I can't get married, and such is the state of our society, we can't even get near the shadow of a girl. So, when it became impossible in every way to keep my mind on my work, I got up and went there, and then I came back.'

I had got out of bed, wrapped the quilt around me and sat down on the charpoy to listen to what he was saying. When I heard his reply I laughed and said, 'You say, "I went there and then I came back," as if you just went to use the toilet and then came back.'

'That's about how I see it.'

Then he changed his clothes, turned out the electric lights, lit the table lamp on the teapoy next to the head of his bed and lay down with a book.

∾

'Where did that pig Dakkhilal go! Get someone to bring me more bread and vegetables.'

I looked up. Bhola had come into the office, his hands smeared with food. I pressed the bell angrily, all the while wondering how he had remembered Dakkhilal's name after hearing it only once. The houseboy who was sitting outside the office came running in.

'Look, where did that lazy boy Dakkhilal go?' I thundered. 'I told him to feed the gentleman and not to go anywhere.'

'Sir . . .' the other houseboy glanced at Bhola in his old tattered clothing, his gaze travelling to Bhola's filthy hands.

I stood up, even angrier. I rushed inside with my hand on Bhola's shoulder, sat him down on the couch and then went behind the bungalow to call for Dakkhilal. I scolded him, asking where he had he run off to when he had been told to feed the gentleman. He started to say something about Rani Ma calling for him, but I refused to listen and ordered him to bring the gentleman more bread and vegetables and not to take them away until he had eaten his fill.

After I had given my orders to the houseboy and patted Bhola on the shoulder, telling him that the food was about to arrive, I went back into my office and sat down. For a few minutes I worked quite diligently. But then my mind started to wander about, drumming up memories of those days spent with Bhola.

≈

When Bhola had first told me about his 'safety valve' I had laughed at his foolishness. 'When that idiot gets the clap and starts boo-hooing over his wounds, he'll figure out the meaning of safety valve,' I said to myself. Bhola had gone to sleep after reading for a while, but I kept thinking about him for the rest of the night, and for the first time I was happy I had married a little sooner than usual and did not have to deal with such a situation. After I fell asleep, I dreamt that Bhola was ill, his nose was runny, his body was covered in sores—and then I saw him, a leper, sitting on a railway bridge, begging—but when I opened my eyes I found I was not sleeping, I was watching all this wide awake.

But when Bhola disappeared again a week later and, on his return, began to recount his exploits, I began to feel quite excited about his adventures; I begged him to take me with him next time, no matter what.

At first he tried to put me off, but when I insisted, he gave in. 'Put fifteen or twenty rupees in your pocket,' he said. 'Let's go.'

'Let's go.' He said it like a true degenerate—one who has spent his entire life trekking across that particular desert— even though there was no way of telling from his face that he had ever been there.

'I'll bring some money, but I just want to take a look,' I said.

'There's hardly a show on there,' he laughed. 'I go when I'm anxious; the exam is coming up soon.'

But when I again expressed great interest, Bhola agreed to take me to see it all the very next day.

'But you'll have to act as though you always go to such places,' he said. 'If they figure out you're just a spectator, not a participant, they won't even talk to us.'

'Don't you worry about that,' I said, 'I won three drama prizes in college. I'll put on such an act, they won't be the least bit suspicious.'

The next evening, I tossed an overcoat over my shalwar kameez, pulled on a nightcap, loafer style, and set off with Bhola. I left behind whatever money I had in the trunk, so I wouldn't have any money on me and wouldn't feel tempted. But I didn't tell Bhola.

First we went to a hotel on Beadon Road. Bhola was familiar with the hotel—so even I couldn't hear what he asked for under his breath when he went to the counter. In response to whatever it was he had said, the butler took us inside to a room with two beds made up in it, and said, 'This room is ready right now.'

'What did you say to him?' I asked, when the butler had gone away.

'I asked him if we could get any goods here, or what.'

'What does "goods" mean? Did he get what you meant?'

'Yes, they understand everything in Indian hotels. If it's an English hotel you ask if there are any "game girls" or not.'

Just then the door opened. Bhola said, 'Look, just make sure they have no idea we're only here as spectators.'

'Don't you worry about that, we'll just take a look, then go,' I said, just to say something, but my heart was beating fast. I did my best to hide any sign of my anxiety.

The butler entered with a girl. The girl was not really a girl, she was a woman, full-breasted. She was fair and ripe, a healthy woman with a beautiful body. She must have been about thirty—she was only two inches taller than Bhola and about the same height as me. Everything about her was fine, but she squinted slightly and that one flaw destroyed all her beauty.

The butler left her in the room and went away. For a moment, the room was shadowed by silence.

And during that one moment, I suddenly wondered, 'Why did I come here? What right do I have to sit here looking at this girl and judging her beauty this way? It's true I don't have any sisters; my wife is sitting at home enduring the pangs of separation while she waits for me to become an I.C.S. officer. She's more beautiful than this squinty girl. But this girl is also someone's sister or wife. Who knows why she was reduced to working at this hotel?'

Then Bhola asked her softly, 'What's your name?' Quickly I recollected my duty.

'Rose!' replied the young lady, pretending to be a little bashful and turning her squinty gaze to the floor.

After that Bhola could not think of what to say. Or perhaps he was thrown into a quandary. The girl lifted her eyes to me, and, a little startled, I managed somehow to gaze at her lustfully—I smiled and recited a couplet:

Roses don't bloom dry on my lover, only
when she becomes a rose does her body smile

'Wah!' The girl's forced modesty turned to a bold smile. She lifted her squinty eyes to me and thanked me for the couplet.

Just then the butler came back and raised his eyebrows in query. Before Bhola could say anything, I motioned to Rose to go outside.

When she was gone I went up to the butler, pulled my hat forward a little more and winked at him, saying, 'Yaar, you could've given a little thought to the difference in age between her and us. Bring us something fresh. What kind of a washed-up hen was that?'

'Right now she's the only one,' responded the butler, a little shortly.

'Okay, so we'll come again. Bye bye,' I waved and I took off, as if I had not come with Bhola, Bhola had come with me.

When we got outside, Bhola said, 'But yaar, the goods were nice.'

'Forget it!' I said with revulsion. 'I was suffocating in that place.'

'But you didn't look at all bored,' Bhola said. 'You put on such an act it was like you'd been playing this game for years.'

'It was an act, that's all, all I really wanted to do was get up quietly and leave. Come on, let's go home now.'

But perhaps Bhola's appetite had been whetted now that he had seen the meal. He said, 'No, no, come on, I'll show you the Grand Hotel.'

'I've seen it before. I've had enough.'

But Bhola's desire had grown stronger. The more I insisted on going home, the more he begged to go to the Grand Hotel. 'You don't have to do anything, you can just watch,' he said, and then with some irritation he added, 'First you insist on coming and now, like a child, you start whining to hurry up and go home. If you're just scared of going to hotels, there are dozens of whorehouses around here.' My enthusiasm had completely subsided, but I was the one who had rooted Bhola out to come here, so it seemed wrong to leave him and go home. I set off with him towards Station Road. I told him he could do whatever he wanted, I would just sit quietly.

'Oh come on, you can come too,' he said. 'When the time comes, I'll send you out of the room. I didn't even say anything back there. Just watch this time! I don't know any couplets, but . . .' and he winked.

But my mind was wandering off on rugged paths. I wasn't listening to what Bhola was saying. After walking about two miles, during which it was only Bhola who spoke most of the time, we arrived at the Grand Hotel. It was about a quarter past nine. The building was quite splendid—the words 'Grand Hotel' were written on crescent-shaped signboards over both gates. Since the bar was closed by now, there was not much light outside and the splendour of the building was all the greater in the semi-darkness. I would never have had the courage to go there by day, let alone at night, but Bhola had already been there once or twice before. He went forward and spoke with a man who looked like a chauffeur, wearing a khaki uniform and a nightcap like mine. Later, we found out he was the hotel's guide. He took us directly from the outside of the hotel into a room where he told us to take a seat, and then he left through an inside door.

The room was not very large. There were two bare beds in it, one dressing table and nothing else except two easy chairs. I was a little tired by then from walking two or three miles, so I sank into an armchair. Bhola sat down on a bed frame.

The next instant, the guide sent in a beautiful plump girl of medium height. She came and stood next to the bed.

I began to wonder how such a beautiful girl had come to be there. But Bhola held her by the arm and sat her down on the edge of the bed next to him. He took her in his arms and asked her name, since that was how he had learnt to start such conversations from his friends who had first taken him down this path.

I don't remember what name the girl told him. I was looking at her face, big and round like the moon, which shone with a strange sort of innocence. She did not seem an actress on this stage at all. She shrank against Bhola in such a bashful manner as she told him her name that the man in him suddenly awoke. All the way there he had been swearing to me that he would tease and flirt a little with the Grand Hotel lovelies and then we could go home; but the next moment, when the hotel guide returned, the girl slid away from Bhola and he, instead of making some excuse to leave, asked with a good deal of enthusiasm, 'How much for a shot?'

'Ten rupees.'

'What are you saying, I come here every day.'

'But take a look at the goods.'

Bhola searched around in his pockets. He must not have had enough money, so he curbed his enthusiasm a little and said, 'Give it to me straight, yaar; no, let's go.'

The guide was a thin, attractive man of medium height. He had a nose like a vulture's beak, and a vulture-like cruelty gleamed in his eyes. He gazed at Bhola narrowly for a moment and the next instant the matter was settled at five rupees.

'Come on Bakhshi,' Bhola said as he followed the guide out of the room.

I got up. All this had happened so fast I was neither able to say anything to Bhola nor could I think of anything to say for myself. I quietly got up to follow him.

But the guide stretched himself across the doorway, blocking my path. 'Why don't you just stay right there!' he said, rather harshly. 'I'm going to bring you even more fantastic goods than her.'

I stopped where I was. On the other side of the door was the great hall of the hotel, with couches and teapoys lined up against three walls and a square space left clear in the middle for dances and balls. To the left, that is, along the back wall, was the bar. It was way past nine, so there were only a couple of lights on in the hall. A door in the back wall led inside to the hotel. The guide had taken Bhola and the beautiful girl through it—perhaps to some other room—and had come back. Another girl was coming out right behind him now. Involuntarily I stepped back and went and sat in Bhola's place on the cot.

The guide left the girl in the room and went away: She was skinny and worn out and looked as though she had come directly from Tibbi Gali, the red-light district.

For a few moments I sat there looking at her quietly. I began to feel intensely disgusted. I had no means of judging what I should do any more. The grandeur of the hotel, my fear of the animal gleam in the eyes of the guide—whose face alone made him look a thug—and the knowledge that my pockets were empty, dominated my thoughts excessively. I asked her the same question as before, without even thinking:

'What's your name?'

'Mukhtar,' she said.

I laughed foolishly, as a pun on her name, which could mean 'secretary', occurred to me. 'Secretary for Water and Dry Land, or for the Heart and Soul?'

'Whichever you prefer!'

And before I could respond in any way, she smiled and sat down next to me. If my pockets had been full and if I had been a regular visitor to such establishments, I would have stood up, grabbed her by the arm and pushed her out of the room. Then I would have called the guide, scolded him and taken off. But I had never been there before, my pockets were completely empty and I was totally overwhelmed by the guide's domineering manner, so I sat glued to my seat. I wondered what I had gotten myself into: I should have gone home directly from the hotel on Beadon Road. I looked a bit dejected by then, but I kept smiling and my hand, of its own accord, touched her shoulder.

I tried to think of a suitable couplet for the occasion. But no matter how hard I tried, I could not recall a single one. I was so nervous that, instead of saying anything, I let my hand slide down, a little below her shoulder, and pressed her arm slightly.

And then, rather than shrinking from me, she threw herself

on top of me, as though she had been waiting for exactly this. Her head dropped on to my shoulder and I felt the unfamiliar touch of her lips in the hollow of my neck.

Before I could jump up, the guide returned. His entrance accompanied the return of my senses. I got up and told Mukhtar to go outside, and then I repeated what I had said at the Beadon Road Hotel, with a few added embellishments.

The guide did not say, 'She's the only one here right now,' or 'I'll show you a different one right away,' or anything like that. He looked at me with a gaze so crooked and disdainful it pierced right through my façade to the core. Perhaps his experienced eyes had ascertained the true situation: 'Why don't you sit outside!' The suggestion may as well have been a command—he walked to the door and motioned towards a couch in the hall.

I felt revived and went and sank into the couch with a sigh of relief.

I assumed Bhola would not come back for some time, so I stretched my legs out on the couch, pulled my hat down over my ears and reclined almost to the point of lying down. My mind began to wander as I thought about the room where Bhola was closed up with that innocent-looking girl.

But I could not have been lying there for more than five minutes when Bhola reappeared, coming from an inside door.

'What happened!' I exclaimed, standing up in confusion.

'That's it, let's go.'

'You finished that quickly?'

'What else! She knew I had only paid five rupees, the bitch didn't let me put my hand anywhere else!'

I cast a sympathetic glance at Bhola and followed him out of the great hall. Just then a car pulled up in front of the porch. After we had gone some distance, I turned and looked behind me. That same innocent-looking girl had rewrapped her sari, just as a hen ruffles her feathers to tidy up after a roll in the dirt, and was now standing in the verandah outside the great hall with the guide, who was settling a price with a passenger standing next to the car.

~

'Sir, that—he's calling for you.'

The houseboy had hesitated after the word 'that'. Perhaps he had been about to use the word 'crazy', but then had tried to finish the sentence some other way.

I went into the drawing room. Bhola had finished eating and was sitting up, wiping off his hands on his coat and pants. I looked angrily at the houseboy.

'Sir, I told him to come with me so I could show him where the washbasin was, but . . .'

'Oh come on, yaar, forget all this hand-washing business,' Bhola said. 'Can't you give me any of your shirts or trousers? This stuff is all ripped up.'

He got up and started wandering around the room. I turned to the houseboy, 'Go on, go inside and tell them to send out a shirt and trousers of mine to give to this gentleman.'

The houseboy was turning away when I added, 'Listen, don't bring anything old or torn. Bring something that still has some wear in it.'

When the houseboy was gone, I asked Bhola, 'Tell me, my friend, do you remember that whore at the Grand Hotel at all?'

Bhola hesitated. For a moment it seemed as though he had travelled somewhere far away. His face was completely devoid of emotion. Then, slowly, the light returned; suddenly his eyes shone.

'You're talking about Shehnaz?'

'I've forgotten the name, but you must remember—one night you took me to the Grand Hotel.'

Bhola's eyes began to sparkle even more. He said, 'Yes, yes, that evening when we met that squinty girl Rose in the hotel on Beadon Road first, and then we went to the Grand Hotel.'

'Yes, yes!'

'She is the bitch who ruined me.'

'How?'

Bhola sat down in front of me. He stretched his legs out on the rug and said:

'You probably remember how the first day we went she took care of me in just two minutes. That really got to me. She seemed so beautiful and innocent—I started having trouble thinking about anything else after that. I thought she'd given me so little time because I hadn't paid very much for her. But the second time, when I gave her ten rupees for an hour, I lay next to her the entire time, but she didn't let me touch her even once and, when the time came to do it, it was just two minutes again!

'Then I thought maybe the reason for the distance between us was the scientific aid I was using to avoid getting the clap. It's only the thinnest rubber membrane, but how can you really satisfy your craving for rice if you eat it with a spoon— even if you eat enough to fill you up! So I gave it up. But she wasn't a girl from a good family, of course—she was an "evil spirit of Tibbi Gali" . . . it was all a part of her profession. I sank so low trying to get her to acknowledge my masculinity! I read every page in the book of Tibbi Gali . . . but I never returned—I stayed below.'

There was such a wilful gleam in Bhola's eyes; I stared at him, transfixed.

'Are you thinking I must be crazy?' he asked suddenly, with a careless laugh.

'No . . . I . . . I . . .' I did not know what to say.

'Do I seem as though I'm in my right mind?' he guffawed loudly. Then he said, 'I'm crazy and there's no cure for me. I've come here by way of Bareilly and Agra. They told me I was fine and let me go, but I know the sickness can never pass from my blood.'

I had no idea what had got into him. He spoke so intelligently that I suddenly found it all quite difficult to believe.

Just then the houseboy brought in the clothing.

Bhola threw it carelessly over his arm and got up to go.

I wrung my hands and said, more to myself than to him, 'But, my friend, you had such ambitions, how did you do this to yourself? You were going to be an ambassador!'

'But I am an ambassador! God has made me his representative and sent me here. I roam around all day and send God the news from here.'

And he turned and went outside. He did not even deem it necessary to thank me or shake my hand as he went.

The Bed

Keshi abruptly looked up from his newly wedded wife's eyes to the cushioned bedstead, in which was framed a round miniature portrait of his mother: she was a lovely woman with sharp features, large eyes and curling lashes. A smile hovered on her slightly parted lips, revealing a row of pearl-white teeth. Suddenly, the outline of his mother's face was filled in with that of his new bride: how closely the two women resembled one another! Keshi's mind grew hazy; a shiver ran through his body. He jerked his head back and tried to take his eyes off the picture. It was to no avail. Until a few years ago, he had lain on his mother's bosom just as he was lying on his wife's at this moment. The memories of those years came flooding back into his mind. Instead of kissing his bride's almond eyes and hungry lips, he slid off her body and lay next to her as though utterly exhausted. He stared at the long strings of jasmine buds that hung like a canopy over his head. His hand fell on the jasmine petals that were spread like a thick carpet over the sheet. He wanted to leap from this floral bed and break out of the fragrant nuptial room in which he found himself imprisoned.

Keshi did not jump off the bed. He lay where he was, still and silent. What would his bride think? It was that fear which kept him on the bed. He shook his head again, even more violently than before. But instead of ridding his mind of the picture of his mother, his head was besieged with myriad incidents that gathered round him like monsoon clouds . . .

~

In this same room, on this same bed, his father and mother are lying side by side; he is lying on the cot in the verandah, staring at them intently. How small, how beautiful his mother looks, lying next to his father.

His mother is doing her hair in front of the mirror. He stares at her from behind the door. She is as beautiful as the fairies that his ayah tells of in her stories. Seeing his reflection in the mirror, his mother asks him to come to her. He goes and buries his face in her lap. She ruffles his hair with one hand and continues to comb her own with the other.

What's wrong with Papa? A man comes to see him every day. He has a pair of snakes with one head that hang around his neck. He puts the tails of the serpents in his ears and touches Papa's chest with their head. Then he sticks long needles into Papa's arm. Papa does not cry, but Keshi begins to howl. His mother clasps him to her bosom and takes him to the next room.

~

Papa is lying on the floor. He does not move. Everyone is crying. His mother is crying; she kisses him and continues to cry. Women help his mother break all her bangles and then wipe off the vermilion in the parting of her hair. They drag Keshi out of her lap. He shrieks and howls, but no one bothers to comfort him.

~

It is the same bed. He is lying in his Papa's place. His mother is beside him. She is dressed in a plain white sari. The morning sun is peeping into the room, but she sleeps on without a care in the world. He stares at her face. Her features are truly as delicate as a fairy's. Her eyes are closed, her hair is scattered about her shoulders. She is like the princess who was woken out of a deep sleep by Prince Charming. He edges towards her and kisses her once on the cheek. His mother wakes up. She stretches out her arms and holds him to her bosom and kisses his forehead, his eyes, his lips.

≈

He lies with his head on his mother's bosom. She is telling him the story of the prince who crossed the seven seas to marry the princess. She finishes the story and asks him, 'Will you marry a princess like that too?'

'I will marry you.'

'Silly boy! Do sons ever marry their mothers?'

She assures him that she will find him a bride just like herself.

'And I'll have this bed too,' he says, looking at his mother's beautiful portrait in the headrest.

'Yes, of course! This bed will be my wedding present to you and your bride.'

And she clasps him to her bosom.

≈

'What's the matter? Aren't you feeling well?' Suddenly his bride turned over, felt his forehead and ran her fingers through his hair.

'It's nothing at all.' Keshi shook his head to break the chain of memories and laughed; it was the kind of laugh that seemed like a long sigh.

His mother had been true to her word. The bride whom she had chosen for him was an exact image of herself: slender and beautiful. Her eyes were large, her features sharp, her lips soft and her teeth glistened like a row of pearls. Even though a large bed had been sent with the dowry, his mother had fulfilled the promise she'd made years ago and laid out her own precious bed for the consummation of his marriage. And not just the bed, she'd even given up her own bedroom for the bride.

The bride was bending over him, gazing deeply into his eyes to see if she could find out why his ardour had cooled so suddenly. But she had no way of getting closer to the truth. Bending over him slightly, she caressed his hair with hesitant love.

For a while Keshi lay still; then he suddenly put his arms around his bride's neck and drew her close to him. For a long time he stroked her hair, her cheeks and her lips, holding her head to his chest, until the cobwebs were swept out of his mind, and the warmth of his bride's soft, fair body, lying against him, poured into his veins. He kissed her softly, laid her beside him and lay down with his face buried in her warm breasts. Again and again he felt he should lift up his head and make love to his wife, but he could not bring himself to face the picture. Without raising his head, he picked up the pillow with his left hand and tried to push it in front of the picture. Then he looked up. It seemed as though the picture had grown even bolder now that it was hidden behind the pillow, and the features of some other face began to replace those of his bride's face. 'No, no, no,' he cried out to himself in frustration and again slid off her and lay flat on his back. Then a whirlwind kicked up in his mind. He jumped up and left the bridal chamber.

The spring full moon was bashfully peering into the verandah through the venetian blinds. For an instant he stopped in the arch of the verandah and quietly stared at the moonbeams playing on the lawn. The touch of the cool breeze soothed his overwrought nerves. But instead of turning back, he went outside. Phlox and verbena bloomed in the flower beds to the right; the dahlias ahead of him swayed in the breeze, heavy with the weight of their blossoms. Beyond the neatly pruned hedge of henna that bordered the lawn, the marigolds bloomed in their bed, and the heaps of nasturtium blossoms planted round the base of the rambler rose were bathed in moonlight. Keshi wandered along between the rows of flowers without thinking, bending over and looking at their colours, touching them carelessly. These flowers that dazzled the eyes with their gaudy colours in daylight now seemed comforting and peaceful in the cold moonlight, like a balm for strained nerves. The bright yellows and pinks had turned pale white, and the deep crimsons, blues and the mauves were repainted in sombre hues. Keshi stopped by the cottage wall where the jasmine blossomed. In the dark shadow of the wall, the jasmine flowers gleamed like petalled pearls. Earlier, whenever he saw jasmine blooming on moonlit nights, it had always reminded him of a line from a song he had read or heard somewhere and he'd start humming:

After many days, at last
The jasmine has blossomed
My courtyard is filled with fragrance,
A heavenly fragrance

But now that his courtyard actually was fragrant, he had completely forgotten that song. Keshi kept walking stiffly back and forth between the cottage and the gate. When he was walking back to the cottage for the second time, he noticed a light in the window of the corner room. His mother had obviously not gone to bed. Perhaps his aunt and other female relations were also awake, discussing him and his bride. What infinite pains his mother had taken in decorating his nuptial bed! The women had cleared the dining room of table and chairs and adorned it to receive the bride. They had carried out all the ceremonies for receiving the new bride, lifting her veil with infinite care. While he sat amongst his friends in the drawing room, they not only rearranged the wedding presents and the furniture which had been received as part of the dowry in his own, adjacent, room, but also decorated his mother's bedroom for the wedding night. The innumerable guests and the hundreds of odds and ends to attend to had given his mother little time for sleep. He had seen her going constantly in and out of her bedroom with his aunt and a young woman who was a distant cousin of his mother's, busy in her task of beautifying the bridal suite. There was no limit to his mother's enthusiasm. It seemed that the sleepless nights, the running about and the endless bother about everything were, in fact, all centred on the embellishment of that one room. Several times he had gone into the room on some pretext or the other to see what his mother and aunt were up to, but each time they had hustled him out; even a casual glance at the bedroom was forbidden until that night.

Keshi's eyes often settled on his mother while he was talking to his friends during the wedding ceremonies, or listening to the women's banter. She was nearing forty, and her twenty-two years of widowhood had hardened her expression and etched dark rings around her eyes, but the wedding of her only child seemed to have wrought a miracle in her. She looked exquisite in her white sari; to Keshi she was the most beautiful of all the women there. The circles around her eyes had magically vanished. She kept slipping out to decorate the bridal chamber in the midst of carrying out the ceremonies and looking after the guests. Not a trace of fatigue showed on her face.

Keshi feared that the fatigue and the sleepless nights would

make his mother ill. Every night before he retired he would go
to her and plead, 'Ma, go to bed now!' But far from going to
sleep herself, she would instead come to his bed and gently rub
oil on his temples and brow until he fell asleep. Then she
would go back to her work.

Keshi had formed a habit of having oil rubbed into his scalp.
During his examinations, when he stayed up all night and
wanted a couple of hours of sleep during the day, his mother
would rub oil on his head. Even then, Keshi, unable to stop
gazing at her, would refuse to fall asleep. His mother would
press the palms of her hands on his eyes, close them and kiss
them. Then she would run her fingers lightly across his forehead,
their soft silken touch laden with a love that gradually made
his lids heavy with sleep, and at last he would fall into a deep
slumber.

Keshi had learnt this art from her. Whenever his mother had
insomnia because she was tired or worried, he would sit by her
pillow and softly rub oil on her temples and eyebrows until she
fell asleep. When he was younger, thirteen or fourteen, his
mother would often pull his head toward her and kiss him on
the lips. When he grew older and got his bachelor's and then
his master's degree, and was appointed lecturer in psychology
at the university, his mother started kissing his forehead instead
of his lips.

~

All through the festivities, Keshi wished he could rescue his
mother from the crowd of women who had come to the
wedding, bodily lift her up and force her to go to bed. But there
she was, as busy as ever, weaving garlands around the nuptial
bed. When the flowers ran out, she sent people all over town to
bring back more. She squandered money as if it had no value.
He wanted to say to her, 'Ma, why all this trouble at the
expense of your health? Your love means more to me than

these ceremonial festivities, more than all these festoons and decorations. You mean more to me than such things. You'll make yourself ill!' But he knew she'd pay no heed to what he said.

'Son, my wedding just sort of happened, that was all,' she'd told him when he tried to protest. 'Your father was only a low-paid clerk; he hadn't yet taken the exam for government service. I don't want your bride to have any regrets. I didn't even get an armlet of flowers. You just wait and see how I'll decorate the nuptial bed for your bride!'

His aunt had pushed him on to the nuptial bed and said with a laugh, 'Now, make sure you don't waste any of your time expounding philosophy.' It took him some time to catch her insinuation.

He'd known this room for a long time and was familiar with everything in it, the bed and the rest of the furniture. His mother's dressing table had been left just as it had always been, her vanity case, her papier mâché bangle box, her table lamp, for which she'd paid a tidy sum in Bombay. What made it look brighter were the garlands of jasmine buds, the first of the season. They were hung in long strings around the canopy frame like a floral mosquito net. They were also spread thick over the bed and his bride lay across them on the virginal white sheet, a flower goddess, her face half-covered by her veil.

Keshi imagined the scene of his mother's wedding. She had been the bride of a low-grade clerk in the canal department. It must have been a hovel, on a coarse stringed charpoy, in the dim light of a hurricane lantern. It all seemed so hazy and dream-like. Later, his father had risen to the post of Executive Engineer and then his mother got everything she'd wanted, but she never forgot the disappointment of her wedding night. She'd adorned her son's nuptial bed as she would have liked her own to have been; she'd fulfilled her desire. But those same decorations had made trouble for Keshi. No matter where he turned his gaze, old images took form before his eyes.

'Make sure you don't waste any of your time expounding philosophy.' His aunt's words and her laughter echoed in his brain . . . Was he caught in a web of his own making? What must his bride be thinking? Several incidents swam before his eyes, in which the man's weakness on the first night had taken a couple's married life down with it. But was it necessary for a man to prove his manhood on the very first night of his marriage? Why do these women get so worked up about this? Didn't every single one of them relive her own wedding night by preparing others for their wedding nights? As had his mother as well—the way she worked so hard decorating the wedding chamber; putting her bed there; decorating it with flowers the way she'd hoped her own wedding bed would look, but which hadn't because of his father's poverty and absentmindedness . . .

Keshi shook his head. What was wrong with him? Why had he said, 'I want this bed'? But he was only a child then; perhaps his mother had been as well.

He had come back onto the verandah. Suddenly he saw his bride standing under the arch.

'Are you not feeling well?'

'No, I'm fine.'

'Did I do something wrong?'

Keshi wanted to burst out laughing loudly. Even his wife was thinking of only one thing. He put his arm around her waist and led her indoors. He decided to lay aside his complex and do what was expected of him. He pushed his bride on the bed a little roughly. He pulled the buttons of her blouse open. He leaned over her, but his bride had put the pillow back in its place: once more Keshi's eyes fell on his mother's picture, once more his thoughts grew hazy. He stood up. He turned to go outside when his bride grabbed his hand.

'What's the matter?'

Keshi glanced towards the door. How much easier it would have been if his mother had decorated his room instead of her own! His room was now stacked with furniture received as dowry and other odds and ends collected for the wedding. He didn't even have the key to his room. Keshi cast a dispirited glance towards the verandah. Moonbeams cascaded through the venetian blinds of the verandah. He exclaimed, 'Look how lovely it is in the moonlight! Let's take a stroll outside.'

The bride got up and readjusted her clothing. She took a quick glance in the mirror, tidied her hair, pulled her veil over her forehead and followed her husband.

They strolled up to the gate and back to the verandah twice, without speaking to each other. Once or twice the bride tried to say something in praise of the moonlight, but Keshi made no reply; the two continued to walk in silence.

The heady spring moonlight did not change their mood. The bride was perplexed by her groom's extraordinary behaviour. From her girlfriends, some of whom were now mothers, she had heard of what happens between newly married couples on the first night. Her husband had started off in the same way and then suddenly changed his mind. She had heard people praise his good looks, his learning and his gentleness. He was a lecturer at the university. Her father had made inquiries about him not only from his fellow lecturers, but also from the students, and had only finalized the marriage negotiations after he was fully satisfied. No one had suggested that the boy was eccentric or slightly unhinged. Yet when she thought of him and his efforts to make love to her, her future looked extremely bleak to her. Glancing furtively at him, she continued to walk beside him, barely noticing the lovely moonlight.

And Keshi felt as though he was stuck in a swamp—he couldn't find any way out of his dilemma. He continued his monotonous pacing with his hands clasped behind him, as if they were chained together. When they came to the gate again he spoke brusquely, 'Come on, let's go out for a while.'

'It's rather late,' she protested gently.

Keshi recalled that one of his friends, when telling him about an amorous liaison, had remarked that the lane between the water tank and the Grand Trunk Road was lonely and shaded, an ideal place for lovers.

'Only as far as the water tank,' he pleaded.

He opened the gate. His bride followed him in trusting silence. Keshi began to explain the landscape: it had once been an exclusive residential area for the senior English officials of the railway; after Independence the bungalows had been taken over by the Indians. When they passed by the flour mill, he explained to her how wheat and corn are ground. At the cold storage plant he recounted how forty thousand maunds of potatoes could be stored there, to be marketed out of season. When they came to the press building, he peered through the window panes and loudly began to explain the miracle of the rotary machine: how a blank sheet went in at one end, and emerged at the other as a newspaper. He was heading for the railway station when he recalled what his friend had said about the lane connecting the water tank and the Grand Trunk Road. They turned towards the gate of the railway crossing. It was closed. Keshi saw the red light and explained, 'This gate is an awful nuisance. There's always some train or the other passing through, twenty-four hours a day. The station's gotten so big, but no one's bothered with this gate. If they put a bridge over here it would avoid many accidents.'

There was still some time before the train would come. They crossed the line by the side gate and came to the water tank. The road on the right hand was open and well lit, the one on the left was dark. When Keshi turned towards the dark one, his wife protested, 'Let's go home; it's very late.' But Keshi put his right arm round her waist. 'Just a little farther,' he coaxed. 'See how the moon shines through the branches!'

'Why not the other side? It's a wide open road.'

'Are you scared?' he mocked gently, bending over to kiss her forehead.

The girl shook herself free in embarrassment, 'What are you doing . . . right in the road . . .?'

Keshi laughed. Once more he put his arm around her waist and exclaimed, 'Who on earth will see us here at this time of the night!' Again he bent over to kiss her, but before he could do so, the headlights of a vehicle caught him in their glare; a truck roared past them. They had barely got the glare of the lights out of their eyes, when another truck came along, followed by a whole convoy of trucks. 'Lonely, quiet road indeed!' muttered Keshi to himself. The romantic mood vanished.

'Let's go back,' pleaded his bride in a tearful voice. 'I'm tired.'

'This is the main road, trucks and cars run at all hours of the day and night,' explained Keshi. 'Let's go to M.T. Lines. The road up to the church should be quite deserted.'

'I'm very tired,' she begged.

He took her firmly by the waist and led her towards the open road leading to the Military Training Lines.

The bungalows on either side of the road were bathed in moonlight, strangely still, as if taken by surprise. Beneath the trees, the patterns of light and shade formed a web-like design. Just then there was a light breeze full of fragrance. Keshi tried to guess where the Queen of the Night was blooming, smiling in its rivalry with the moonlight, and spreading its fragrance into the atmosphere with its every breath. He twined his arm round his wife's waist and guided her to the shade of the trees.

'Are you very tired?' he asked.

She didn't answer, but instead put her head against her husband's chest. He drew her face to his and kissed her on the lips.

A beam of torchlight flashed from across the road; the couple sprang apart. Keshi went pale; his heart began to beat rapidly. He remembered that no one was allowed to come to the M.T. Lines after midnight.

A group of soldiers in olive green uniforms came by singing a song from the latest film they had seen:

Whether you're the full moon, or the sun
Whichever one, I swear by God
You're matchless in your beauty

Despite the moonlight, they flashed the light of their torch on the couple.

Keshi had wanted to take his bride in his arms, look into her eyes and repeat the opening lines of the song:

Whether you're the full moon, or the sun . . .

But the bad manners of the soldiers quelled his surge of romantic feeling. He remembered an incident involving a friend and his sister who had come to dine at a bungalow in the M.T. Lines. They hadn't realized how late it was and were unable to find a rickshaw. When they were walking home at half past twelve, they were stopped by soldiers. They had to go back to their hosts to prove they were brother and sister.

Before his bride could say anything about going back, Keshi turned his steps towards home. When the soldiers had flashed the torch on his bride's face, Keshi had felt roused to such a temper that he wanted to get one of the fellows by the collar and slap him on the face. But if there'd been a scene and if anyone had asked what the lecturer and his bride were doing at that late hour in a deserted lane, what could he have replied? Instead, all his anger boiled up at his mother, at the bed she had given him and at his own impotence.

He walked back at a brisk pace; his bride followed, dragging her feet, a few steps behind him. He slowed down when he entered through the gate. The girl, clearly annoyed, went ahead at a quickened pace, straight to the bedroom and threw herself on the bed. When Keshi came in, he saw her lying on the nuptial bed, her feet dangling over the edge, with one end of her sari trailing on the floor and her low-cut blouse revealing the contours of her soft, warm breasts. He wanted to go down on his knees and put his head in her lap. But once again—and without any volition on his part—his eyes travelled from his bride to his mother's portrait.

He stood in the centre of the room, lost in thought. The girl stared at the ceiling, her eyes brimming with tears. Keshi glanced at the door to his room. 'Isn't that door locked from the outside?'

'Yes,' she replied, her gaze still fixed on the ceiling.

Keshi walked around the room twice. 'Where's the key?'

'Probably with Auntie; she had all the furniture put inside.'

Keshi went out to the other end of the house. The light in his mother's bedroom had been switched off. The other women had obviously gone to sleep too. Should he wake up his mother? If his aunt happened to wake up too, she would make fun of him. He came back and walked about the bedroom for a while. He stole a glance at his bride. She was still gazing stonily at the ceiling. He went to the door of his own room and put his shoulder against it. The bottom latch was firm and would not yield. His mother always used the bottom latch. If it had been the upper latch, he could have smashed the glass pane on the top of the door and undone the bolt.

He stepped back and examined the door. Both sides had three panes of glass each and some woodwork. If he broke the third pane he could reach his hand to the bottom latch. He wanted to smash the glass with his fist; but the thought of waking up his mother dampened his enthusiasm like a cold shower. With his fists clenched behind his back, he paced back and forth, deep in thought. He went around a few times and again stopped in front of the door. He looked at its base. The right side was somewhat damaged. He peered at it more closely. A crack showed clearly through the paint. He squatted on the floor, rested his back against the bed and pressed his heels against the crack with all his strength. The bed slid backward, but the door did not yield.

The bride lay stiffly on the bed, her gaze fixed on the ceiling. She seemed to take no notice of the bed sliding. Keshi stole a glance at her. She turned towards him. Their eyes met. Was there just a trace of sarcasm in her eyes? Did she look at him as if he were a little mad? An insane impulse possessed Keshi; his rational faculties vanished into thin air. He leapt up, and with one powerful blow smashed the third pane of the door. The glass splintered and fell on the other side.

The bride sat up with a start. A look of astonishment appeared on her face as she rose and stood by her husband. 'What on earth are you doing?' she asked irritably.

Keshi did not reply. He didn't even look at her. He put his arm through the broken pane and undid the latch on the other side. The door yielded to his weight. Holding on to it with his left hand, he carefully withdrew his right arm. Even so, his elbow got scratched and blood began to ooze through his torn sleeve.

'Hai, what have you done!' the girl cried. Her voice was at once full of concern and recrimination. She looked around to see if she could find something to bandage the cut.

Keshi paid her no heed. He pushed the door open with both his hands and went in. He knew where the light switch was, and turned it on. The room was packed with wedding presents and dowry furniture: a sofa set, a dressing table, an almira, a sewing machine; a trunk and suitcases full of clothes, trays of sweets and dried fruits. The bed that had been sent as dowry was there as well. It was loaded with all kinds of garments. He bundled them up in both his arms and flung them on the couch.

The bride had come in behind him. In her eyes was not bewilderment but fear. Keshi turned around and put his hands on her shoulders. He gazed into her frightened eyes and then drew her to him and kissed her. Through her fear she felt her husband's indifference change to passion; she felt his hot breath on her ears. Her petrified limbs relaxed in his warm embrace and she began to caress his hair.

～

Early the next morning, Keshi's mother woke up and went to the bridal chamber. She was alarmed when she saw the door open, so she tiptoed in and parted the curtain. What she saw made her gasp. The decorated room was as empty as a mausoleum. Her eyes fell on the other door and the splinters of glass on the floor. Was there a robber in the house? She crept forward to see for herself. On the threshold she stopped dead in surprise. The newly-weds lay fast asleep on the rough unmade bed, with just the cushions of the sofa beneath them.

The Dal Eaters

Morning had dawned in Pahalgam with a beauty and splendour slightly more alluring than even the day before. White clouds floated about the snow-covered peaks of the mountains. The Lidder was looking very nice indeed, frothing and crashing against the rocks at dawn, through the world of countless tents large and small pitched along its banks. I picked up my walking stick and set out for a stroll by its shores.

I must have walked only a few steps from the hotel when someone put a hand on my shoulder. I started and turned, 'Oh, Mr Chopra! When did you get here?'

'We've been here seven days, Artist Sahib, when did you come?'

'I came the day before yesterday. I was quite tired out, so yesterday I just rested. Today I thought, why not go and take a look at the Lidder from up close.'

'Isn't the Lidder something!' exclaimed Mr Chopra, gazing out at the river as it crashed noisily on to the rocks in its path, its foaming waters changing to an eerie light colour from its usual bezoar-stone tint. 'If it weren't for this, there would be no Pahalgam! You know, we bathe in the Lidder, we wash our clothes in it, we spend our afternoons there.'

'How long are you thinking of staying?'

'Oh, Artist Sahib, we did come here with the intention of staying only two or three days, but this brother of ours, our Bhai Sahib, won't hear of us leaving.' And turning suddenly, he introduced me to the man with him. 'You don't know him?' he asked, pointing to me. 'He's a very famous artist from Delhi, his pictures should be in the President's Mansion, but he doesn't even care, he just makes them and hands them out to his friends. But believe you me, whoever has a painting of his has in his hands a fortune worth thousands of rupees.'

His 'brother' greeted me. I grinned sheepishly. Then, introducing him to me, Mr Chopra said, 'And this is my brother, my Bhai Sahib, he works in the visitors' bureau here, he's quite a gentleman. We're staying at his place. We don't even feel as though we're away from home.'

I greeted him. This time it was his turn to grin.

'Where are you staying?' Mr Chopra asked me, stepping forward.

'I am in room number three in this very hotel,' I said, turning and pointing to the hotel across the way.

'Why don't you pitch a tent?' Bhai Sahib asked.

'I've just come for a few days, I didn't bring the servant with me, so I've landed up at a hotel.'

'Okay, Mr Chopra, you've found friends,' said Bhai Sahib, tapping Chopra on the back. 'I'm going now, I have to get ready to go to the office. Why don't you take a walk along the Lidder with him!' And then, turning to me, 'I'm very pleased to meet you. I dabble in painting a bit myself. I'd like to show you a few of my pictures, if you'd be willing to give me some of your time . . .'

'Of course, please bring them by.'

And he pressed his hands together to bid us good day.

∼

'Tell me, Artist Sahib, how do you like Pahalgam?'

Mrs Chopra was approaching from behind. As soon as the other gentleman had gone, she came forward. I greeted her and said, 'Actually, I have just got here. How do you like it, what have you seen?'

Their ten-year-old daughter skipped forward and grabbed my finger. I pinched her on the cheek and asked her fondly, 'Tell me, Munni, what did you see in Srinagar?' The girl shrank back shyly.

'What could we have seen—Mr Bhalla put us through such hardships.'

'Oh yes, where is "Gop Sahib"? He hasn't come to Pahalgam?'

'He did come; he stayed two days and then left.'

With the mention of Mr Bhalla, several images passed before my eyes: the bus trip from Pathankot to Srinagar, our companions on the bus and, most of all among these, Mr Bhalla's massive body and the faces of his wife, his sister-in-law and his children.

Sitting on the first, second and third seats of the bus were my son, my wife and I. Across from us, were Mr Chopra and his wife. Behind them sat Mr Bhalla and his wife, each with a little daughter on their lap; and behind us sat Mr Bhalla's sister-in-law and this same little daughter of Mr Chopra's. Behind Mr Bhalla, a businessman from Delhi, a Mr Garg, was seated with his niece, whom we mistook to be his young wife, married in the error of old age. There were other people in the bus as well, but these were the passengers who attracted our attention and whom we later met. And of them all, Mr Bhalla was the most noteworthy.

We might never have noticed him if his sister-in-law had not been sitting behind us; if his daughters had not left their Mummy and Daddy behind and come to sit by their Auntie; if I had not dozed off quite soundly; and if Mr Bhalla's little girls had not been intent on outdoing one another as they attempted to follow in the footsteps of Lata Mangeshkar, the Melody Queen.

One of Mr Bhalla's daughters was four and the other was around five or six, but Mr Bhalla had not bought tickets for them. And the Bhallas, husband and wife, had seated the girls in their laps. My seats were reserved. A friend had asked us to stay in Pathankot for two days. His servant had stowed our baggage and everything for us. We had tarried over breakfast, arriving five minutes before the bus would leave. When the bus had set out and I saw that Mr Bhalla was seated uncomfortably, I had advised him to put one of his daughters on the other seat with my son, and the other on the seat behind me, next to her Auntie. Mr Chopra also offered, out of formality, 'Yes, yes, my daughter is sitting here, why don't you have one of yours sit with her!' But Mr Bhalla shook his head. 'No thanks, these two refuse to sit near anyone else, they always stick with us,' he said, and as he spoke, he glanced towards the conductor.

But the bus must have gone only a short distance when both the girls came and sat behind me, next to their Auntie. This Auntie of theirs—that is, Mr Bhalla's sister-in-law—was, according to reports, a B.A., but neither her voice nor her dress imparted any evidence of this. Her voice was strangely crude and nasal. From behind us, we could hear her continuously delivering sermons on various subjects. And then, the thing which bothered me the most was that when the sun shone on her, she would put Mr Chopra's daughter next to the window and sit in the child's place herself; and when there was shade from the shelter of the mountain, she would exchange places with Mr Chopra's daughter once again, all the while providing a continuous running commentary on the changing sights, the interesting bends in the road, the rising peaks and the flowing rivers. Although our friend from Pathankot had spared nothing in assuring our comfort, I had not slept well, partly because it was a foreign place and partly because of the heat. My eyelids kept dropping shut, but the commentary of that charming lady just never seemed to end. And then Mr Bhalla's little girls came to sit with her. But instead of seating them next to her and making her seat a little narrower, she stood one of them near the window and the other behind me so that she would be able to see the view from the front.

For a moment those two young maidens silently stared out the window, then suddenly one of them began to sing in a loud, hearty and untrained voice:

You are my moon, I am your moonbeam

And the other, looking outside, interrupted her in a lisping tone:

My heart knows no affection, no affection

For a little while both of them continued to sing in this manner and then suddenly the first one screamed, while still singing, '*That little car is coming . . . that little car is coming . . .*'

I woke up once, wanting to give the girl a smack on the head, but the car had perhaps disappeared around a bend—the girl fell silent. I dozed off.

But then maybe the other one saw a steamroller driving along and she began to sing, '*That big truck is driving along . . . that big truck is driving along . . . that big truck is driving along . . .*'

And perhaps the car too reappeared around the bend and the other little girl began to clap, '*That little car is coming . . . that little car is coming . . .*'

And in my half-dozing ears I heard something like this: '*That little car is coming . . . that big truck is driving along . . . that little car is coming . . . that big truck is driving along . . .*' I stood up, enraged, and growled softly, 'Shush!'

I again tried to sleep.

The girls fell silent, or perhaps the car and the truck had disappeared around another bend. But a little while later, the two of them, figuring I had fallen asleep, began to shriek:

Even if there's no more moon,
nor even stars, I'll always be yours

Finally I got up, wiped my hand across my face and, turning around, I remarked to Mr Bhalla, 'Your girls sure can sing, sir!

You should enrol them in some school where they can get a chance to explore their genius.'

Mr Bhalla looked over at me and said, 'That's what I think too, but right now they just get their education from the movie theatre nearby.'

Mr Chopra chuckled when he heard what Mr Bhalla had said. Perhaps he too, like me, was trying to sleep, and the awkward, harsh voices of these little Melody Queens were rattling his sleep. He laughed and, turning around, he looked at Mr Bhalla and said, 'Why don't you send them to the All India Radio Children's Programme?'

This time, it was Madam Sister-in-law who responded, 'Actually, the Radio Programme Assistant lives right near us. The girls sing all day long. When he heard their singing, he said they would turn out to be truly great radio artists, but Brother-in-law won't listen.'

At this, Brother-in-law, a smile on his face, plump and round as a thick Punjabi kulcha, remarked, 'Our home is a little far from the Radio Station. If we get a Hillman I'll send them there.' And pulling the smaller girl lovingly to him, he put her in his lap and said, 'Sing us that song, sweetie, you know—

Far off someone sang, I heard this rhythm—
without you it is false, there are neither instruments
nor flutes.'

And his daughter, gleeful and encouraged, began to squawk away.

I beat my head with my hands. Completely abandoning the idea of sleep, I began to gaze at the changing sights outside.

We arrived at Batote at around six o'clock in the evening. I was quite tired; not only had I had trouble sleeping the night before, but then the hour or so I might have shut my eyes in the bus had been destroyed by the ear-splitting vocal stylings of those little Lata Mangeshkars—Mr Bhalla's daughters. The bus stopped in front of a hotel where I arranged for a room for one night. There were two charpoys, a verandah and not a lot of light. It wasn't very open, but one could get warm water in the morning. One didn't have to go far to get tea or to eat, and the price was only two-and-a-half rupees. So we decided that we would stay right there and ordered tea.

Mr Bhalla got out a little later with his sister-in-law and daughters, but he thought it necessary first to look at the other nearby hotels. He also took Mr Chopra and his family along with him. We had already had our things put away in the room and had drunk half a cup of tea, when, hands in pockets, he came climbing up the stairs of our hotel, leading the rest of the group. He was a fair, plump man of medium height; his big round cheeks shone as though he massaged them every day with butter. He was wearing a shirt with an open collar and dark green corduroy pants. If he had not been accompanied by his middle-aged, completely old-fashioned wife, his sister-in-law who looked illiterate despite being educated, and his dirty-faced little girls, he would have looked like some kind of fancy officer. But he had said that thing about buying a Hillman car—when I recalled that, I thought he must be a newly rich businessman, one who had himself become a bit polished, but whose household was still turning somersaults in the same old mud.

'Tell me, Artist Sahib, where have you taken a room?' Mr Bhalla asked, as he climbed the stairs.

'Oh, for the time being we are drinking tea,' I laughed. 'When we get our strength back we'll look for a room.'

'But it's getting on towards evening.'

'And if we don't find anything anywhere else, we'll just stay right here,' I said in a tired tone, 'we've had our luggage stowed here. Upstairs, you can get rooms for two-and-a-half rupees each.'

Mr Bhalla rushed upstairs taking his party with him; a little while later, he came back down, and raising his eyebrows and putting his nose in the air, he remarked, 'They are very dark and dirty rooms, how ever did you end up here!'

And he continued on ahead with the idea of looking for some nice, airy and open hotel.

As soon as he had gone, my wife complained, 'You're just sitting there. If you had had a little nerve and looked around, wouldn't we have found some nice cheap room?'

'Madam, those people will come right back here no matter what,' said the hotel owner, when he heard what she had said. 'The Rest House is full. The tents are a bit farther. But for one thing, it's cold in the tents, and for another, it costs three rupees to rent one. You're not going to find a cheaper or more comfortable hotel in Batote than this. If you experience any inconvenience we are ready for every kind of service; but they want a room for one and a half rupees. They were upstairs bargaining for ten minutes. They can walk all over Batote, but they won't be able to find a place cheaper than our hotel.'

And what the hotel owner had said turned out to be true. After about an hour or so, Mr Bhalla came back with his party. In an ingratiating tone, he said, 'Now look, Artist Sahib, we've decided to stay here too.' And then, motioning towards Chopra and the rest, he said, 'These people wanted more airy and open rooms, but I told them that one should always stick together on a journey. So I thought that we should stay where you were staying too.'

And he took the hotel owner to one side and argued with him for fifteen or twenty minutes in whispers. At one point we heard his voice, 'So we'll go across the way, the rooms there are much larger than yours.'

But the hotel owner wouldn't budge, so, finally, Mr Bhalla took one room.

'And if you require any charpoys you can get them at a fee of four annas each,' the hotel owner informed him when he returned.

'We'll remove those from the room,' replied Mr Bhalla as we went upstairs towards the room. 'We can't stand bedbugs.' And then, looking at me, he said, 'You had better roll your bedding out on the floor as well, Artist Sahib.'

Mr Chopra worked in the editorial section of a well-known English daily in Delhi. He received good pay. I thought that Bhalla and Chopra had taken separate rooms, but in the morning I found out that Mr Bhalla had persuaded Mr Chopra into sharing the room with him. 'What, brother, you want to sleep on charpoys? You sleep in the inside room. We are going to roll out our bedding on the verandah—we actually prefer the open air,' he had said and forced Mr Chopra to spend the night with him. And in this manner, the two of them had happily spent the night on three quarters of a rupee each.

They didn't eat at the hotel either. When we told them that one could get very good food at that hotel, they replied carelessly that they had brought a brazier and coals, so they could fire it up and make parathas; one could get chicken cheap, so they'd make chicken and rejoice.

∼

Up to Banihal I was a little jealous of Mr Bhalla, but when I got to Verinag I realized how full of hot air he was. Verinag is home to one of Kashmir's most beautiful waterfalls. The driver of the government bus had agreed to swing the bus by the falls for an extra rupee from each passenger. When we arrived there, Mr Bhalla struck out in front of everyone else, as before, to see the Verinag Spring, the source of the Jhelum River. There was a small temple as well, by the tank. When we were just outside the spring, a pundit also joined up with us, as a guide. He took Mr Bhalla to be the richest of all of us and began to walk right behind him, telling him all the things worth knowing about the Verinag Spring.

The spring is surrounded on all sides by an octagonal tank. Its source is extremely deep and from the surface of the tank one can't tell that water is constantly spurting up from below, but so much water comes out of the spring every minute that not only does the large canal which becomes the Jhelum flow from it, but also smaller streams which irrigate paddy fields.

Mr Bhalla entered, following behind the guide, as did we. If you throw a piece of bread into the pure water—the colour of bezoar stone—countless fish, black and long, appear, gliding up from far below, greedy for the rotis or biscuits which come with the arrival of new visitors, and slip back and forth at lightning speed.

Walking along with great pomp in front of the guide, Mr Bhalla learnt—as did we, thanks to him—all the details about the spring: what year Jahangir had the tank built; when Jahangir had come here, where he sat; how deep the spring was, and so on.

Having shown us the splendour of the spring, the guide brought us back outside. There he showed us one more spring next to the garden. The Jhelum flowed through the middle of it. On both sides there were grassy fields. There were colourful flowers, all sorts of flowering trees, and it was here that we first set eyes on the sky-kissing poplars. The guide showed us each thing in the garden—lotuses the colour of blood, the plum, cherry, apricot and apple trees. And then he took us to the other side of the garden to show us the waterfall. At the end of the garden, the Jhelum actually cascaded downward in the form of a small waterfall and that sight was very beautiful to behold indeed.

We walked around the garden, ate the plums and picked flowers. Mr Bhalla bathed in the water, cold as ice, and bowed down to the image of Shiva, but he neither made an offering, nor gave any tip to the guide. When we all started walking towards the bus the guide fell behind him asking for baksheesh. He sent the guide over to me. The entire time, the guide had been walking only with him, but thanks to him we had also learnt every single minute detail about the beautiful spring of Verinag. I gave him eight annas. He asked me if this was on behalf of everyone or just from me? I told him that this was from me and to take theirs from them.

By that point, Mr Bhalla had gone ahead and was sitting in

the bus. Right up until the bus drove off, the pundit continuously asked him for baksheesh, but he didn't give him even one paisa.

Someone had given Mr Bhalla the nickname 'Gop' when they saw him bathing, like a cowherd, in Verinag, and from then on, everyone called him 'Gop Sahib'.

∼

And thus, with the mention of Mr Bhalla, all the memories of the hours spent with him during the bus journey to Srinagar's Amira Kadal swam before my eyes. My friends had written some letters to Srinagar's artists, and when the bus arrived there, Mr Kachru, Mr Butt and Mr Santosh—all three young artists from Srinagar—had arrived at the bus station. We took our time in getting the luggage unloaded, chatting and enjoying tea in the waiting room.

As we were going in a tonga towards the Tanki House, where Mr Kachru lived, we saw 'Mr Gop's' caravan coming along near the Amira Kadal—he himself in front with his wife, then his sister-in-law and daughters, then the Chopra family, then the uncle and the niece from Delhi. It appeared he had taken all of them under his leadership.

As for us, we stayed with Mr Kachru for two days and then moved to a houseboat, and we didn't encounter Mr Gop again; but one day, in Gulmarg, we suddenly ran into the uncle and the niece—they were staying at the same hotel we were. When Mr Bhalla came up in conversation, the uncle, Mr Garg, laughed and said, 'You know, the first day he led us around so much, my legs still hurt to this day. He convinced us he would get us a nice cheap room and dragged us through half the hotels in Srinagar. I have rheumatism, it's hard for me to climb up and down again and again; he found fault with something in one place, and then with something else in another. Frankly, we got bored. Finally we told him, "Listen, we refuse to stay in a hotel. Sure, we might get ripped off, but we can't stand this hotel game any more ... so we've found ourselves a houseboat."'

I suddenly recollected the uncle's story as we were walking along the banks of the Lidder, so I asked Mr Chopra: 'So what hotel did Mr Bhalla end up staying in?'

'What hotel!' Mr Chopra twirled his walking stick with a guffaw and whacked a tiny pebble so hard it flew up and fell far off in the waters of the Lidder. 'When Mr Bhalla had seen every hotel from Residency Road clear across to Amira Kadal and none was to his liking, and Mr Garg had gone to a houseboat with his niece, we too gave up hope. But the friend who had invited us to Srinagar, his house was outside the city, so we thought we would just stay at a hotel one or two days. That was why we ended up with Mr Bhalla. Finally, we said, "Yaar, just arrange any room at all, we're tired out; the little girl is tired." Then Mr Bhalla took us to a laundry—he had brought a letter from Delhi addressed to its proprietor. The laundry people gave us the addresses of two or three hotels, but we had already been to all of them. Then Mr Bhalla said that he had also brought a letter addressed to another laundry person ... but, Artist Sahib, we had got tired of all this. We took a tonga and went out to our friend's place.'

'But how come Mr Bhalla was friends with all those laundry people?' I asked suddenly.

'Why, being a laundry man himself!' Mr Chopra chuckled. 'He runs a big, popular laundry in Delhi.'

'Your wife was saying that he destroyed your life, so did you all stay together?'

'Oh my, where could we stay, Artist Sahib!' said Mr Chopra, kicking another pebble. 'We stayed with that friend of ours for two days, but that place was so far from the city we tired of it quickly; then we met up with another friend whose house is in Amira Kadal. He had two rooms empty. He insisted on bringing us to his place. One day we ran into Mr Bhalla with his wife and sister-in-law; I asked him, "Tell me, what hotel are you staying at?"

'"We're spending four annas a day and having a great time enjoying Srinagar," he told me.

'When I expressed astonishment, Mr Gop told me that he had spent two days in the Gurudwara at Amira Kadal. When the Granthi had absolutely refused to allow them to stay any longer than two days, they went to the house of a laundry friend of theirs near the Majestic Hotel, in Maisuma Bazaar. His laundry is on the second floor. It has a small balcony; he just stuck his luggage there. The shops there close at nine o'clock. Kutchery Gate is out that way; it closes at six o'clock. At night Mr Bhalla would sleep below on the footpath. In the morning he would give two annas to the coolie, who took the bed upstairs and put it in the balcony. Two annas in the morning and two annas in the evening, he got everything done for just four annas.

'When Mr Gop had finished explaining this, his sister-in-law boasted, "Just tell us where you'll find such a cheap hotel?"

'"Yes, you can't find anything that cheap in all of Srinagar," I said, praising them, "but you must have had trouble with bathing and washing and relieving yourselves."

'"Oh, what does it matter here? Even in a big city like Delhi we get up early and go out into the fields," remarked Mr Bhalla proudly.

'"But there aren't any fields that close by here," I objected.

'Then Mr Bhalla told me that his entire family is in the habit of waking up at the crack of dawn. If either his or his wife's eyes don't open, then the little girls wake them up. After getting up at daybreak, they trudge two or two-and-half miles to Shankaracharya. They do everything there and they also take darshan of the God Shankar. As they come up the mountain, they also bathe in the Dal Lake and that's where they wash their clothes as well.

'"But why do you go so far," I asked. "Why don't you bathe in the Jhelum?"

'"The water in the Jhelum is so dirty," responded Madam Sister-in-law, turning up her nose.

'But the very next day the sister-in-law let slip that only Kashmiri boatwomen can bathe in the ladies' bathing house next to the Jhelum. Outsiders would not be able to bear it.

'And then I found out that she sometimes bathed there herself.'

I listened quietly to what Mr Chopra was saying. Although I had seen some of the true colours of Mr Bhalla in the bus on the way, I still had trouble believing it all. 'But he told me they would stay in a houseboat in Srinagar,' I observed. 'They would roast chicken every day and order tandoori parathas.'

'My God, since when does he eat chicken? His grandfather and great-grandfather probably never even tasted it!' retorted Mr Chopra, with irritation. 'He stayed with me for ten days, I know full well what he eats.'

'He stayed with you?'

'What happened was that one day he came to see us at our place. I had two rooms. Actually our friend was expecting some guests who were delayed by fifteen days or so, and our friend had insisted on inviting us there for fifteen days. The rooms were very spacious and open. Gop Sahib's eyes popped open when he saw them; he said, "You're having a great time here." For some reason, I replied, "If you're having trouble over there, feel free to come here. These rooms are mine for ten more days. Why don't you take one?"

'I just said it casually but Gop Sahib immediately went off and brought back his luggage. He wanted to do his cooking right there as well, but there was no kitchen and I didn't think it appropriate to make improper use of my friend's generosity, so I didn't even let him light a coal grill. He also proposed that we cook below on the footpath. He tried to explain that this was where the fun of a picnic lay, when the food was cooked right out in the open road. Although I myself believe in this type of simple living, his cooking downstairs on the street

seemed tantamount to an insult to my friend. So he went to
Pyarasingh's dhaba across the way and ate one five-anna thali
in the morning and one in the evening. The husband and wife
and sister-in-law would order three thalis and feed the children
with them. They took us there too several times but, my friend,
we just couldn't get ourselves to eat there. We ate at the
Majestic. Whenever we ate at Pyarasingh's dhaba we always
told Gop Sahib, "Listen, order us parathas and the special. We
just can't take this urad dal."'

'We have also eaten at Pyarasingh's dhaba,' I said. 'The
chicken there is quite good. You can get half a plate for eight
annas and, for two and a half rupees, a whole roasted chicken.'

'I asked Mr Bhalla,' said Mr Chopra, '"Why don't you get
some, you can get it for cheap here." But he was of the opinion
that one could get chicken in Delhi as well; in Kashmir one
should eat fruit.'

'Maybe they ate some fruit at a store at some point,' Mrs
Chopra laughed. 'We, Artist Sahib, never saw even an apricot
in his hand.'

We all burst out laughing.

'But Gop Sahib is very fat,' I observed.

'He's bloated from eating urad dal,' retorted Mr Chopra
brusquely.

~

For a few moments we continued to walk along silently. A new
bridge was being constructed over the Lidder. It rested on
thick iron ropes and the government order was that only one
person could cross at a time. We walked across, one at a time.
Below, the Lidder's water flowed wildly—knocking against
the rocks, tossing foam in the air, free! There was no trace of
blue or green in the water. The Lidder churned like a molten
moonbeam as it flew along the breast of Pahalgam.

When we arrived on the other side of the bridge, I asked,
'Where did Mr Bhalla stay in Pahalgam?'

'Where did he stay!?' Mr Chopra asked. 'When we started out for Srinagar, he didn't want to vacate the room at first; he kept saying, "You're going; we'll stay in your room." But our friend's guests had arrived; he had told us before that he couldn't give us a room for longer than fifteen days. So, after much persuasion he consented to leave—but when he heard that we were going to Pahalgam and that we hoped to get a room or two there, he immediately fixed upon a plan to go as well. He started by saying, "Pahalgam is a wonderful place. What's the point of going to Kashmir if you don't see Pahalgam—otherwise, there's no point in coming to Kashmir. We plan to stay there for twenty days." The Deputy Director of the Visitors' Bureau in Srinagar had become my friend; he had said that his subordinate was a clerk in Pahalgam and owned a house there. "I will arrange a room there for you," he had told us. When I mentioned to Mr Bhalla that I had plans, he pretended to have already made a plan himself.'

'How did the Deputy Director come to know you? Did you know him from before?'

'No, sir,' laughed Mr Chopra. 'It's a very amusing thing. We actually didn't even have a settled place to stay in Srinagar. It's true that a couple of friends had invited us, a couple of other friends had given us letters addressed to their Kashmiri friends as well, but we had no way of being sure what place would be right for us. So I had given out the address of the Visitors' Bureau as our mailing address. When I got off the bus, I found out that the bureau office was right across the way, so I thought I would go over there first. The chaprassi directed me to the Deputy Sahib's room. A rather young officer wearing a suit and lace-up shoes was sitting at the table, chatting with two or three persons who were either officers or officers' relatives. When he had finished with them he picked up a newspaper and began to read. He had taken no notice of my arrival. The thing was that my clothes were looking a bit filthy after the long trip. You people had changed your clothes after bathing in Batote, but I just can't stand bathing in that cold water so early in the morning. . . .'

'But you could get a bucket of warm water there for four annas,' I interrupted.

'We were actually about to order two buckets of warm water, but Mr Bhalla stopped us. He said, "We'll bathe in the Verinag Spring—it's such healthy water, the Verinag's; even terrible diseases in advanced stages can be cured with that water." But when we got to Verinag I put my hand in the canal in the garden—it was freezing! Mr Bhalla did bathe in that water and change his clothes, I just didn't have the courage . . . My clothes were quite dirty. So I said to the Deputy Sahib in English, "Sir, can I trouble you for a moment?"

'He replied without lifting his eyes from the newspaper, "What is it?"

'Then I said what I had to say. "I am very busy," he replied, and told the chaprassi to take the gentleman to the clerk.

'My blood boiled; I asked, "What work are you busy with?"

'He pushed the newspaper away. I continued, "A friend of mine had nothing but praise for the Visitors' Bureau in Kashmir. I didn't know that the officers here were so uncivilized that they considered lifting their eyes to look towards some visitor an interruption to their work."

'I'm the editor of an English-language newspaper. I know English like the back of my hand. He was quite surprised when he heard my fluent English and said with some irritation, "Did your friend also tell you that the Visitors' Bureau does the work of the post office?" I replied, "If any visitor mistakenly understood that to be the case it should be the duty of the office to help them as much as possible. Such a duty could be given to a clerk. I regularly send accounts of my travels to my own newspaper. I had thought that I would start out by praising the Visitors' Bureau, but it seems that . . ."

'The Director Sahib's face changed completely.

'"Please take a seat!" he said, half-rising from his chair. His entire manner had changed. When he found out that I was in the editorial section of the *Delhi Times*, not only did he guarantee that he himself would handle my papers, but he also served me tea.

'After this, I met with him several times. We became pretty close. He gave me all the details about his work and the difficulties he faced. I even wrote an article about it. When I expressed a desire to go to Pahalgam he promised to get me a room. At first, his plan was only to give me a letter. Then he decided to go to Pahalgam himself and returned only when he saw that I was happily settled.'

～

We had walked back quite a distance along the other bank of the Lidder. The path ahead was closed due to a small brook flowing down from the mountain. The water had flooded the banks. We descended a bit and made our way forward, jumping over the rocks. Mr Chopra was silent for a short while, so as not to fall while chatting. When we crossed the brook, he resumed his story:

'Now listen to what happened when we got here. Gop Sahib stayed in a Gurudwara when he came here as well. They have that same rule here about staying for two days . . . He begged on his hands and knees, but the Granthi here wouldn't budge either. Then he came to me. He said, "My friend, this room is very large, why don't we come here too?" I told him plainly, "Bhai, this is not my friend's home, it's the home of a friend of a friend; how can I keep another family here?" He responded, "You may think of us as 'other' but we think of you as our own." I said, "That's fine, but other people may not think of it that way . . ." and I put forth another argument: "In Srinagar there was a second room, here, there's just one room. You will be inconvenienced and so will we." Then he started saying, "Don't worry about our inconvenience, but, yes, you will definitely have difficulty because of us." I said, "It's not a matter of difficulty, this just doesn't seem right. The Vazir Hotel is very close, you can get rooms there for a rupee each. If you want I'll make arrangements there." He turned up his nose and said, "The rooms at the Vazir Hotel are very small and musty. If we stay in a hotel we'll stay in the Pahalgam Hotel. Yes, it costs five rupees a day, but the rooms are very open. And right behind it, there is quite a beautiful view of the Lidder." I asked him, "What is this room in comparison with the Pahalgam Hotel?"'

'Then where did he go?' I asked suddenly.

'Why, Artist Sahib, they're dal eaters. Dal eaters!' Mr Chopra guffawed.

'Dal eaters?' I asked with surprise.

'That's right, Artist Sahib, the Kashmiris contemptuously call tourists like them "dal eaters". The Kashmiri term is "dali-visitor", but what they mean is just "dal eater"—people who take pleasure in the paradise of Kashmir while eating only tandoori rotis that come with free dal. If only tourists like them started coming here, who would buy all these Kashmiri almonds and walnuts, peaches and apricots, apples and pears, shawls, woodcuts and papier mâché?'

'You've got a point there.' And at this point, I also laughed with Mr Chopra.

'What can I tell you?' Mr Chopra was on a roll now. 'He made me feel ashamed in Srinagar too. While he was staying with me, he suggested one day, "Why don't you come with us? We'll take you around by Nishat and Shalimar." We got ready. At the height of the season, no groom was prepared to take anyone there for less than thirteen or fourteen rupees. After a lot of bargaining he fixed the rate with a pack-saddle groom at ten rupees. First Shalimar, then Nishat, then Chashme Shahi, and on the way back we also went to Nehru Park. When we arrived back at Amira Kadal it was already nine o'clock at night. The groom dropped us off and we were standing in the street taking out our money. He kept saying, "Sir, I've worked very hard, I should get some baksheesh as well." Mr Bhalla took a five-rupee note out of his pocket and put it into his hand, so the groom thought that he would also give him a ten-rupee note, but when Mr Bhalla turned to leave he asked for ten more. Although it had been settled for just ten, he had worked very hard. But Gop Sahib said, "Arré, go away then, I have given one rupee more. Last Sunday we went for four rupees."

'"Four rupees, Sir, is what they take for going up to Nehru Park. I took you all around the world and back," replied the groom angrily.

'There was a lot of wrangling, but Mr Bhalla would not budge. The bazaar was nearby, so a lot of people had gathered at the embankment. Then Madam Sister-in-law took a two-rupee note out of her blouse and threw it at him. She said in her nasal voice, "Take this baksheesh. Now go."

'How could he go? He grabbed Mr Bhalla's sleeve. Mr Bhalla said quite shamelessly, "We don't have any more, do whatever you want." And he turned his trouser pockets inside out.

'It was hard for me to just stand there. I took three rupees from my pocket and gave them to him and then walked on ahead.

'When we got home, Gop Sahib told me, "You were wrong to give him more money. My trouser pockets were empty, but I had five one-hundred rupee notes in the inside pockets of my coat. These bastards loot their passengers. If you hadn't interfered he would have gone quietly on his way.'"

≈

We had already arrived at the second bridge over the Lidder. A group of Kashmiri Gujjars was coming along from the other direction—they wore very long firans and their knees were bare. A young woman—very beautiful, but quite filthy—was walking boldly along, openly holding her child to her naked breast. Perhaps there was work somewhere and they were all headed in that direction.

We stood to one side to give them room to pass. Mr Chopra again picked up the thread of his story:

'If they had planned to stay at the Pahalgam Hotel would they have stayed at the Gurudwara?' he asked. 'The very next day he started saying, "We're going to leave Pahalgam." I remarked, "I thought you were going to stay for twenty days." He responded carelessly, "We did take rooms at the Pahalgam Hotel; everything was fixed for staying there, but last night suddenly the Mrs came down with a stomach ache. I was also feeling a little under the weather. The water here doesn't suit us." And so he cut short a twenty-day trip and went back.'

'But it seems as though he's pretty well off,' I said.

'Oh, he is well off. He has his own house in Delhi; he just had it built last year for fifty thousand. It's in the same colony as ours, just as big as our house.'

'You have a house too?'

'Oh yes, we had it built in Patel Nagar, for forty-five thousand. We live upstairs; we take in two hundred rupees rent from the lower level.'

When the Gujjars had gone by, we crossed the bridge. On the other side, some people were washing clothes at the river bank, while others were doing oil massages or bathing. Over here, there were no tents, but there was quite a crowd of people bathing and washing their clothes. Mr Chopra told us where he bathed and where he washed his clothes. He also advised us to come there and bathe and wash our clothes.

'But the dhobi takes a two-anna fee per item,' I said, 'and that's the same rate as in Delhi.'

'Oh, no, Artist Sahib, these people add bleaching powder,' said Mr Chopra, glancing at me in a very teacherly manner. 'It shortens the life of your clothing. We don't get them washed even in Delhi. We just wash them at home and press them ourselves.'

Near the Vazir Hotel he said goodbye. I shook his hand and asked, 'How much longer have you decided to stay?'

'We had just come for two or three days, but we have become like a family to this friend, he won't let us leave. We think we'll stay seven or eight more days. If we find some good companions, we'll go as far as Amarnath and the Kolahoi Glacier.'

~

In the evening we were about to go out when Mr Chopra's friend, the artist from the Visitors' Bureau came by—he was very gentlemanly and very honest. He showed me some of his pictures and asked my opinion of them. Mr Chopra's name came up in conversation. 'He has nothing but praise for you,' I told him.

Suddenly Mr Chopra's friend exploded. He said, 'That's actually what I've come to see you about. I'm a poor man. If I rent out one or two rooms during the season, the expenses of the house get paid. This gentleman came with my supervising officer; he said he would stay two days. It's been seven days by now and he isn't even considering leaving. I keep giving hints, but he doesn't understand. Please advise me, how can I get rid of him?'

The Cartoon Hero

Vimlesh was enjoying the silent, deserted atmosphere outside the window that stretched far off to the horizon: the railway lines, gleaming at intervals as they spread out into the distance, criss-crossing one another like a maze; the railroad cars standing quietly at a little distance to the left; the electric wires sparkling in the dark, straight ahead; the windows of the houses outside the station yard peeking through the thickets of trees; the light from the floodlights cascading down on to the trees, the wires, the railroad tracks and the railway compartments, which stood quietly, visible through the dust and smog in the distance off to the left; and farther off, the hissing of the shunting engine. The darkness, the lights, the silence and the roar of the shunting engine combined to create this eerie atmosphere. It was as if even he, seated in his compartment, had become a part of this atmosphere. Just then, in an extremely harsh tone of voice, someone threw a question at the back of his neck, like a rock.

'Is this lower berth empty?'

Turning around, Vimlesh saw a party boss dressed in handloom clothing—big-boned, robust, a wrestler-type in spite of being middle-aged—standing in the middle of the compartment. Behind him was a porter with his luggage.

It was very hot in the compartment. Vimlesh felt extremely exhausted, but he had been unable to completely separate himself from the atmosphere outside. Instead of answering, he just glanced at the bedding spread out on the opposite berth as if to say, 'See for yourself. It isn't empty.'

'Yours?' the man asked, pointing at the bedding.

'No, sir, but the seat is reserved,' Vimlesh replied unwillingly. 'The gentleman just set his things down and went back outside.'

'I had said to book me a lower berth.'

Vimlesh felt as if he were accusing him of something. He was going to say, 'No, sir, you didn't say that to me.' But the party leader didn't pause to hear what he had to say. He ordered the porter to set his bedding on an upper berth and rushed back out.

Vimlesh put his head back out the window. But for some reason all the beauty of the atmosphere had evaporated. It was summer, the month of June. The compartment was already an oven, but the quiet atmosphere outside which previously had been refreshing to his eyes had now also vanished into thin air. Outside, everything was the same as before, but even though Vimlesh was staring at it all, he didn't see it any more. The face of that homespun-clad despot of a party boss had come and occupied that space. Vimlesh felt as if he had seen him somewhere before. Then he realized he had seen that face in R.K. Laxman's cartoons in the *Times of India*. Whenever Laxman depicted the kind of tyrannical Congress Party boss who was always beating up his colleagues, everything about him looked exactly like this man: his build, his sleeves rolled up to show his strong hairy arms, his jowly crooked jaw, his thick distorted lips, his teeth bared in an angry expression, everything. The cartoonist surely must have seen this leader somewhere, otherwise how could there be such a similarity! He thought of this, and several of Laxman's cartoons flashed before his eyes.

~

Vimlesh was always very nervous when it came to travelling. He would start getting obsessed with a trip two or three days in advance. Even if his seat was confirmed he would still reach the station an hour ahead of time. Just two years ago, after Partition, he had come to Allahabad. In Punjab, his father had had a business and he himself had written poetry to his heart's content. But not only had everything been destroyed during Partition, he'd also become deprived of his father's protection and now the weight of the household had fallen on his own shoulders. Now he had to go Lucknow on some business connected with his resettlement in Allahabad. Since he was ill, his wife had decided to book his seat on the train that left Allahabad at 10 p.m. When she went to the station to reserve his seat, she had found out that they no longer booked second-class seats. The government had withdrawn first-class compartments, substituted second-class ones in their stead and raised the fare a bit. Intermediate class had been changed to second, thus making the question of reservations moot. The trip to Lucknow was essential, so his wife had been forced to book a first-class seat. For him, these were days of financial crisis. It bothered Vimlesh even to travel second class, but after his wife explained that it had cost only a little more and he had got a lower berth, he stopped worrying.

Nevertheless, despite having a confirmed seat, he reached the station forty-five minutes early, a slave to his habits. His wife figured that since the seat was reserved and the station wasn't far away, he would get there in plenty of time even if he left at quarter to ten. But he had been fussing since early evening. His luggage packed and his essential documents secured, he was ready to go by 8 p.m. At nine o'clock he ate dinner and at 9.15 he took a rickshaw for the station. His wife would have got bored waiting all that time, so he made her stay home.

The train reached platform no. 6—called the donkey line by Allahabadis—a full hour in advance. Even though some friend of his had told him that First Class was written with chalk on the second-class compartments, Vimlesh realized the moment he entered that his seat had been reserved in a real first-class compartment, one left over from the old days. Someone had ripped off all the vinyl from the front seat and the hideous, naked seat was showing its stuffing. When he read the number and found out it was his seat he wished he could get the other, undamaged one instead. He looked at the reservation card stuck on the outer door of the compartment and discovered that that seat wasn't empty. He thought of looking for an empty seat in some other compartment, but he was already tired from having walked so far. So he just told the porter to spread out his bedding on the seat. He said to himself, 'When the bedding is spread out the stuffing will be covered and no one will know the vinyl is tattered.' When the bedding had been laid out and he'd sat down and made himself comfortable, he started to realize how hot it was. It was June. A hot wind blew all day and the nights were humid. The compartment was like an oven. After the porter left, he switched on the fan. But the fan remained motionless, like a yogi deep in meditation. He stood up and shook it. Then he realized that paying second-class fares (actually a few paise more) didn't give one the ease of first-class travel. Whoever had ripped the vinyl off the seat had also ruined the fan. He thought he'd go look around in the second class; if there was a seat there he would take it. He felt pleased with himself for coming early; if he'd come at the last minute he would have had to make the journey in this compartment.

However, when he went and saw the second-class compartment he found it was only an intermediate one. All they'd done was cross out 'Inter' with some chalk and write in 'Second'; and even though there was still half an hour to departure time, the compartment was already jam-packed. Yes, he would be sitting under a fan, but Vimlesh just didn't have the strength to sit up all night. He would lie down on his own berth and, once the train started moving, there'd soon be a breeze and it wouldn't be any problem at all. He thought of this as he went back to his compartment. At first he figured he would wander around on the platform until the train left, but he didn't really feel up to it. So he got a glass of water from a clay pot, and went back to his seat. After a little while the occupant of the opposite seat came in, set his bedding down and went outside again. He wasn't in the mood to read and, besides, the light in the compartment would only brighten when the train started moving. So, folding his pillow in half, he propped himself up on his elbow and, half-lying, half-sitting, began to stare at the tracks stretching out into the distance behind the train.

Watching that scene had wiped away all his annoyance and, lost in thought, he even forgot about the heat in the compartment. But, following the Congress Party leader's enraged exit, the magic of that scene had now vanished, try though he did to recreate it. How could a man who looked like the owner of some gambling den, a gang leader, or the proprietor of some disreputable hotel be in the Congress Party? Time and again this question passed through Vimlesh's mind. In addition to his strong physique, he had a jaw that sagged a little to the left, thick paan-stained lips and teeth which protruded from the left side of his mouth over his lips, which seemed permanently twisted. All in all, he was a fairly terrifying individual. Staring out the window, Vimlesh felt as though he were actually looking at him.

Vimlesh was lost in these thoughts, his head sticking out the window, when the party boss stormed back into the compartment. Behind him was the conductor.

The conductor came inside, checked the seat number against the chart in his hand and then pointed at the upper berth, 'This is your berth.'

'But I asked for a lower berth!'

'Well, it says upper here.'

'Can't I get a lower berth in some other compartment?'

'Not a chance!'

The conductor got down from the compartment. The party

boss was climbing down right behind him when the gentleman who had the lower berth climbed inside and greeted him. Without even paying the slightest attention to his greeting, the party leader rushed out after the conductor and started arguing with him outside on the platform.

The man with the lower berth silently started to spread out his bedding.

'Who exactly is he, sir?' Vimlesh asked him.

'Until yesterday he operated a grinding mill and a silage cutter. But now he's a committee member.'

'Of the Congress Party?'

'His brother spent years in jail for the Congress movement. After Independence this guy joined the Congress Party too. Nobody even cares about his brother anymore; he got frustrated and joined the People's Socialist Party. But this one is still in the Congress Party. Whenever some official comes to town, he's always on the reception committee. He's on several committees and runs a transport agency with twenty trucks and buses. In the next election he wants to try for a seat in Parliament. If he wins, he figures no one will be able to stop him from becoming a cabinet minister.'

Just then the guard's whistle sounded from somewhere nearby. The party boss quit following the conductor around and rushed back to the compartment. Grumbling, he started to spread his bedding out on the upper berth: an old duffle bag, a dirty mat, a cotton pad and an off-white homespun sheet. When everything was set he turned towards the fan.

'It's very hot in here. Sir, why didn't you turn on the fan?' he thundered at Vimlesh as if he were some servant or volunteer worker of his. Vimlesh felt like telling him the fan was out of order, but he kept quiet.

Stepping forward, the party boss fiddled with the switch. When the fan wouldn't start he grabbed it from below and jerked it back and forth. When, even after getting a good shaking from those strong hands and iron wrists, the shameless

fan still refused to budge, he tried to stick his finger through
the wire casing to rotate the blades. But the casing holes were
narrow and his finger fat. Unable to decide what to do next,
his glance suddenly fell on a guard standing outside on the
platform, signalling with the green light in his right hand and
preparing to blow the whistle in his left. The party boss lunged
at the door.

'Listen, I'm travelling in first class. The fan is out of order.
Please get it fixed.'

The guard blew his whistle, waved the hand with the torch
in it, then took the whistle out of his mouth and replied, 'It's
departure time now. It might get fixed at the next station.'

The train moved; the guard turned away. A puff of hot air
drifted into the compartment. Vimlesh propped himself up on
his pillow and lay down with his feet out the window.

For a second, the party boss just stood there silently between
the two doors. Usually a first-class compartment would have
contained an easy chair, but since this was a converted second-
class compartment, the chair had been removed.

After standing there a moment, the party boss stepped over
to Vimlesh. 'You came ahead of time.'

'I always come half an hour to forty-five minutes early,'
Vimlesh responded, propping himself up on his elbows, as if he
had done something special by arriving ahead of time.

'Didn't you notice the fan?'

'Yes, I did.'

'So why didn't you get it fixed?'

'I figured I would say something if a workman passed by.
But the train was on the donkey line; maybe that's why no one
came.'

Even though Vimlesh had completely forgotten about the
workman while engrossed in the view from the train, he said
all this about the donkey line to defend himself. He figured the
party boss would realize from his choice of words that he was
a resident of the city too, and would soften his tone. But
instead, he responded in the same irritable manner:

'You should have gone and reported it to the station master. A first-class compartment with no fan!'

'I'm ill. I wasn't up to walking so far,' he replied. 'Besides, when I got here the compartment was empty. Who would I have left the luggage with?'

From the expression on the party boss's face it was apparent that he was placing sole blame for the lack of a working fan in that compartment on Vimlesh. Shaking his head in exasperation, he started to deliver a speech from right where he was standing on how this was what was wrong with Indians: they hadn't learnt how to stand up for their rights. If it had been an Englishman in his position he wouldn't have rested until the fan was fixed. Vimlesh had the lower berth so he would get some air, but he should have thought about the people in the upper berths too. 'We were slaves for so long,' the party boss thundered, 'that we can't see beyond our own narrow self-interests. We don't know what the rights and duties of a citizen are. We learnt to endure every indignity. We don't realize that just obtaining freedom is not enough. We will have to fight for our rights every step of the way. Bureaucratic machinery will constantly need to be lubricated with the oil of loyal opposition. Now we'll see just how these people don't fix the fan!'

Who knows what got into Vimlesh. Softly he said, 'That's not quite the way it is. The truth is that our government is a government of the people and it wants to enlighten first-class passengers by means of these small inconveniences about the realities of the common man's travel in third class.' And he showed him the torn vinyl on the seat underneath his bedding. Whether or not it was ripped up, it was still better than a third-class seat! 'I've also heard,' he continued, 'that the government is going to install fans in the third class and remove them from the first.'

For a second, the party boss stood over him, glaring, trying to figure out if he was making fun of him or not. But Vimlesh just sat there, looking innocent and completely serious.

'You heard wrong,' the boss replied, looking even more disgusted. 'The government definitely wants to erase the difference between high and low, but that doesn't mean they will remove the fans from the first class. Do they give people like me first-class fare so that we can broil in the heat on our way to committee meetings? We too used to travel without fans in the third class.'

Vimlesh wanted to add that Mahatma Gandhi had travelled only by third class even to take part in big important conferences, not just ordinary committee meetings. His glance, however, fell on the party boss's face, distorted with anger, and he realized that, who knew, this man might become a cabinet minister some day. And R.K. Laxman's cartoon party boss flashed before his eyes and he felt as if the man might knock him down on the compartment floor and start jumping on his chest at any moment. He kept quiet.

~

When they passed through Prayag station, the speech was still in progress. When the train slowed down at Phaphamau the party boss went and stood by the window. When the train had stopped, he jumped out on to the platform and ran towards the guard shack. But he probably hadn't even reached the guard's compartment when the engine whistle blew. The next minute, he came rushing back. The train had started to move by the time he climbed in. After getting back, he informed them that the train only stopped here for a couple of minutes. He would talk to the guard at the next station.

When the train started moving a nice breeze began to drift in. It was almost eleven o'clock, so Vimlesh lay back down. He usually rested in the afternoon, but that day—like any other day when he had to travel—he had been too nervous to relax. Now he wanted to get up and turn out the light, but the party boss was still pacing around like an angry, caged bull, so he put a handkerchief over his eyes instead to keep the light from hindering his sleep. But just then the gentleman from the opposite lower berth, who had gone to the bathroom, returned in his pajamas, his clothing draped over his arm. He quietly hung them on a peg, then put his hand on the light switch and said, 'Sir, I am turning the lights off. Please turn your own berth light on.' He definitely was getting his revenge for having his greeting ignored.

The party leader turned around, startled. Grabbing hold of the chain on his berth, he put one foot on the lower berth and climbed up. Resting on his elbows like Vimlesh, he turned on his night light. The man opposite had turned out the lights and stretched out on his berth.

But it was stifling in the upper berth. The next moment, he took his kurta off. Vimlesh felt like telling him, 'Sir, just forget about the fan. It's a first-class compartment, with a clean, spacious floor. Spread out your bedding down here in the open space between the two doors. The windows on both sides will provide cross-ventilation. You can sleep in comfort.' But he was afraid to come straight out and say this. So, pretending to talk to himself, he said, 'Once, years ago, I was travelling in the first class. I had an upper berth. It was summer, as it is now, and the fan was broken. I couldn't stand lying up there, so I spread out my bed right on the floor between the two doors and slept soundly. That's the advantage of the first class; seats are reserved. There's no worry of someone coming in from the outside. The floor is wide and clean. When necessary, a man can easily spread his bedding out.'

The party boss glared down at him for a moment, but his face was in the dark. His eyes were implying, 'What a stupid thing to say! Spending money for a first-class ticket just to sleep on a bare floor.' But he didn't say it aloud. What he did say, however, also as if talking to himself, was in reply to Vimlesh. Lying flat on his back, as if speaking to the ceiling, he said, 'Actually, it's really nothing special. I've slept in third-class upper berths all my life. But I have to participate in an urgent meeting in the Agricultural Ministry tomorrow. It would be great if I could get some sleep!'

Vimlesh said, 'Sir, you seem to be an important leader. Why don't you speak to the Railway Minister and stop this nonsense: a trip in the summertime, a first-class compartment and a broken fan!'

Clearly Vimlesh wanted to dispel the party boss's irritation with him.

'Don't worry. I'll catch hold of that guard at the next station.'

Vimlesh wanted to tease him and say, 'Don't worry. My seat is getting plenty of air,' but he kept quiet. Gusts of wind, the jerking train, his tired body: Vimlesh fell asleep.

∾

Suddenly, he opened his eyes and found that the train was standing at some small station. The party boss was standing in the compartment door arguing with someone down on the platform.

Raising himself up a bit Vimlesh peeked out the window. It was the guard, a Sikh, and he was showing the green light for the train. Who could guess what the party boss had said, but these words of the guard's reached Vimlesh:

'Report it to the station master at Pratapgarh. This is a flag station. There's no repairman here. You come running to me at every stop! I'm not a repairman, I'm a guard!'

The train started to move so he closed the door, chained it, locked it and returned to his berth. It was so humid that even in the moving train the breeze barely reached the lower berth. Vimlesh lay right next to the window, sometimes stretching his feet outside. In the upper berth there wasn't even a trace of air. The party boss removed his kurta, which he had again put on. He hung it on the hook and lay down again.

∾

It must have been about one o'clock in the morning when Vimlesh was awakened by a racket outside the train. Just then, someone scrambled aboard. The light came on. The gentleman opposite just rolled over but otherwise didn't move. Vimlesh noticed that behind the party boss was the station master and a workman.

The workman turned the fan switch on. He opened its casing and jiggled it. Joining some wires together he tried to get it going. Then he said, 'Sir, this fan is broken. It will have to be replaced, but the job can't be done here. It can be done only in a workshop. This compartment looks condemned anyway. I don't know why they're using it!'

And the workman picked up his tools and left. Right behind him went the station master. Outside, the guard blew the whistle. Standing in the doorway the party boss screamed, 'But I'm a first-class passenger! I can't travel in this heat without a fan! I won't let the train leave. I'll pull the chain!'

The station master said, 'Sir, it's not our fault. You should have reported it back there in Allahabad.'

Just then the Sikh guard walked up, swinging his torch. The party boss thundered at him, 'I told you to get the fan fixed back in Allahabad, but you wouldn't listen.'

'You told me right at departure time. What was I supposed to do then?' the guard responded sharply. 'Where were you before that? Now just go and relax. The train's late as it is.'

'I'm not letting the train leave! What are you thinking? Do you think I got a reservation in first class just so I could roast in this train?'

'Please make your complaints to the authorities.'

'You attach another compartment. I'm going to pull the chain.'

'You pull the chain and I'll have you arrested.'

'What's your name? I'm going to report you to the railway minister.'

'If you're such a big leader why don't you also tell the

railway minister that before initiating new programmes every fourth day, they ought also to figure out how to carry them through so that short-tempered passengers like you won't be inconvenienced.'

'You are very rude!' the party boss lost control of himself. 'What's your name? I'll have you dismissed!'

'My name is Sardar Banta Singh. Please make a note of it. I don't know any ministers. I am subordinate to the district superintendent and he knows my work. He is also familiar with complaints from people like you. If he were to listen to you people the whole railway staff would be dismissed. Have me fired if you wish, but right now please go and relax. It's after one. Please think of the other passengers.' And he blew loudly on his whistle and waved his torch. The train started.

Fuming, the party boss shut the door, turned off the lights and climbed up on to his berth. This time he even took off his undershirt.

~

Vimlesh went back to sleep. Since it was so late at night, the air was somewhat cooler. He had completely forgotten about the party boss's predicament. If he created another fuss in Rai Bareilly, Vimlesh wasn't conscious of it. He was sound asleep. When he opened his eyes the next morning, the train was entering Lucknow station. The compartment light was on and the man opposite was rolling up his bedding. The party boss's berth was empty. Vimlesh saw him when he sat up; he was asleep over on the left by the door, half-naked, his bedding spread out in the middle of the floor. His dhoti was rumpled and his snores reverberated loudly in the morning silence.

Mr Ghatpande

Mr Ghatpande changed his clothes and sat down on the bed. 'You needn't worry,' he said. 'Of course, some ten or fifteen years ago, T.B. was considered a dreadful disease, but since then, science has made great strides; and now even the most hopeless cases are cured.'

I coughed violently and spat up some clots of blood. Then I told him in my feeble voice that I was like a sinking ship. My family was trying to save me in vain. It was written in my fate that I should sink deeper with each passing moment.

'Nonsense!' Mr Ghatpande cut me short. 'You just don't know enough about this disease. The doctor who sent me here is a renowned T.B. specialist from Poona. Would you believe it, he has an artificial lung made of steel? That's right, steel! He was operated on in America. It is my belief that methodical treatment is not as important in this disease as the patient's self-confidence. Never pay any attention to what others say and have confidence in yourself. When I was diagnosed with T.B., I weighed only eighty-six pounds, and now, after a month's rest, I've gained twenty-five pounds; my sediment is normal now and my fever has vanished completely. I wouldn't have come here, but it was getting so hot in Poona, I thought, why not use this as an excuse to visit Panchgani. Mahatma Gandhi used to come here all the way from Wardha and, living as I do so close to this veritable Ganges of health, I thought, why not take a dip myself!'

I wanted to say something, but I had another coughing fit and spat up more blood along with a lump of mucus. Mr Ghatpande was not fazed by this and continued with the same zeal:

'To tell you the truth, when the doctors suspected an infiltration in my left lung it alarmed everyone at home. They thought, there! Now he's finished. But a great man once said that you should never allow sickness to get the better of you; and you should always maintain strong self-confidence. To tell you the truth, when my relatives had lost all hope of my survival, I consulted the doctors and girded myself to fight this disease to the finish. Four things are considered necessary for gaining victory over T.B.—rest, a nutritious diet, clean air and freedom from care. But, in the light of my experiences of the past month, I can add a fifth item as well, which is extremely important when it comes to this illness. As you may know, Marshal Stalin once said when speaking about the security of his country's new-found freedom, "Comrades, I believe that there are three things necessary for the defence of our nation: first, military power; second, military power; and third, military power." If anyone were to ask me what it takes to beat T.B., I would say, just as Marshal Stalin did—three things: first, will power; second, will power; and third, will power. Will power is that veritable cure-all . . .'

But Mr Ghatpande did not get an opportunity to expound on his views regarding that veritable cure-all—will power—because Sister Blake came into the room and broke in on his oration, caring little that some poor person was drinking in his every word as though it were nectar.

'Sir!' she pounced upon him like a mother jackal. 'This is rest time. You must rest; don't disturb others.'

Mr Ghatpande's enthusiasm subsided like hissing soda bubbles, to the point that he lay down flat on his back. Then the sister turned to me:

'Your case is quite severe, sir! You shouldn't talk, you

shouldn't get up, you shouldn't sit up. You must rest all day. If you need anything, ring the bell.'

Then she placed a little brass bell, the kind that vendors use, on the teapoy near my bed, and went back inside the ward, muttering to herself.

I plucked up my courage and threw a glance at Mr Ghatpande. He was lying on his bed with his eyes closed. Fifteen minutes later, his nostrils, by way of soft snores, began to give evidence of that strong will power of his, the exertion of which had caused him to fall into a deep sleep, unmindful of the sister's scolding.

∾

We had both been admitted to the sanatorium that day. Mr Ghatpande had arrived two hours after I had. As a rule, newcomers were first sent to the Acute Ward. If they didn't run a fever for nine or ten days, they were sent to a different ward. If a patient in another ward showed signs of developing a fever, he was transferred back to the Acute Ward.

Summer was on with all its fury, and every day more and more patients poured in. The doctors and the nurses usually entered the ward through the verandah, but the main ward was full to capacity by now so we had been given beds there. The beds were set along a wall with two lattice windows of glazed glass that could be opened and closed. Initially, I had been given the bed which Mr Ghatpande now occupied. After I had been put in the bed there, and the sweeper had placed the spittoon and the chamber pot next to my bed, and the sister had instructed me to rest, and my family had left for home after trying to buoy my spirits with words of encouragement, my eyes—exhausted from a sleepless night and the long journey—dropped shut, despite my fever and coughing. But I had scarcely closed them when I was awakened by the pathetic coughing of a patient lying on the other side of the window, inside the ward. The patient, as I came to know later, was from a wealthy Bohra family of Bombay. He had been lying in the sanatorium for the past five years and his condition was very serious by now. He had great difficulty coughing. The phlegm hardly ever moved from his throat. He could only spit it out with great effort. He coughed as though he were a rickety whimpering baby. All of a sudden I could no longer sleep. Even though my own condition was extremely serious, he was even worse off than I was. It made chills run up and down my spine. *How will I be able to sleep right next to this pathetic coughing*, I thought; and, overwhelmed by a natural spirit of self-defence, I asked the ward boy to get my bed changed. When the sister came, she saw that I was lying on a different bed. She glared angrily at the ward boy, so he said, 'This gentleman's eyes are sensitive; over there, the light was shining directly into his eyes.' After the sister had gone away again, I placed four annas for tobacco and paan in the ward boy's hand as a token of my gratitude and I promised to always keep him happy.

Although the sun was fairly high and everyone was walking around with their shirt collars open, I had started to feel cold, being terribly weak, and had fallen asleep with the blanket pulled up to my neck. I don't know how long I slept, but I was suddenly awakened by the sister's harsh voice. I opened my eyes and saw her coming in from outside; close behind her was a healthy-looking young man, followed by a coolie carrying a suitcase and bedding on his head. A few steps away from the verandah, the sister called out loudly to the ward boy, 'Gannu!'

Just as she entered the verandah from one direction, Gannu came running in from the other. A new bed was made up in minutes. My anxious eyes strained to look up through the window. I thought the patient would be carried here slowly on a stretcher, as I had been. But no stretcher came and, a few minutes later, an older man wearing a good suit came walking slowly towards the ward. I thought this must be the patient, and the young man who accompanied the sister was his son, and he had come to leave his father off here. Two more men came in with him. The old man went over to the sister and told her in English that he had just met with the Residential Medical Officer and made the appropriate arrangements.

The sister said to him, 'It's rest time right now, why don't you go? You must be tired, why don't you rest a little. You can come in the evening after six-thirty.' The old man replied that he was returning to Poona by the next bus and would come again the following Sunday. Turning to the young man, he told him not to worry at all, and if there were any problems to tell the sister or the R.M.O. If he needed anything, he should write to him and he would bring things from Poona on Sunday.

It was then that I learnt that the young man hadn't really come to leave someone off, but was himself a patient, and that the older man was not the patient, but the patient's father. The young man was Vinayakarao Ramarao Ghatpande. He introduced himself while changing his clothes soon after his father and the sister had left.

~

On the ward side of Mr Ghatpande's bed—on the other side of the window—the Bohra patient continued to cough pathetically. The thin sound of his coughing hardly reached my bed, but I thought that the moaning cough must be incessantly hammering away at Mr Ghatpande with all its intensity. However, it appeared that Mr Vinayakarao Ramarao Ghatpande was actually sleeping quite peacefully on his side of the room. I envied his peacefulness. I was in much worse shape than he was. I suffered from insomnia. If I did manage to fall asleep, I was visited by horrible nightmares, in which I felt as though dying of tuberculosis was similar to descending slowly, step by step, into a vast chasm veiled in darkness. One day, my feet would touch the bottom. Whenever I felt my feet reaching that final step, I woke up instantly. The thought that one day I would no longer live in this world kept stabbing at my heart like an invisible dagger. I always took a deep breath and turned over, perhaps to get the sense that I was still alive.

Mr Ghatpande was snoring away comfortably. I turned over quietly. The invisible dagger had been stabbing at my heart only a moment earlier. Clouds were peeking out from behind the tall silver oaks above the cottage across from the verandah; there was a gentle breeze now; a flock of nightingales materialized from out of nowhere with a flutter of wings. They divided into pairs, some perching on the electric wires, some on the long branches of bougainvillea and some on the henna hedge. So many nightingales! I started watching them to see if any pair among them was fighting. Everyone loves the song of the nightingale, but I love to watch them fight. When ordinary birds fight they fall down on the ground, but nightingales keep flying straight up, higher and higher into the sky, striking one another with their tiny beaks. Such beautiful fighting! I kept watching them for quite a while, but they didn't chirp or fight, and then, one by one, they flew away.

I felt strangely lonely. I missed home. When death is inevitable, home is infinitely better than the harsh and loveless ward of a hospital or a sanatorium. I wanted to die with my head in my mother's lap. Why had she thrown me out in this condition? A whirlwind of anger rose in my heart against my brothers and sisters and my father. My eyes grew moist like a tiny child's when I thought about my mother's warmth and affection. Just then, Mr Ghatpande gave a loud snore and his earlier oration echoed in my ears, and I remembered how he had said that the best cure for any disease was to not allow it to get the better of you. I don't remember when my eyes closed as I tried to console myself and to rouse my dormant will power.

～

'Tell me, are you just going to keep on sleeping? Your tea is getting cold.' I was awakened by Mr Ghatpande's voice.

The ward boy had put my cup on the teapoy, but I was not allowed to sit up. I rang the bell. The ward boy came and raised the head of my bed slightly. I picked up my cup. Mr Ghatpande was sitting down, facing me. He asked, 'So, how are you feeling?'

Since I was not allowed to speak, I made a gesture to indicate that I was all right.

Mr Ghatpande replied: 'I have had a sound sleep. Perhaps you don't know that with this disease it's best to sleep as much as you can. Sleep is a sign of feeling carefree, and feeling free of care works like a cool and efficacious balm to the wounds. That's why I sleep soundly and I don't let worry come anywhere near me. I don't even read the newspapers. After all, what else is in them but fighting and war and poverty and disease? It makes one feel depressed and uneasy. I never even pick up a newspaper and look at it, and I don't listen to anything anyone says. What can I tell you: you know how friends and relatives, when they hear that you're sick, come to console you supposedly; but by the gestures they make and the way they talk, they frighten you so much that you wonder what's going to happen to you. In my heart of hearts I just say to myself: look, my friend, you have T.B. Now, what could be worse than that? And then I start having thoughts—quite gloomy ones, really—but I exercise my will power, drive them all from my mind and fall into a deep sleep . . .'

Mr Ghatpande finished his tea. He had propped himself up with two pillows and stretched his legs out luxuriously. I was coughing less, lying with my head slightly raised. I listened to him attentively. Perhaps he was about to expand upon his ideas regarding will power, which, because of the sister, he had not been able to discuss in full earlier, but at that very moment another patient made a dramatic entrance from the ward, asking, 'Tell me, gentlemen, did you just arrive today?' He greeted both of us respectfully with a nod of his head, and then he began to examine the chart which was hanging from my bed.

Although he was able to walk about and even had a smile on his face, tuberculosis had etched the marks of its friendship into his form. He was six feet tall, but emaciated; his chest was broad but sunken, his fair complexion was yellowish, or actually almost black from T.B., and since his cheeks were hollow, his nose jutted out and looked longer than it actually was. In fact, other than his nose, nothing was noticeable about his face.

When he glanced at my chart, he made a face as if to say it was just as he had expected, and mumbling, 'Bilateral!' to himself with satisfaction, he turned to Mr Ghatpande's bed.

But Mr Ghatpande's chart was empty. Since I had come very early, the doctor had already examined me and filled in my chart, and had also given me Calcium Gluconate and Congored injections. The doctor had left by the time Mr Ghatpande came in. He was to undergo pathology tests in the evening.

When the man with the long nose found Mr Ghatpande's chart blank, he gave him a questioning look.

'I just have a mild infiltration,' Mr Ghatpande told him with an air of nonchalance.

'Right side?'

'No, left.'

'Do you take A.P.?'

Mr Ghatpande told him that he had been taking A.P. for two months and had responded well to the treatment. He had had a nice 'collapse' and his lung had shrunken to just this much: he showed him the size with his fingers.

'Do you come from Bombay or Surat?'

Mr Ghatpande laughed. 'I come from Poona,' he said, with that same carefree air of his. 'In fact, in my case, it wasn't entirely necessary to come here, but since the weather was unendurably hot there, I decided to come. It's only a mild infiltration and I'll test negative in a couple of months.'

'It doesn't matter if it's mild or it's serious,' the man with the long nose retorted. 'T.B. is T.B. When I was admitted to the sanatorium, I was C-minus, but now look at me. It's well over

a year since I came here. First it was fluid, which eventually led
to pus. Every week they pierce me with a needle this long to
take it out.'

He raised his shirt on the left side to show the spot on his
ribs from where they removed the pus. Two big patches of
sticking plaster sealed the wound.

Mr Ghatpande went white in the face. He asked him
anxiously, 'What the hell is fluid?'

'With A.P., ninety out of a hundred people run the risk of
getting fluid in their pleura,' said the gentleman with the long
nose. 'The A.P. air is transformed into water. You think you'll
be cured within two months, but it could take two years.
When the doctors send their patients here they just say things
like that. Mr Manilkar is in the cottage opposite the ward.
He's been here for two years. Last year he tested negative, but
he got fluid three times.'

'He might be a particularly bad case,' Mr Ghatpande said,
'but I gained twenty-five pounds in one month.'

'That's immaterial,' said the patient with the long nose.
'This Bohra, who's lying parallel to you on the other side of the
window, has been here for the past five years. He managed to
get up to a hundred and sixty pounds, but look at him now.
The weight we gain is just body fat. It'll burn off in just four
days if you have a fever.'

Just then the Bohra patient coughed pitifully. A cold shiver
ran down my spine.

He spat with great difficulty and called out from inside the
ward in his broken voice, 'Everyone's fate is different. It's not
as if it happens to everyone.'

The man with the long nose felt that he was losing ground
with the Bohra patient's statement. He became excited, and
pulling his legs up on to the chair to sit cross-legged, he said,
'Admittedly T.B. can be said to be the result of a man's ill-fate,
but fluid is the result of A.P. Ninety per cent of the people who
take A.P. are susceptible to it.'

He laughed pointlessly. Mr Ghatpande sank back into his pillow and I began to console myself with Mr Ghatpande's own words: *since I already had T.B. and both my lungs were affected, why should I be afraid of fluid? One should not pay attention to what others say. When the doctor comes in the morning to give me my injection I'll ask him about it.*

'You didn't come here at the right time, my friend,' the man with the long nose said. 'In another fifteen or twenty days the monsoon will start and there's a particular risk of fluid in the rainy season. By about the fifteenth of June nearly half the sanatorium will be empty.'

He would have continued to augment our knowledge about T.B. and fluid for who knows how long, but by then the doctor had arrived in his office and Mr Ghatpande was called in to see him.

The man with the long nose turned to me. But acting on the instructions of the sister, I remained absolutely silent. He glanced at me and said, 'You should try to get plenty of rest. You shouldn't talk at all. Talking would just unnecessarily tire out your lungs. If A.P. works in your case, that's all very well and good, otherwise they'll give you P.P. No need to worry, P.P. turns out to be successful in many cases and people who take P.P. don't run the risk of fluid.' He smiled at me and left.

For a moment I was surprised. I wondered why he had been so sympathetic towards me but had said no words of comfort to Mr Ghatpande. Perhaps he was jealous of Mr Ghatpande's good health, whereas he would have no reason to envy me.

∼

When Mr Ghatpande returned after about half an hour, he burst into a loud guffaw. 'I just asked the doctor about fluid,' he said, 'and he told me that the chances of my getting fluid are about the same as getting run over by a car.' Mr Ghatpande laughed again and continued, 'The doctor told me, "Nobody ever thinks about getting run over by a car, so why are you worrying about getting fluid in your lungs?" My case is quite mild. There's hardly any chance I'll get fluid.'

Saying this, he sat down comfortably on his bed. He rested his back against his pillow and then he laughed again. The colour had returned to his face. 'The doctor was telling me,' he said, 'that as a rule here, they examine the new patients for seven days in this ward, and if they don't run a fever, they're transferred to another ward and even allowed to walk around a little.'

I heaved a deep sigh because I knew for sure that the chances of my ever being transferred from this ward were very slim.

'You have no reason to worry,' Mr Ghatpande told me. 'You should never listen to what other people say. Have faith in yourself. You know what Napoleon once said about self-confidence?'

Mr Ghatpande was about to reveal to me Napoleon's views on self-confidence, when a patient with a shaven head came out of the inner ward. He wore a khaki shirt and trousers, and was of medium height and lanky. He had a broad chest and a rather large face, but his cheeks were sunken and there was a kind of a crazy look in his eyes. They seemed peculiarly hollow, straying constantly from one object to the next, resting on nothing.

'Just think, gentlemen, you've arrived today and today I'm leaving.' He bared his teeth in a grin and greeted us from the door. Walking on to the verandah, he first cast a glance at my chart and then at Mr Ghatpande's.

Mr Ghatpande laughed and asked him, 'Are you too afraid of fluid?'

'Well, yes, fluid is definitely worth fearing,' he said, 'and then, it's been a year since I came here and my condition has not improved a bit. My fever hasn't gone down and there hasn't been any decrease of "G".'

'I myself will be leaving the sanatorium in a couple of

months. My doctor says . . .' Mr Ghatpande started to say, but the other man cut him short: 'All the doctors say that. That's exactly what they told me and, now look, I've been here a whole year. You did the wrong thing, coming to this sanatorium. Who cares about the patients here? This is just a goddamn business. I'm going to Miraj. The doctor there is the most renowned specialist in T.B. You did the wrong thing by coming here. If your case gets worse here, there's no way you'll get any better. It will rain here incessantly for weeks and months while the weather will be wonderful at Miraj.'

He went outside and sat down on a recliner. I thought Mr Ghatpande would continue with his discourse, but he kept silent and looked sullenly out the window. In the inside ward the Bohra patient began to cough pathetically as usual. I felt some comfort as I reclined on my bed. I turned my eyes towards the outdoors. Evening was beginning to close in. A cool breeze was blowing and the silver oak leaves rustled. A bird came and perched on a thin branch of the tree opposite the ward and began whistling long, melodious notes. Just then the man with the long nose came in, bringing an Irani fellow with him, whom he introduced to Mr Ghatpande.

The Irani was a pale young man, short of stature, with a cheerful disposition. His name was Hasan. In both English and Hindustani his pronunciation was quite entertaining. He looked at me and said, 'Doan warry my friend. You'll be arright. I been here the past year. I come in C-minus. I get fluid and that turn into pus. They prickled such big needle in my ribs. Oh my God! You'll see how much I scream. Tomorrow they prickle me with the needle again. You hear it in here even.'

'Could anyone explain to me what this bloody fluid really is?' asked Mr Ghatpande suddenly.

Mr Hasan turned towards him and said:

'You know when the steam touches a cold surface, and drip-drip, it turns into drops of water? Same with the A.P. The air drip-drip, turns into water if it gets cold.' He motioned with his fingers to show how the drops of water 'drip-drip', trickle into the pleura and become fluid. Then he said, 'During monsoon most people here they get the fluid. I got a delicate chest like a goddamn balloon. I got to watch out about catching the cold.'

Who knows what other information he would have shared with us if the dinner bell had not rung from far off in the club room. The man with the long nose went away and took Mr Hasan with him.

～

The ward boy brought my meal, but I couldn't bring myself to eat a single bite. When he left after tidying up my bed, I began to regret that I had ever agreed to come here. Already there was no strength left in my body and now I would have to be stuck full of needles. If I developed fluid and if I got pus, then I would be stuck full of even bigger needles. To die of tuberculosis was terrifying enough in itself, but to die getting stuck full of needles? My eyes filled with tears. But then Mr Ghatpande's words echoed in my ears: Have faith in yourself. Exercise your will power and don't listen to what other people say! The ward boy had switched off the lights at about 9.30. The night was especially dark with the waxing of the moon. I didn't know if Mr Ghatpande lay awake or if he was sleeping. I wanted to talk to him. But I couldn't even hear him shifting around in his bed. 'He is the master of strong will power,' I thought, trying to console myself. 'He must have gone to sleep.' Then I tried to soothe myself with the help of his words: 'Will Power, Will Power, Will Power!' I don't know when I finally fell asleep as I lay there awakening my will power, soothing myself, listening to the 'drip-drip' of the A.P. fluid.

When I woke up in the morning there was a great commotion in the ward. It was discovered that Mr Ghatpande had been missing since dawn. The man with the long nose had come to wish him a good morning and turn their acquaintance into a deep friendship, as soon as he got up that morning. He had seen that Mr Ghatpande's bed was empty. He thought Mr Ghatpande must have gone to the bathroom. After half an hour he returned. But he was still not there. When he went to look in the bathroom he was not there either. The newly admitted patients were not allowed to use the bathroom even to relieve themselves. He went and conveyed the news of Mr Ghatpande's disappearance to the nurses' quarters. And thence arose all the tumult. Even the head doctor was informed. After a good deal of running around, a telegram was sent to his father. The old man arrived that evening. Laughing with embarrassment and begging everyone's pardon, he told the doctor that Mr Ghatpande had arrived in Poona by the first bus that morning. Certain patients had made his son feel frightened that he would get fluid and who knows what else, and he was not prepared to return for any reason. Mr Ghatpande's father got a refund of his one month's security deposit, foregoing the charges for not giving fifteen days' notice and took away his son's belongings.

The R.M.O. came into the ward as soon as he had left. He reprimanded all the old patients and threatened that if they did not tell him who had spoken with Mr Ghatpande and who had misguided him, he would throw everyone out of the sanatorium within twenty-four hours. He reprimanded the doctor and the sister and gave orders that if any new patients arrived who had already had some treatment, they were never to be put in the Acute Ward if their health was reasonably good and if they were not running a fever, etc., etc.

～

Mr Ghatpande was gone. Perhaps he had no recollection of me, but I could never forget him. I stayed in the sanatorium for three years. I was given A.P. injections in both my lungs every eight or ten days. I also had P.P. injections in my stomach. I underwent an Adhesion operation in both lungs, and both times, after the operation, I got fluid. I had a number of close calls. The Bohra and a few other patients died during that time, but I never forsook the company of that great cure Mr Ghatpande had explained to me, citing Marshal Stalin as an example.

Three years later, when I was leaving the sanatorium, the R.M.O. shook hands with me and said, 'I feel that in your recovery your will power has played a greater role than our treatment. I congratulate you on getting well. Though we got disheartened at times, you never did!'

~

Today, five years later, all these events suddenly passed before my eyes again. I am completely healthy now, but I always go to the mountains during the hot season. This time, I have come to the Dharampur Sanatorium. A few hours ago, a patient arrived in the cottage next to mine. Just for the sake of it I went to see who it was. He was in a lamentable state. Both his lungs were affected. Only a skeleton! I heard the Doctor-in-Charge saying:

'Mr Ghatpande, you should have some faith in yourself. There's no need to go to so many sanatoriums. The treatment is just about the same everywhere. What you need to do is to make use of your will power and stick with one treatment.'

Translated by Daisy Rockwell and Upendranath Ashk

Formalities

'Come my friend, relax and make yourself at home.'

(This is what one sincerely feels, all the while hoping to God to avoid getting ensnared by such a friend!)

Rashid Bhai came out on to the balcony after reviewing with his wife all the arrangements for tea and snacks. He had smoothed out the wrinkles in the rug; he had shaken out the colourful teapoy cover and spread it out again; he had rearranged the cushions on the bamboo chairs; he had cleaned the frames of the pictures hanging on the wall. Stepping back a bit, he cast a critical glance over the balcony's simple yet engaging decorations and heaved a sigh of relief. At last, he sank into a chair and, stretching out his feet on the railing, he began to wait for Director Qadir and his wife.

Rashid Bhai was a stout man of medium height. He was stout, but he wasn't flabby. His cheeks, neck, arms, stomach, thighs, calves—all were fleshy for his height, but his flesh didn't sag anywhere. Not on his round cheeks, not on his neck, not on his stomach, nor anywhere else. Perhaps this was because he possessed an unmatched work ethic, despite his weight. He wrote songs for the movies; he also wrote stories, dialogues and scenarios; when he had the chance he even acted, and he didn't shrink from all the running around that such activities require. But despite all his dedication and labour—and despite the fact that his income continued to flow—he had not come across any suitable formula for fame. His genius—this is what he thought—was sinking into a mire of stunt films, and he devoted all his time to the effort of saving it. He longed for the chance to write the story—or if not, at least the dialogue—for some 'social picture'. If he could just once get the chance, he hoped to escape from the mire of stunts forever. And then . . . Then . . . His dreams, like the dreams of everyone who works in the film world, would travel via directorship, and arrive at the pinnacle, producership.

There was a knock on the door. Rashid Bhai leapt up as though rigged to a spring. A slightly ingratiating, fawning smile formed about his lips and, with a pounding heart, he opened the door. He was about to bow with a respectful greeting, when his gaze fell upon the fruit-seller, who, on seeing him, managed to produce a voice from some portion of his throat and asked, 'Do you want oranges or bananas, sir?'

That smile of Rashid Bhai's, in which a sugary welcome and buttery fawning were combined in mysterious proportions, disappeared from his lips in an instant. Turning completely harsh, he looked down the hall to the kitchen and called out to the servant in a grating voice, 'Boy, tell Mem Sahib, if she wants any fruit or anything, to come and get some.' He closed the door and went and sank into the chair as before.

≈

He had first met Director Qadir at a party given on the occasion of the birthday of Miss Shameem. Director Qadir was a successful director at Ratan Limited. He had actually started out life as a professor, but he had met with success in the film line. He had four hit films to his credit and now he was in demand everywhere. The previous year, he had suddenly fallen ill with T.B. and gone off to the sanatorium at Miraj. Now that he had grown a bit healthier and had returned, he had a very full schedule before him; even in the depths of his illness, he had written stories and scenarios for three films, and as soon as he had got back he had also signed a contract with Bombay Talkies. At their first meeting, Rashid Bhai had made such an impression on him with his critical praise for his first films that Director Qadir had agreed to come with his wife to Rashid's house for tea. And Rashid Bhai had been so pleased by Director Qadir's acceptance that his enthusiasm and excitement had prevented him from sleeping the previous night. Again and again, he instructed his wife about what she should prepare for tea.

'If they don't come, then . . .' Suddenly the thought occurred to Rashid Bhai as he sat there in his chair, and his heart froze with anxiety. Just then, there was a knock at the door. Rashid Bhai got up. The possibility of disappointment had snatched the smile from his lips, but even now there was still a trace of enthusiasm playing about them. When he opened the door, he saw Director Qadir and his wife standing before him. Rashid Bhai suddenly panicked. He forgot to lower his head in respectful greeting. He rubbed his hands together, clenching his teeth and giggling. 'Please come in, please come in,' he urged, as he brought them out to the balcony and positioned them in the chairs. Then he went inside and, returning with his wife, introduced them all to one another. Rashid Bhai's wife, like him, was heavy-set and cheerful. She smiled and came and sat opposite Mrs Qadir.

'Tell me, are you feeling better now?' asked Rashid Bhai, for the purpose of starting the conversation.

'I am fine,' Director Qadir said. 'But if either we or Miss Shameem don't move somewhere else soon, I'm sure to get worse.'

Rashid Bhai's mouth dropped open with surprise. After a moment, he asked, 'But the house where Miss Shameem is staying is yours, isn't it?'

Director Qadir laughed, despite his seriousness. 'Yes it is,' he said, 'but we can't get her to move out. You are aware of whatever drawbacks the house may have. Even when I was sick I continued to pay the rent and I didn't let anyone else move in. Shameem came to see me in Miraj. She had just come from Lahore. She was having a great deal of trouble finding a house. I mistakenly suggested to her—who knows why—that if she couldn't find a house for some reason, she could just stay at our place. And now I'm paying for that bit of formality. When she returned from visiting me in Miraj, she went straight to my house, and to this day she hasn't budged.'

At this stage, Mrs Rashid got up to see about serving tea to the guests.

'But surely Miss Shameem has made some arrangements for you?' Rashid Bhai asked.

This time it was Mrs Qadir who answered. She was a serious woman of medium height, lean yet vigorous. She had a B.A. and a B.T. If Director Qadir still looked a professor, she looked no less than the headmistress of some school.

'Made some arrangements!' she exclaimed in a bitingly sarcastic tone. 'What could she give us out of a three-room flat? We have one room. How can we be comfortable like that? And He is ill. He needs a separate room all His own!'

'Even if there isn't more than one room,' said Director Qadir, running his hand over his balding head, 'there should be some peace and quiet. Over there, we feel as though we were sitting in a fish market twenty-four hours a day!'

'All day long we hear nothing but "Ha ha, hee hee, ho ho",' said Mrs Qadir, building her case. 'Shameem has created such an impression since coming here to Bombay that the whole town is gaga over her. Dancing, singing, parties, flash and rummy drives! There's not a moment of peace. And He has to work, too. What does she have to do? Just go to the set, say four words the wrong way and come home. The real tragedy is for Him; He has to consider the story, scenario, shots, dialogues and even the camera and sound. For such matters, one does have to think a little. And there's not even a moment to hear oneself think there.'

Director Qadir kept quiet. But the lines of helplessness on his face grew more pronounced. At that moment, Rashid Bhai felt as though there was nothing he wouldn't do for him; if he could, he would huff and puff until a house appeared into which Mr Qadir could move with his family, and all their troubles would be over. 'I have only these two-and-a-half rooms,' said Rashid Bhai, 'that is, if you could call this balcony a room; otherwise I would have asked you to come here.'

'Thank you so much for your kindness!' said Mrs Qadir, smiling. 'It's not a matter of space, it's a matter of peace and quiet. If a person is good, polite, then forget about a room, one can easily make do with a storeroom. But what can one do when no part of the camel stands straight!' Miss Shameem was a tall, languid young lady. Mrs Qadir smiled while comparing her to a camel, and then continued, 'For the sake of appearances, Her Highness has set up a dining table, but she doesn't know even the ABC of table manners. She dresses as though she had just graduated from college, but at the dining table she's worse than a peasant. While drinking or eating, she makes such a noise, God help me! She gets gravy all over her hands and face. And then all kinds of tabla, sitar and sarangi players and new-money businessmen come and sit at the table, and eat in such a way that one begins to feel nauseated. Sometimes there's such an uproar, one feels like simply *dashing* one's head against the wall!'

Just then the servant came in behind Mrs Rashid, carrying the tea and snacks; and Mrs Rashid, with her simple smile, began to pour out tea for the guests. Rashid Bhai took advantage of this opportunity to bring up the topic of himself; how he himself had had a good deal of trouble finding a house; how when the ship had crashed in Bombay and people had begun to flee for fear of an attack by the Japanese, he had acquired this beautiful seaside flat. Talking about his flat, he brought up his experiences in the film world and told Director Qadir which films he had worked on, and for which he had written stories, dialogues and songs. Not finding this topic interesting, Mrs Qadir, after drinking one cup of tea, went with Mrs Rashid to look at the flat. Rashid Bhai took advantage of this lull to praise Director Qadir's genius: he expressed his opinion that if Director Qadir gave him an opportunity to work with him, he would meet with success in the film world, and so on and so forth.

Director Qadir listened to what Rashid Bhai was saying with great seriousness, an unfathomable smile playing on his lips; eventually, he made one of those vague promises to the effect of: 'Why not, why not, I'll definitely help you, why don't you write a story and show it to me.' Then he called out to his wife that it was getting late; Producer Vadilal was coming to meet with him and they should go soon.

When Mrs Qadir came back on to the balcony her face was radiant. 'Oh my! Your flat is so beautiful and so open!' She said to Rashid Bhai, 'It has made me so happy to see it!'

Rashid Bhai stretched out his hands in a dramatic fashion and exclaimed, 'Please, your wish is my command!'

For an instant Mrs Qadir stared at him silently, and then, realizing what he meant, she laughed, saying, 'You are so very kind! I was just admiring your flat.'

'No, if you like it, please come. It would make us so happy to live with you, even if we occupied only the balcony. And here, even if there were other inconveniences for you, at least there would be no mental disturbance. Really!'

Mrs Qadir only laughed gratefully in response. As she walked down the stairs, she suggested to her husband that he get Rashid Bhai to write the dialogue for his new picture. And when Director Qadir got into the taxi he shook Rashid Bhai's hand and promised him that he would propose Rashid Bhai's name for the dialogue right away when he met with Producer Vadilal.

When Rashid Bhai returned from seeing them off, he ran up the stairs, taking not one, but two and three at a time. He hugged and squeezed his wife enthusiastically and announced to her that, God willing, he himself would write the dialogue for Director Qadir's next picture; he wanted praise for his cleverness.

'You can't even imagine how cleverly I extracted a promise of work from Director Qadir. In the film world, no one cares about qualifications. I've learned that secret after years of getting kicked around. You have to have cleverness and dexterity to go along with qualifications. There are actually plenty of people who aren't qualified at all, but are only aware and clever. Now, you tell me, if I hadn't invited Mrs Qadir to come here and live with us, would I have got this job? Never! But I know what should be said, where and when! Those people would hardly leave a nice flat like theirs and come to live with us, but this small offering of mine did have an effect on them and I have just tasted its fruit . . .'

And leaving his wife astonished at his savvy and dexterity, Rashid Bhai set off enthusiastically to meet with the producer of his company so he could impress him with this news and get a good contract from him for the next picture.

～

When Rashid Bhai returned in the evening he was a little drunk. He couldn't meet with his producer, so he had gone and grabbed his friend, the stunt film hero, Shahbaaz. When Shahbaaz had seen him a bit happier than usual and wanted to know the reason, Rashid Bhai made him promise first that he would not tell anybody; then he whispered in his ear that he was going to write the dialogue for Director Qadir's next picture. And then, without Shahbaaz even saying anything, he promised him he would try his best to get him a role in the picture—preferably the hero's and, if not, then of the second hero or the villain. To celebrate, Shahbaaz took him to Dadar Bar and the two of them tossed back two small pegs of scotch each. Shahbaaz was short of cash, otherwise Rashid Bhai would have had to be escorted home by friends. But he invited Rashid Bhai to meet him at Dadar Bar after one week and assured him that in the meantime he would arrange preferably for a bottle of scotch, but if not, a bottle of dry gin.

The tide was coming in. The waves advanced and collided with those returning from the shore, a sort of a wall of foam continuously forming in both directions for a long way off. A slice of moon among the stars in the sky cut a shining Milky-Way-like path into the vast bosom of the sea with its light. Rashid Bhai felt slightly buzzed. He wanted to wander about on the beach in this pale brilliance; to get wet, to stand on the sandy beach and gaze at that path of light illuminating the sea as far as the eye could reach; to go and sit on the covered cement cylinder drains pouring the Dadar water into the sea; to stretch his feet out above the waves of the advancing waters—just high enough so that the spray from the waves hitting the drainage cylinders would sometimes splash on his legs. Just then he felt a cold gust of wind. Rashid Bhai recalled his warm soft bed. The thought of his bed reminded him of the warm, soft, ripe body of his wife and, abandoning the allure of wandering on the beach, he went upstairs, climbing the steps, not one, but two and three at a time. He then impishly extended one finger and pressed the bell for a long time.

He imagined that his wife would come and open the door— her flapping, Gujarati ghaghra-like dress dragging along the floor as she made unsuccessful attempts to hide her voluptuous bosom in her dupatta. Fretting but smiling, she would scold him sweetly, 'Stop it, stop it! Why are you pressing the bell like a child? I'm not deaf!' But Rashid Bhai jumped back a step in alarm when, instead of his wife, Mrs Qadir opened the door and, piercing him through with her naked sword of a gaze, she said harshly, though she was trying unsuccessfully to be gentle, 'Oh, it's you! I thought some urchin boy must be making trouble! Do you ring the bell like this every day?' Then she softened her voice and made room for Rashid Bhai to come inside. 'So, we've come,' she said, laughing. 'After fixing things up for you with Producer Vadilal at the studio we arrived home to find an incredible hullabaloo. People from who-knows-where-all had come to congratulate Miss Shameem on her birthday, believing in "Better late than never". And He is ill. And then I just started feeling so suffocated by the uproar. I called for a taxi, packed a few essential items and we came here. This will be an inconvenience to you, but . . .'

In the midst of this, Rashid Bhai's buzz had evaporated. His facility for reason had returned; his hesitant steps had moved forward and the high-flying kite of his imagination had received the shock of reality and touched the earth. Laughing foolishly, he responded, 'Heh, heh, what inconvenience? As I said just this morning, this is your home . . . heh, heh, this home is yours. Have you all eaten already? Where is Suraiya?' Suraiya was the name of Rashid Bhai's wife.

'We waited for you until quite late. But—' and here Mrs Qadir spoke very softly—'you know, He is a sick man; He should eat and sleep on time. We have eaten. Mrs Rashid is probably in the kitchen.' And directing Rashid Bhai's attention towards the kitchen, she added, 'For now we've settled in just this room; why don't you eat? I'll go take care of His sleeping arrangements. Don't worry, I don't believe in standing on formalities. I have taken everything I need and will continue to do so—and I won't hesitate to cause you any inconvenience either.'

With this, she went into the inside room.

~

In only one week, Rashid Bhai found out that Mrs Qadir was in no way one of those people who say one thing and do another. She literally did exactly whatever it was she had said she would. In those seven days she did not stand on formalities whatsoever and she did not hesitate the least from causing inconvenience to Rashid Bhai and his wife. In Rashid Bhai's absence she had already taken over the larger of the two rooms as soon as she arrived. Under her own supervision, she had Rashid Bhai's bedding and belongings set up in the middle room, which was Mrs Rashid's dressing room. She was extremely helpful to Mrs Rashid in setting up the room so that two beds could fit into it, as well as the ladies' and gents' dressing tables, and not even look bad. With great informality, she had dinner cooked without even waiting for Rashid Bhai. She showed absolutely no hesitation in instructing the servant as to how many eggs should be in the omelette or the halwa, and which vegetable should go into the curry with the meat. In fact, she planned the menu for how many times her husband should have milk, eggs and soup starting from the next day— 'Eating is the only important thing with a lung condition, that's why!' She had ordered the servant to bring food to her in the room, eaten it and busied herself with her husband's sleeping arrangements.

Up to this point, well, Rashid Bhai hadn't experienced too much inconvenience. When he regained his composure after the initial shock, he felt honoured and proud to find Director Qadir in his home, knowing that he had not only relieved his favourite director of heavy mental stress, but had met with the opportunity he had sweetly imagined for years as well. To his wife, sitting in the kitchen with her head resting on her knees, he presented scores of arguments, explaining that Director Qadir's arrival in their home was a wonderful opportunity for them both in every way.

But from that point on, the same mental stress from which he had saved Director Qadir's life now began to eat him up.

It was night and he was lying in bed with his wife. He was thinking about how he had imagined that it was he who had trapped Director Qadir with his savvy, but now he realized that it was Mrs Qadir who had trapped him with her own savvy. The moment this thought occurred to him, he chuckled at his own foolishness. Just then a tap came on the door from the inside room. Mrs Rashid jumped up and went and sat on her own bed and he called out, 'Come in!'

Mrs Qadir entered the room on tiptoe with her finger to her lips. 'For God's sake, please laugh softly,' she whispered. 'I have finally managed to soothe Him to sleep by massaging His head with oil!' And she retreated, closing the door gently behind her.

After this, Mrs Rashid did not have the courage to get into bed with her husband again.

The next day, Mrs Qadir, with great informality, had a charpoy removed from Rashid Bhai's room and placed in the balcony, and she had Director Qadir's table put in its place. This was because the bedroom was not appropriate for work, and then they also had a small daughter, who was now thick as thieves with Rashid Bhai's son, and no work could take place in all the noise. 'At night we'll put the charpoy back here again,' she explained to Rashid Bhai. 'Right now, you people sit at this table and work.' With that, she went into her room and busied herself with straightening up.

Rashid Bhai sat down at the table and discussed the dialogues with Director Qadir for a few minutes. That was all the encouragement he got. For the rest of the day, all sorts of people kept coming to meet Director Qadir. Rashid Bhai got up and went out to the balcony, where he talked with his friends, and Mrs Rashid sat in the kitchen all day. There is no need to mention that the people who came all day to meet Mr Qadir used the other charpoy as a sofa and, by evening, the freshly washed bedclothes that Mrs Rashid had spread over it were filled with scores of wrinkles.

There were two bathrooms in the flat, one for bathing and so on, and the other for the dishwasher to come and scrub the pots and pans, and so forth. Mrs Qadir, without any hesitation whatsoever, took over this second bathroom on the third day and told the dishwasher to scrub the pots and pans in the kitchen.

On the fourth day, after a good deal of thought, Rashid Bhai devised a plan whereby the second bed would be brought out to the balcony as well and set up there, and the things in the balcony would be put in the middle room, which would be turned into a shared drawing room. Mrs Qadir praised him to the skies for this suggestion. The result was that that room also slipped from his hands, and Mrs Rashid again remained locked up in the kitchen most of the day as before, because, when Qadir Sahib was speaking with the people who had come to see him, it was impossible for Rashid Bhai to sit there himself, or seat the people who had come to meet him, let alone speak to them. So Rashid Bhai was, as before, forced to sit and work in the balcony and meet his visitors, and Mrs Rashid spent the day in the kitchen.

On the fifth day, the dressing table also arrived in the balcony. In this way, the balcony became their sleeping, sitting and dressing room, and his earlier comment to Director Qadir, 'It would make us so happy to live with you even if we occupied only the balcony,' had been made a complete and happy reality by Mrs Qadir with no qualms whatsoever.

On the sixth day, without any sort of hesitation, the Qadirs removed Rashid Bhai's things from the storeroom and set up their own kitchen there. 'You know Him,' Mrs Qadir said to Mrs Rashid. 'He has lung trouble. What does it matter if He's negative today, He could be positive tomorrow. I even keep Naazli's and my pots separate from His. You have a delicate little child. That's why I'll be cooking in a separate kitchen.'

Thus, she was extremely helpful to Mrs Rashid in arranging the things which had been removed from the storeroom and placed in the hall, making a temporary storeroom for them and unhesitatingly giving priceless advice on the subject.

There is no need to mention that as soon as the kitchen was finished, Mrs Qadir took over Rashid Bhai's cook and dishwasher, forcing Mrs Rashid to cook with her own hands until a new servant came.

On the seventh day, when Rashid Bhai arrived at the Dadar Bar at Shahbaaz's invitation, Shahbaaz saw on his face not even a hundredth part of the elation that had been there seven days earlier. He had let his beard grow and his clothing was unclean. His face which, despite its fleshiness, was usually full, taut and shiny, now looked saggy.

All Shahbaaz knew was that Rashid Bhai was writing the dialogue for Director Qadir's new picture, so he had brought a whole bottle of scotch and was waiting for him to come so that he could ask if he had done anything to get him a role or not; but when he saw Rashid Bhai's mood, he kept quiet. He called to the waiter and ordered a mutton chop and kababs, and then he poured the pegs out into the glasses. He popped the corks from the soda bottles, poured the soda into the glasses and held out a glass to Rashid Bhai.

In the midst of this, Rashid Bhai sat with his elbows on the table, resting his chin in his palms. With his eyes he chased the doe fleeing across the picture on the facing wall: it was difficult to tell whether it was leaping or stretching, because there would be the same amount of space between the front and the back legs for a leap or a stretch. The artist had perhaps glimpsed the stretch of his lover in the stretch of the doe. Who knew? One couldn't even figure out what the average man was thinking, and here he was contemplating what was going on in an artist's mind. As far as Rashid Bhai was concerned, his mind was in a state completely opposite to that of stretching. It had contracted so much that perhaps he was not thinking at all. His eyes were glued to the doe as though willing her to leap. Or if she would not leap, he might at least bore two large holes into her.

For a few moments Shahbaaz waited for Rashid Bhai, of his own accord, to take a look at the bubbles rising in the glass, but when the foam rose and then began to subside again, and

Rashid Bhai's desultory gaze had not yet moved from the doe, he asked, 'What's wrong? Pick up your glass, why don't you? Look, the fairy who jumped into the glass is eager to touch your lips!' And he laughed hollowly.

'Just leave me alone! I'm not in the mood today. Why don't you drink it! I only came so that you wouldn't have to sit here waiting for me.' And he placed his glass next to Shahbaaz's glass.

'But what's wrong? Didn't things get nailed down with Director Qadir?'

For the first time Rashid Bhai smiled a little. 'Forget getting nailed down, this thing has become a millstone around my neck! I keep wondering how I'm going to get out of this.'

'What do you mean?'

In reply Rashid Bhai told him the whole story of his misfortune.

The waiter set the mutton chop and the kababs on the table.

The liquor was sitting in the glass, the nice warm mutton chop was staring invitingly up from the plate; to Shahbaaz, all sorrow seemed tawdry before such pleasures. 'Forget about it!' he said. 'Why are you wasting your time thinking about such little things! Your big wish has come true. Lift your glass, let's throw back a few pegs to that!'

But there was great pain in the line of a smile which had formed on Rashid Bhai's face.

'This seems like a little thing to you? Now I know that I've fallen into hell when I was sitting in heaven. If Director Qadir or Miss Shameem doesn't find a house in two months, I'll be ruined.'

'Oh come on, just lift your glass; if it's causing you so much inconvenience, come to my place,' he said, picking up his own glass.

Rashid lifted his glass and responded dejectedly, 'But you just have a single flat. Where would you go?'

Shahbaaz clinked his glass against Rashid Bhai's and finished it off in one gulp; he said, 'What does it matter to an easy-going guy like me? I'll roll out my bed on the stairs!'

~

The next day, at around eleven or twelve, when Shahbaaz opened his hung-over eyes, he saw that his room was packed full of luggage and that the only empty space was where he himself was sleeping. He blinked a couple of times to make sure he wasn't dreaming. Just then, Rashid Bhai appeared in the doorway. 'Well, I see that you sleep as much as you drink!' He remarked, 'Get up, wash your hands and face, and have something to eat. Then help us set up our stuff. My wife is making something to eat in the kitchen. Your servant is really great. If it weren't for him, we could never have gotten so much luggage up to the third floor.'

And he began to laugh and laugh.

~

That night, when the clerk who lived on the fourth floor came home a little later than usual, he noticed as he was climbing the stairs that it wasn't just the servant from the third floor who was sleeping on the stairs, but also his master, who was lying on his bedding, staring fixedly at the ceiling.

Some Suds and a Smile

Hariya was sitting happily on the square embankment under the water pipe, wearing a khaki loincloth—perhaps just the remnant of a pair of shorts—his skinny legs stretched out contentedly, his head bowed down a little, and Lallan was vigorously scrubbing his body with soap.

Professor Malhotra usually went this way when he was going to his friend Professor Sen's house. Even though he could just as easily go by the street that ran along the train tracks, or even by South Road, he really liked that piece of road that went between the two-storeyed Railway Living Quarters. To the left, there were the Living Quarters, where a community water pipe had been installed for the servants who lived at the corner, and to the right were ten rooms set aside for the lower-caste servants, who sat and did nearly all their housework at the small door in front of the Quarters: the women dried their hair, put on their clothes, did their make-up; lay their naked children upside down or right side up on mats and rubbed oil into their bodies; strained and sifted the grains; cooked the food; fought and quarrelled. Professor Malhotra didn't know why he enjoyed this exhibition of private life in the open market. But then, Lallan, their new, young sweeper, lived in the last room in the row. Although, by now, Lallan had worked for them for a long time, she was still new, compared to Sharbatiya.

Sometimes when Malhotra passed by on his day off, at

129

around twelve or one o'clock, Lallan would be bathing at the water pipe. Sometimes she would be walking towards her room, hiding her blossoming body in a wet sari. Malhotra would half-glance in her direction. At times, her husband Hariya would be sitting in front of their room, smoking a bidi. His Chinese moustache drooped down his shrivelled-up face on either side of his mouth, just like in photographs. When he saw Malhotra, a helpless-looking smile always spread across his lips. Wrinkles appeared in his sunken cheeks, changing from parentheses to brackets, and he would greet him, hiding his bidi in his fist. There was something about that smile that awoke in Professor Malhotra a sense of weak hostility. Sometimes Malhotra remained silent in response to Hariya's greeting; at others, he nodded his head a little, and at others he laughed, and said, 'Tell me, Hariya, my brother, how are you?' But he never stopped to hear his response; he always kept walking.

From a distance, Professor Malhotra's gaze slipped from Hariya's soapy body to Lallan: her complexion was now even darker, dishevelled locks of hair hung about her face, shadows had crept below her eyes, and yet she must be only twenty-five now, give or take a year ... And then, the last four years passed before Malhotra in the blinking of an eye, and he remembered that first afternoon, when Lallan had come into his room, following behind Sharbatiya.

∼

It was early afternoon, probably around three or three-thirty. Malhotra was sitting in his study looking at a thesis when his wife came and said, 'Sharbatiya has brought a new sweeper.' Then she turned and called to her, 'Come in, Sharbatiya!'

Sharbatiya was their old sweeper. A few days earlier, she had unexpectedly given notice, saying she was returning to her village, and to kindly let her leave. Malhotra thought perhaps she wanted a raise, but when she didn't change her stance even after he tempted her with a raise of a rupee or so, Malhotra came to believe that she really was going to the village. He told her that if she gave her place to some other trustworthy sweeper, they would let her go.

Sharbatiya lifted the curtain and came in, and behind her, right behind her, came a thin, graceful young lady with a wheat-coloured complexion; her face was round and her big round eyes were rubbed with kohl; she wore a freshly cleaned printed sari and a silk blouse, and she glittered in her silver necklace and earrings. Sharbatiya was extremely tall and fair. She too was beautiful and young. But there was a strange slackness to her. This young lady, because of the build of her body, the wideness of her round eyes, her taste in clothing and her unusual poise, looked much more beautiful than Sharbatiya, despite her darker colouring. If she had not come in with Sharbatiya, Malhotra would have taken her to be the wife of a merchant from some good home, or a paan seller's wife.

'She is going to do the work of a sweeper?' he exclaimed to himself, but aloud he asked, 'What's your name?'

'Lallan!'

'But you're so dressed up, will you be able to do all this work?'

Lallan was embarrassed. Sharbatiya was the one who replied.

'Sir, she got married just a month ago, but she's a smart worker. Don't worry.'

'But you know, Sharbatiya, at our house everything is in the open, we need a trustworthy sweeper.'

'Don't worry, sir, you won't have any complaints.'

'All right, you explain everything to her, what work she'll have to do and how many rupees she'll get a month.'

And the two of them went away. Malhotra signalled to his wife to stay behind.

'Such a dressed-up girl. I doubt she'll do good work,' he said. 'It would be so much better if that useless Sharbatiya would stay on.'

'But she can't stay,' his wife said. 'Anyway, she has assured me Lallan is a fast worker and she's trustworthy. She's her sister-in-law by some distant relationship.'

His wife went away. Malhotra got involved with reading the thesis again, but Lallan's large, round, kohl-lined eyes, the generous curve of her waist and her sparkling earrings continued to shimmer before his eyes. *There's no way such a woman can do the job of a sweeper!* he thought to himself.

∼

But his suspicions proved totally baseless. Not only could Lallan do the work Sharbatiya had done, but she also started cleaning the rooms inside the house. She swept and mopped Malhotra's study, arranged the things on his table and put his books back in their places on the shelves. She polished shoes for Malhotra, his wife and his children and washed their clothes every day. The more work she undertook, the more her wages increased. After cleaning the toilets she always washed her hands and arms with soap up to the elbows before touching any clothing. Before returning in the early afternoon she always bathed and changed into a clean sari. It wasn't just she who was always clean, she kept the house neat and tidy as well. Mrs Malhotra was so happy with Lallan's work that, when she found out Lallan went home to bathe and cook after she had done her morning work, she gave her two new saris. That way, when she went back to her own home, she would always return in the afternoon wearing a freshly cleaned sari. One day, Mrs Malhotra even went so far as to tell her husband that if Lallan ever wanted to stop being a sweeper, she would put her in charge of a higher level of work in their house.

It had only been four or five months since Lallan had started when Professor Malhotra became severely ill. It was the month of February, but the sunlight was quite strong. One day, he had to teach a class at two o'clock in the afternoon. At around twelve o'clock he felt so warm that he took off his long-sleeved sweater. When he left for the university he wore only a coat over his shirt. He thought he would teach one period and then come home while the sun was still out, but instead he got caught in a university meeting. During the meeting, clouds gathered in the sky from out of nowhere and it began to drizzle. First the cold, then the rain, then a strong breeze. He got extremely wet. Although he took off his suit as soon as he got home and put on a fresh shirt and pants, a long-sleeved sweater and even an overcoat, he continued to feel a piercing pain on the right side of his chest. All night long he coughed. When he tried to get up in the morning he simply could not. His head hurt, his throat was swollen and his whole body was aching. When he took his temperature he found he had a fever of 101. They called for the doctor, who said it was influenza.

But this influenza took on such a complex form that Malhotra ended up staying in bed for two months. He grew extremely weak. Exactly when Lallan started pressing his feet he could not remember.

In the afternoons, when he felt tired but was not able to fall asleep, and when his feet and calves felt oddly restless, and his body ached all over, he would get extremely fidgety and ask his wife if she would just press his body a little. His wife was the beloved only daughter of her executive engineer father; her body was fair and plump, soft and delicate, and her hands were fine. She would try to press his legs, but her hands always started to hurt and Malhotra ended up feeling no relief whatsoever, which made him angry.

One evening, when Lallan came for the second time in the day to do the cleaning, Mrs Malhotra asked her, 'Lallan, would you mind washing your hands and coming over here to press Professor Malhotra's legs?' And so Lallan started to press his legs.

But that had all happened in the early days of his sickness. In the end Malhotra just asked Lallan directly.

Lallan was slender, but there was iron in her hands. First she would press his calves, then his ankles, then his heels, then the soles of his feet, then his toes and toenails. After that, she would crack his toes and press his feet and then his legs. Sometimes she would press his knees and even his waist. The knots of pain scattered with the touch of her hands, as if they had been smashed to pieces. While she worked, she talked about this and that in such a sweet voice, that he often fell asleep just listening to her words.

One day Lallan returned in the afternoon wearing a colourful, freshly washed sari. Perhaps she had bathed with turmeric ointment that day. Her face was shining. There was a huge vermilion bindi on her forehead and her lips were red from the juice of the paan she was chewing. That day it seemed to Malhotra that his wife was right when she said that if Lallan were to quit working as a sweeper she really could be given a higher position, and while she was pressing his feet, he mentioned that desire of his wife's to her.

'I'd come, sir,' Lallan said with seriousness, 'but the Sweeper wouldn't let me.'

And she told him that the Sweeper—that is, her husband Hariya—was a no-good alcoholic and gambler. All the expenses of the house were paid out of what she earned at their house. He didn't give her even one coin from his salary.

'Your father didn't arrange your marriage carefully?' Malhotra felt a sudden pang of sympathy for her.

'I was only four years old, sir, when I got married. They have only recently brought me to my husband's house.'

'So he doesn't even give you his salary?'

'What does he ever give me, sir? It's just the opposite, he asks me for money. If I don't give him anything, he beats me.'

'On what does he spend your wages?'

'He's a real bastard, sir. He drinks and gambles,' Lallan said. 'Yesterday he kept asking for my necklace, so he could pawn it. When I wouldn't give it to him, he tried to pull it off.

I was cooking. I grabbed a piece of burning wood from the fire to get him to take his hands off me. I threatened to break his arm. After he took his hands off me, he started cursing me. I've kept all my money at my mother's house, sir.'

Malhotra turned over to lie on his stomach and asked, 'Lallan, could you press my back a little?'

'Can you let me go now, sir? I still have to do all the rest of the work. If I'm late the Sweeper will yell at me.'

'Just press it a little bit,' Malhotra said very softly. 'This sickness has sucked out all my blood, I don't have any power left at all.' Then he laughed a little. 'Anyway, my life is drawing to a close, I've grown old.'

Lallan laughed too, 'Oh, sir, how can you be old, my Sweeper looks much older than you.'

'How old is he?'

'He's four or five years older than me.'

'Then how did he get older than me? I'm past forty.'

'Oh, sir, what do numbers like forty and fifty mean? You could still get married twice more,' and she laughed.

'If I can manage just once, that's no small feat,' Malhotra also laughed.

Lallan quietly began to press his back. The knots on each side of his spine slowly started to subside under the pressure of her hands: his waist, his buttocks, his thighs; Lallan kept pressing, and Malhotra wanted her to keep pressing, for the knots of pain to keep melting, for his body to keep feeling this sweet relief . . . when suddenly she withdrew her hands.

'Sir, I'm going.'

'Oh, please, just crack my toes!' He turned over.

There was a strange shame in Lallan's eyes and her cheeks were glowing.

'No, sir, I'm going now.'

And she hurried off.

≈

One day, when Malhotra was returning from his walk in the evening, he heard a racket from the direction of the storehouse and the kitchen.

His health was somewhat better than before. His fever had broken fifteen or twenty days ago. He had even started to eat solid food and to go out walking a little after resting in the afternoon for a couple of hours. When he heard the noise, he went to the yard behind the bungalow. Lallan was standing on the verandah of the storehouse, behind one of the columns, and a skinny feeble man was standing outside screaming at her.

Malhotra could tell who he was, but even so, he asked in a threatening voice, 'Who are you? Why are you screaming?'

'Sir, I'm Hariya.'

'Which Hariya?'

'Sir, your sweeper.'

'Then why are you yelling?'

'Sir, Lallan . . .'

From behind the column, Lallan cried out, 'Sir, when I come home from working here, sometimes I'm a little late and then this man curses me and hits me.'

Hariya was going to say something, when Malhotra thundered, 'Don't talk nonsense, get out of here.'

Feeling more confident of support, Lallan emerged from behind the column, 'Hit him, sir, beat him up.' And then she said to Hariya, 'I'm not going, I'm staying here. Get out of here, run, go!'

Malhotra lifted his eyes and looked at her. He didn't think it was wrong of her to threaten her husband, but he didn't think it was right for her to tell him to beat him up. Then his gaze returned to Hariya: the bones of his shrunken chest showed through his shirt with its broken buttons. He had a dirty lungi wrapped around his waist. His head and feet were bare. Malhotra's eyes rested on his Chinese-looking moustache and his shrivelled-up face and his dark red teeth . . . He felt oddly disgusted; and whereas earlier, he had been on the verge of getting angry with Lallan, he now felt only sympathy for her as he cast a glance at the two of them. He scolded the sweeper for beating his wife, not giving her any money for food and throwing away his earnings on alcohol: how could she stay at home? If he didn't get out of there immediately he would beat him to a pulp and then have the police called and get him arrested.

Hariya immediately fell at his feet. He entreated him piteously, insisting that he wouldn't say anything to Lallan— he would bring all his salary home and put it directly in her hands and he would quit drinking completely.

Now that the sweeper had fallen at his feet, Malhotra could not think what to say. He told Lallan to go home, and that if Hariya bothered her again she should tell him. Lallan refused a couple of times, but after Malhotra had reasoned with her, she went home with her husband.

Malhotra went and sat down in his study and put his feet up on the table. He leaned back in his spring chair. His wife came in behind him.

'If Lallan comes to live here I really will get another sweeper,' she said.

Malhotra asked carelessly, 'Where would she live?'

'In the verandah of the storehouse.'

'Wouldn't she get cold?'

'There are only a few days left of winter, next month people will start sleeping outside. But she won't get cold, we'll put up a curtain in the verandah.'

'But how can she live in our house?' Malhotra asked. 'A sweeper . . . our relatives . . .'

But Mrs Malhotra interrupted him. There was a Muslim cook at the home of her executive engineer father. She said, 'Are all these bearers and cooks from the high castes? They got converted into Christians out of low-caste Pasis, Chamars, Julahes, or Mehtars. When I look at the landlord's wife, I can tell she was definitely a sweeper who became Christian. Mr Holden may be English, but that black-as-pitch wife of his is definitely a sweeper by birth. How is Lallan any worse than her! And we even drink tea at Mrs Holden's house, and we eat there too. If Lallan quits this kind of work, I'll definitely keep her on.'

His wife said all this in one breath. Professor Malhotra didn't reply. *How silly these women are. They totally reject reality in the face of sentimentality. They don't look at what's right in front of their noses*, he thought. For an instant he closed his eyes. His wife's words echoed in his ears: *If Lallan comes and lives here I'll get another sweeper . . .*

If Lallan comes and lives here . . . If Lallan comes and lives here . . . Neat and tidy, attractive Lallan, who is highly skilled at pressing a tired body, who heedlessly melts away knots of pain, who is sweet-spoken (no matter how much she quarrels with her husband, she always speaks softly in their house), whose big round eyes are rubbed with kohl and who has somehow learnt to stand in exactly the same pose as the young women of Ajanta. When Malhotra had seen those dark-skinned young women (who were princesses) in that pose in Ajanta, he had thought the pose was only a flight of the artist's imagination, but here was Lallan . . . this illiterate village sweeper sometimes looked just like those young women of Ajanta. All it would take was for the bun of her hair to be more like theirs, then there would be no difference at all. . . . *If Lallan were to come and live here . . .* and in his imagination Lallan came there and began to live in their home. His imagination took another leap . . . but then a shiver ran through his entire body and he started and sat up straight. His legs went beneath the desk, his back straightened and he pulled a copy of a thesis in front of him.

His wife was still standing there. 'Don't be ridiculous!' he said, without looking at her. 'It doesn't matter how neat and tidy Lallan is, how good her work is, how little belief we place in caste. If she came here to live, not one of my relatives would eat in this house.'

And Professor Malhotra busied himself with the thesis before him.

～

Lallan ran to their house again one evening, a few days later. When Malhotra talked to Hariya, he claimed that since that evening, he had not drunk any alcohol, but even so, Lallan still always quarrelled with him: 'Now, sir, I'm just a poor sweeper,' Hariya said. 'How can I wear clean clothes every day, how can I wash my hands and feet all the time?'

Lallan told Professor Malhotra that Hariya had hit her again, and then snatched her earrings and pawned them.

This time, Lallan's father came and reasoned with her too, and finally took her home with him.

The next day, in the early afternoon, Lallan was pressing Malhotra's body, when he asked, 'Lallan, why do you quarrel with Hariya every day?'

'Sir, he drinks, he takes my jewellery and pawns it, and if I say anything about it he hits me.'

'But he says he has quit drinking.'

'He hasn't quit anything, just yesterday he fought with me in the evening and then came home really drunk.'

'What happened?'

'Nothing, sir!' She fell silent.

'So then?'

'Sir, he always wears such dirty clothes. Whenever he talks, he curses. He says: "Why don't you just go over to your master's house, tell him to build you a bungalow," and then he comes home really drunk. There's only one bad habit, sir . . .'

Lallan was pressing his calves with great concentration. Malhotra was silent for a moment, and then, laughing slightly, he said, 'So if you don't let him come near you, he won't quarrel, he won't drink and he won't curse your master in front of you either?'

'No, sir, how can he curse you? How can he have the right to?'

Malhotra acted as if he had not heard what she said; he laughed again, and then asked her softly, 'So then what's wrong, Lallan, do you hate him?"

Lallan hesitated, then she turned up her nose, and whispered, 'Sir, he smells!'

Malhotra couldn't think what to say to that. He laughed hollowly, and said, 'Take a piece of sandalwood soap from the bathroom. Make him bathe with that. He'll improve.'

'I'm not going to bathe him with soap, I'd rather have him run out of town!' Lallan said. 'If he keeps bothering me like this, I'll pack up and go to my mother's, then I'll call a Panchayat Court and get rid of him. My father says, "You'll have to give him two hundred rupees." Mrs Malhotra says, "Lallan, you come and live here." If Mrs Malhotra gives me a little help, sir, I'll get rid of that bastard.'

'Yes, get divorced from him and set yourself up in the home of some other companion you prefer.'

'Sir, if I can't find happiness with my own fate, where will I find it? All the men in my caste drink, curse and beat their women. Sir, if you help me get rid of him, I'll work for you here.'

And Lallan began to press Malhotra's knees with great devotion. She pressed both sides of his kneecaps, and then started pressing his thighs a little above his knees. Malhotra began to feel great pleasure from the pressure of her hands. She had leaned over more to press the thigh on the other side of the charpoy and was pressing with great involvement, when suddenly, Malhotra drew his legs back. 'Lallan, you can go now, you'll be late.'

'No, sir, I'll just keep pressing, you go to sleep!' And she pulled his feet to press the soles.

'No, Lallan, you go. If you're late your Sweeper will yell at you. I'm fine now, I'll go to sleep.'

Lallan had begun to crack his toes when he pulled his feet away, 'Enough, now, go!'

He pulled the blanket up to his chin and he turned over.

~

After that day Malhotra did not ask Lallan to press his feet again. She always swept his room in his absence and she brought the paan box in to him when he was there. Malhotra never looked at her and remained absorbed in his work. A few days later he found out from his wife that Lallan had gone to her father's house. Then he found out that Hariya wanted to call a Panchayat Court. His wife suggested that they give Lallan two hundred rupees so the poor thing could get rid of that boozing gambler! Malhotra heard what his wife said, but then again he did not hear it, and remained absorbed in his work. Some days later, he found out that Hariya had called the Panchayat. Then he heard that he had given his word in front of its five leaders that he would not drink and he would also give back all Lallan's jewellery, and when the five leaders and her parents insisted, Lallan unwillingly went back with Hariya. A short while later they heard that Lallan was pregnant.

~

Lallan had a son. She did not come to work for a whole month. During that time, her mother and her sister-in-law came to do her work. Both of them were dirty and raggedy. Malhotra's wife did not let them come into the house. They just did their work outside and went away. One day, Malhotra saw Lallan's mother. Even though she quickly pulled her veil over her face, he caught a glimpse of her fair colouring, her sharp features and her blue eyes. *There is definitely the blood of some Englishman in her veins,* he thought. *Before Independence, only English people lived in this area. Even if Lallan didn't get the English skin colour, she certainly inherited their haughtiness.*

And he smiled slightly.

After a month Lallan started coming to their house again. In the mornings she left her son with her mother. In the evenings, sometimes her sister came and held the baby in her lap, and sometimes Hariya came with the baby on his shoulders. Mrs Malhotra hated the very sight of Hariya's face. She would not even let him come inside the house. He would sit near the gate, on the drainage pipe outside the bungalow, with the child on his shoulders. Sometimes, when Malhotra returned from the University at that time of day, Hariya would stand up with the child and greet him, spreading the wrinkles of a smile across his shrivelled-up face to reveal his dark red teeth.

Malhotra would say, 'Tell me, brother Hariya, what's going on?' and continue without waiting for his response. Sometimes when he saw Lallan on the path, or when she came to take the paan box away from his room, his gaze would happen to fall on her and he would be amazed that even after becoming the mother of a child, Lallan looked no different: under her tight-fitting blouse, her waist was just as slender, her stomach was just as flat and taut, the swell of her bosom had increased only slightly and her colouring had cleared up . . . And then the image of his own wife would come before his eyes: after the birth of only one child her waist had lost all its elasticity.

But his wife never again expressed the desire to keep Lallan at their house as an ayah. It really greatly irritated Mrs Malhotra that Lallan brought her child along with her to work. But now and again, Malhotra wished that Lallan would press his feet again. On summer afternoons, when his calves felt restless and he couldn't get to sleep, this desire became even stronger. But in the afternoons, her Sweeper would come with her and then her child always lay outside crying, and she would be in a hurry to finish work quickly and go and feed her baby; and so Malhotra continued to toss and turn.

Even though Lallan's body hadn't changed particularly after the birth of her child, she didn't dress up any more. Malhotra didn't like that child of hers one bit. A child was a child, whether it was a sweeper's or a leather worker's. Even a donkey's child could look beautiful when it frolicked about, but Malhotra didn't like this child of Lallan's at all. He took after neither his mother nor his grandmother. It was his father he took after, or maybe his father's father, because Hariya's features were also sharp, like Lallan's. This child's nose was incredibly flat and wide and his face was incredibly heavy. Lallan had very lovingly named him Ramdulare. When this Ramdulare turned one year old, Lallan started bringing him with her in the mornings as well. She would spread a piece of mat on the ground and put a dirty mattress over it and lay him down on top of it. She made her little sister sit next to him and then she went and did her work. Ramdulare cried all the time. He rolled over and wallowed in the dirt beneath the mat and the mattress. His nose dripped all over his face and then he got all dirty; Malhotra felt a great aversion towards him. At first Lallan always put him on the porch outside the study, but when Malhotra asked her not to, she started putting him on the verandah of the storehouse behind the bungalow. Whenever Malhotra looked at Lallan, the image of her child came before him and he averted his eyes. When Lallan was at their house, he never went behind the bungalow and, if he ever happened upon her with the child in her lap, he turned his face away.

This child of Lallan's was three years old when he came down with the measles because of the changing seasons. Instead of taking him to a doctor or giving him medicine, she took him to the Kalyani Devi temple so they could prostrate themselves there. Then, she went to bathe in the Ganga. The child caught a cold. Instead of the measles going away, they went inside him and when she thought the measles were disappearing, the child actually had pneumonia. The pneumonia turned into double pneumonia, and in less than a week the child had flown out of her hands.

Whether Lallan cared about Hariya or not, she had loved

Ramdulare very much. Out of love for him she had even more
or less forgotten her anger towards Hariya. She had stopped
worrying about whether or not Hariya gave her any money for
the household. Night and day she was involved with her
Ramdulare. She was deeply depressed by the death of her
child. She half-wasted away from crying. Her eyes grew sunken
and her body sagged.

~

The hot season that year was intense. There had been several
deaths in the city the month before because of the heat.
Malhotra too had a heatstroke one day and for several days
burned with fever. By the time the fever abated he felt extremely
weak. Even though it was the hot season, his calves started
aching. The weakness bothered him even more. His spirit was
quite broken. One day he asked his wife if she would just press
his feet a little, so his wife told Lallan to do it; and thus, Lallan
started pressing his feet again. This time, Malhotra felt that
some of the iron in Lallan's hands had softened. When he told
her to press his calves harder, she said, 'Sir, I'm too old now. I
can't do that any more.'

And she laughed a feeble sort of laugh.

'Tell me, how is your Sweeper these days?' Malhotra asked
with a smile, to change the direction of the conversation, 'He
doesn't beat you and steal from you any more?'

'Now he doesn't even come home at all!' There was so much
sorrow in Lallan's voice, it touched Malhotra's heart.

'Where does he stay?' He asked.

'He goes over there, to Bai ke Bagh.'

'Who's in Bai ke Bagh?'

'There's a Mr Collis. He teaches in the Christian College.
His sweeper is such a whore, sir, he's under her spell. As soon
as he finishes work, he goes over there. He gives her all his
wages, he eats and drinks there.'

Malhotra sensed a thin flash of jealousy in Lallan's eyes and voice.

'So, is she a beautiful woman?' He asked.

'How should I know, sir, I've never gone over there. As far as I've heard she's ten or twelve years older than me. She's a whore, sir, she's snared him. The Sweeper has been living over there for the past year.'

Malhotra also got a faint sense of longing from her voice. She kept quietly pressing his feet and Malhotra thought about that other woman.

~

He did know Professor Noel Collis, because he too was a history professor. They weren't friends; they were acquaintances. One evening he went to Professor Collis's house with his friend Sen. While they were drinking tea, he lavished praise on Collis's bungalow and his garden. After tea, Professor Collis took him into his garden. 'Flowers just don't flourish in the summer the way they do in January and February,' Professor Collis said, 'but I've planted so many kinds of petunias that flowers of different colours are in bloom all day long. And then, perhaps, nowhere else in the city would you find such a large jasmine as I have here at my home.'

To encourage him, Malhotra praised the tiny little plants that looked like bamboo, which were planted on both sides of the crescent-shaped path along the edge of the lawn, and asked their name.

'Those are called "puchiya", or peacock's feathers,' Professor Collis explained enthusiastically. 'Take a look at this, all the plants look the same. None is the slightest bit taller or shorter than the others.'

And he began to explain how he had sorted out these identical-looking ones from five hundred other plants and then planted them in rows.

He kept going on about his jasmine, pearl jasmine, champa, sunflowers, blue verbena and who knows what other kinds of plants. Malhotra didn't hear a thing. He just kept nodding and murmuring in response. When Professor Collis took them behind the bungalow towards the servant's quarters to show them more of the grounds, Malhotra's interest was suddenly piqued. He praised to the skies that habit the English had of making room for their servants in their bungalows and always putting the kitchen far away from the house, and then he enumerated the many good qualities of that system.

Professor Collis told him he had four servants: the cook, the bearer, the gardener and the sweeper, and that they all lived in the bungalow.

Malhotra was walking in front of the servants' quarters when he suddenly stopped in front of one of the rooms. The door was open, and Hariya was sitting inside with a small earthenware cup in front of him, next to a fat, coarse woman. As soon as he saw Malhotra he pushed the earthenware cup under the cot.

'Why, Hariya!' Malhotra cried out, pretending to be astonished. 'What are you doing here?' And he darted inside.

The parentheses turned to brackets on Hariya's shrivelled-up face and he quickly got up and greeted him.

Malhotra did not reply to his greeting. His gaze moved from Hariya to the coarse, fat, dirty, raggedy sweeper woman beside him. Lallan had said she was ten years older than her, but she seemed to him to be about the age of his own mother.

'What are you doing here?' he suddenly asked Hariya.

Hariya looked at the floor, trying to figure out how to answer Malhotra's real question. Then he said, 'She's my relative.'

'Come here a minute!' Malhotra went outside. He told Collis and Sen that this was his sweeper and he had to tell him something important.

He took Hariya a little distance away and scolded him for

leaving such a good wife and going after this witch. He would not let Lallan go, but he would not give her happiness, either, it seemed. Malhotra threatened that if he ever saw him there again, he would have him sent to jail on some charge. 'You know, the chief captain of police is my friend. At the police station they'll see to it that all your carousing is leashed in and stopped forever. For one thing, you'll go to jail, and for another, you'll have to wash your hands of your job.'

Hariya listened quietly, his gaze fixed on the ground.

'What do you say?' he asked, thundering. 'If you don't agree, would you rather I told Professor Collis that this witch has opened up a brothel here?'

'I'm just a sweeper, sir, and Lallan talks like a rich lady,' Hariya complained.

'Oh, come now, she probably tells you to keep clean. If she bothers you, tell me. I'll reason with her!' Malhotra patted him on the back and turned away.

~

And two days later, Lallan told him as she pressed his feet that Hariya had come home, and she asked Malhotra for five rupees so she could have a kurta-pajama sewn for him.

'You've got your man under control,' he told her, giving her a five-rupee note. 'I told you before, too, that if he doesn't stay clean, you should clean him up yourself. If he doesn't wash his clothes, you should wash them. It's better if he eats and drinks in front of you than if he eats and drinks outside the house.'

After Lallan had pressed his feet and gone away, he heard her asking his wife for half a bar of the 'English' soap that was in the bathroom.

~

All these events flashed before Malhotra's eyes when he reached the water pipe. Then Hariya saw him. There was nothing but suds all over his body, and on his face there was a kingly smile, in which he sensed neither the old helplessness nor hostility. Hariya greeted him from where he was sitting.

Malhotra did not reply to his greeting. He glanced briefly at Lallan, her head bent down in great concentration as she scrubbed Hariya's back and ribs with soap; and there had been a day when she had said, 'I won't scrub him with soap, I'd rather have him run out of town.'

Malhotra smiled in spite of himself.

The Aubergine Plant

Mahiram has uprooted the aubergine plant, and yet, as I cross the vegetable field, walking on its narrow boundary to my house, that dry plant and the yellow, shrivelled aubergine that dangles from it still swim before my eyes.

~

It was some time since the brief winter day had come to a close. I had taken a long, after-dinner walk, sporting an overcoat and a scarf, and under that, a warm achkan and kurta, a thick khadi shirt and undershirt. Flashlight in hand, I was absorbed in the clicking of my steel-heeled Flex boots, my ears hidden in the collar of my overcoat to protect them from the sharp, cold, dry wind of the month of December. When I entered the verandah of my house, I was astonished to see an old man seated there on a dirty charpoy, coughing. He was decrepit, filthy as the dark night and wrapped in a black quilt.

'What is it, my friend? What's the matter?' I asked, pulling my overcoat tighter around me.

'Nothing, sir,' he said, 'I'm Mahiram's man.'

'You're Mahiram's man, fine, but why are you out here, on this open verandah?'

'I have enough clothing to protect me, sir.'

Silently, I opened the door to my room. I had left the large line-fourteen Ditmar table lamp burning, and although both the transom windows were open, the room had grown warm. The moment I entered, a smell assailed me which was warm, yet sharp, redolent with kerosene. My friends have often advised me not to leave the lamp burning like that. 'What's the point in leaving behind the pollution of the city to live in the fresh air,' they ask, 'if you don't leave your bad city habits behind?' And they inform me that keeping a lamp burning in a closed room is extremely harmful, according to doctors: dirty air enters the breathing path, it affects the lungs, and the lungs are weakened. I often feel that way myself, but what can I do about it? In the end I'm forced to leave the lamp burning in the closed room every day. Whenever I sit with the door open and a sharp gust of wind comes in, and my hands become motionless, and my pen refuses to move, I get up and close the door. Just the way a cigarette smoker grows fond of the cigarette's dizzyingly bitter, pungent smell, I have, after a fashion, grown fond of the smell of kerosene in my room.

I hung my hat on the hook, took my scarf and wrapped it around my head and ears, and sat down to work.

But my attention was still focused on the verandah.

≈

I had seen that old man before. I had seen him just that morning. He was pruning the aubergines, and when I was returning from the dining hall, I had even asked him why he was doing that. He had explained to me that aubergines bear fruit twice. If they are pruned once, they get even larger and plumper. I glanced at the dry, flowerless plants. A yellow aubergine, shrivelled and desiccated, hung from one of them. My gaze shifted from the aubergine to the old man. It was difficult to tell how old he really was, but he looked extremely aged. Though he had a thick cotton shawl to shield him from the cold, his yellow, stick-thin hands, his legs, skinny as bamboo stalks, his dry, pinched face and the sockets of his eyes were all

completely exposed. Then a strange thought entered my head—
even when an aubergine plant dries, it produces fruit again
after it is pruned; the drumstick tree also grows after pruning.
There are certain kinds of trees and plants that grow even
more after pruning. Why didn't the Unseen Creator make man
the same way? But on the other hand, someone once said that
the vine of mankind is also immortal: men and women, children
and old people are its fruit and flowers, leaves and branches.
Death is its pruning shears. When people rot or dry up, those
shears cut them away and, in their place, leaves, flowers, fruit
grow ever outwards, always fresh, full of green, shouting with
the excitement of life, laughing, dancing, singing.

But why was this old man outside in the biting cold? Did he
have no home of his own? And starting slightly, I looked out
and asked him, 'But who are you?'

'Sir, I'm Mahiram's man!'

'Yes, you are Mahiram's man, but just how are you related
to him?'

The old man was about to say something when he had a
coughing fit. After coughing ceaselessly for a few moments, he
brought his breathing under control with some difficulty and
told me that he wasn't related to Mahiram in any way. He was
from his village. His family was very large. He had five small
children, a wife and two daughters of marriageable age, and he
had come here with Mahiram to earn a living.

As I sat and worked, I found it hard to concentrate when I
thought of the tenderness of his voice. Not only was I wearing
a great deal of clothing, I was sitting in a warm room with a
blanket pulled over my trousers, whereas that poor man was
lying outside in the cold. All he had for bedding was a thin
blanket, ragged and filthy, and an ancient black quilt.

'Why don't you lie here, inside—it's so cold outside,' I
suggested to him tenderly. 'The verandah is open on two sides.
Why are you sitting out there?'

But just then the sound of heavy shoes stamping on the

cement floor reached my ears, and the next moment, Mahiram—that six-foot-three employee of the contractor Gopal Das—appeared, standing at the door. He was wearing a huge turban, a thick black blanket, a dhoti down to his knees and, on his feet, shoes weighing two or two-and-a-half pounds each. Once he had chased a man all the way to the press for stealing nothing but six radishes and, when he'd caught the thief in the field, Mahiram had given him such a beating he had never turned his face in that direction again.

'I told him to sleep here myself, sir,' he said. 'I don't know who the bastard is who robs the fields at night. It's been going on for two or three days. Yesterday, ten heads of cauliflower were missing. In the whole field you wouldn't find such nice cauliflowers, and the day before yesterday, someone picked some ripe tomatoes. You know, we also have to supply the kitchen, and then, sir, there's the two hundred-rupees rent. All that has to be made from the produce.'

'But who steals the vegetables?' I asked. 'I've never heard of any stealing here. My house is completely isolated, there's no other house nearby; but I'm gone for hours at a time, and I leave the door open. It's probably some outsider.'

'No, sir. An outsider wouldn't come in this cold just to take ten heads of cauliflower.'

'But that other time there were the radishes too . . .'

'That was something different, sir; he was just a passer-by. While he was going by, he dug them up and took them. But this is someone from here. I'm going to catch the bastard and teach him so he'll never lay his hand on anything again for the rest of his life.' And he smiled, his thick lips spread wide and his pockmarked face stretched tight.

'But, why don't you let this man sleep inside? It's very cold.'

'No, sir,' Mahiram replied. 'The cold only affects rich people like you. We don't feel the cold. I'm having him sleep here like this only as a blind. I'll be on guard, sitting behind those jasmines. As soon as he thinks the old man has gone to sleep, he'll come and then I'll swoop down on him.'

And he laughed.

'But he has no clothing to . . .'

'He has enough clothing, sir.' And he went away.

The old man had another coughing fit.

I again became engrossed in what I was doing. But I soon found I just couldn't work. A picture of the employer of these two men sketched itself before me. Contractor Gopal Das—whose cheeks, because of his wealth, prosperity, offspring and lack of worries, were as pink as a rose even now, at the age of fifty—was probably warm from the glowing brazier, lying under a thick quilt, gossiping happily in his room, or amusing himself with playing cards or chess.

Musing thus, my eyelids began to droop—I had eaten too much, I had weighed myself down with clothing, and my room was warm. I got up. I took some important papers along with pen and ink to my bedroom. I thought I'd get up a little early the next morning. Then, when I was going back to lock the office, I asked the old man if he wanted me to leave the office door unlocked. But when he said, 'No, sir, no, I have enough clothing,' I locked the door and went into my warm, cosy, little bedroom. The bed was already made and all I did was put another blanket over the quilt, change my clothes and lie down. The bed was cold as ice. I drew in my feet and then, after a while, I slowly stretched them out again. My mind started to wander through a number of different thoughts—disordered, disconnected and uncontrolled—but my eyes had grown heavy from the warmth of the quilt and, slowly, they closed.

As I slept, different faces came into my mind: sometimes Mahiram's, sometimes the old man's, and sometimes that of their employer, the contractor.

I dreamt that Mahiram had caught the thief and taken him to the nearby village, Vairoke, beating him all the way. Gathering all the villagers around him, he announced that whoever stole our vegetables would meet with the same punishment. So saying, he beat the thief some more. The thief looked towards him with pathetic eyes and I was astonished that it was none other than the contractor—the same polished head, the same blooming cheeks, the same flat nose.

I opened my eyes. I saw that the quilt had slipped off my legs. My chest felt a little heavy from eating too much and my throat felt dry.

I drank some water from the pitcher at the head of the bed, pulled the quilt back up and, tucking it under my legs on each side, I lay down again. Outside, the wind was lashing at the walls, and the trees were shrieking fervently, contending with all their might against its intensity. From far away came the thundering of the clouds and the crack of lightning. But my body grew warm again and then relaxed. I fell asleep.

This time I dreamt that it was raining heavily. A strong wind was blowing. Hailstones were falling, as big as half a pound each. All the vegetables were destroyed. Their beds were full of water. Only that yellow, shrivelled aubergine was left standing. Then, right before me, the aubergine started to grow larger and I saw that its face had become just like the old man's—his arms were stuck to his chest and wrapped around his knees, he was shrunken, naked, hanging from that very same plant by his braid. The hailstones hit him on the head, but all the same he hung there, swinging . . .

Then I saw that the plant had become a big, tall tree, perhaps a rose apple or a mango. A crowd of people was standing under it making a lot of noise—the old man was dead . . . The old man is dead . . . The old man hanged himself and now he is dead . . .

And then only voices saying, 'He's dead . . . he's dead,' reached my ears.

I woke up and heard someone knocking loudly on my door. I put on the warm socks I had placed next to the head of my bed, and a warm hat and, wrapping the blanket tightly around me, I got up and opened the door.

Outside, the secretary of the colony was standing with a few other people. It was raining: as far as the eye could see, there was nothing but water, and it was well after sunrise.

'What's the matter?' I asked.

'The old man died on your verandah last night.'

I saw that the old man was lying on that same black charpoy, bent over, wrapped in his quilt. His quilt was completely soaked and the rain had drenched the entire verandah.

'Last night I told him . . . to . . .' I tried to say.

The secretary said, 'I was going to the kitchen to get some milk for tea, when I saw him here, wet. I called out to him, but he didn't move. When I came up close I found that he was stiff.'

And he told the contractor's men to arrange to remove him.

〜

Two days later, I called out to Mahiram as I was going to the kitchen, 'For God's sake, get rid of that yellow aubergine plant!'

Mahiram stared at me, astonished by the strangeness of my tone, and then he said, 'Very good, sir!'

Furlough

It was the second week of June when Kaviraj decided to go to Shimla. He told Chetan to get himself ready for the trip and then come to his pharmacy.

Chetan didn't have much to get ready. All he had was the soft, warm quilt he had received as a wedding gift. Somehow he managed to scrimp and save and get two pairs of homespun cotton pajamas and shirts stitched. He had absolutely no coat to speak of, so he brought along the old government-issue overcoat which his older brother had been wearing for quite some time. In those days, the custom was that after three years, a station master was issued a new coat and then the old one would belong to him. This particular coat, having finished its term as Chetan's father's, had been handed down to Chetan's older brother; and after he had exploited it fully for three or four years, he had very kindly given it to Chetan. Chetan had had it altered, but despite the new cut, it still looked like an item purchased from a junk shop. Even so, when Chetan wore it over his freshly laundered clothes it didn't look too bad with his collar open and his long curly hair.

For Chetan, a trip to Shimla was no less momentous than a trip abroad. He could not contain his excitement. For a junior editor working thirteen hours a day in that fire-breathing weather, the very thought of Shimla's diversions during the hot season was no less than a sweet dream.

~

The train was heading towards Shimla. Kaviraj, his wife and his children were travelling in the Intermediate Class and Chetan was in the Third with Kaviraj's clerk Jaydev, his servant Yadram and Yadram's wife Manni.

Chetan was so happy that even though there was enough room in the compartment to lie down, he did not feel sleepy. At Amritsar station, a young man from his city came and sat with him. He had recognized Chetan and greeted him. Chetan didn't actually recognize him but when he found out he lived in Jalandhar near the neighbourhood he grew up in, he told him quite proudly that he was going to Shimla to improve his health and he also asked him, if it wouldn't be too much trouble, to go to his house and inform his mother and his young brother Nityanand that he was well. 'Tell them,' Chetan instructed him, 'that you ran into Chetan in the train on his way to Shimla. He will stay there for three or four months and return when his health has improved.'

After he had said this he began to search for a reaction of envious respect on the face of his companion.

The train arrived in Jalandhar at around one o'clock in the morning. Yadram—six feet tall, young and well-built—had stretched his body across the bare seat and fallen asleep. His wife was dozing sitting up, her veil pulled down slightly over her face. Chetan did not feel sleepy at all. He stuck his head out the window and looked at the station that was so familiar to him. He scanned the platform in both directions to see if any ticket checker of his acquaintance came into view so he could give him the news that he was going to Shimla, but he didn't see anyone he knew for quite some distance.

Some clerks, eyes drowsy, were wrapped up in their work at chairs and tables set up on the platform. For them, it seemed, none of this was of terribly great importance: the comings and goings of the trains, the passengers getting on and off, the shriek of the engines, the whistling of the guards. Though they lived squarely in the uproar of the world they were as engrossed in their labour as yogis who live far removed from earthly matters. Chetan felt overwhelmed with compassion as he watched them. How could they know that, as they leaned over their tables, their clothing dripping with sweat from the humidity, a young man seated in the train right near them was about to go and revel in the cool breezes of Shimla?

It occurred to Chetan that he might get down at the station and saunter a bit, walk just beyond the platform; if possible, he could get a drink of cold water at the familiar station well. But he remembered that the night was already half over, the well would be empty and the person who served water on the road would probably be relishing a sweet or bitter rest.

The train set off. Chetan averted his gaze from the scene outside. Although Yadram's wife was dozing, the veil had slipped back from her face. Chetan glanced over at her, furtively at first, then openly. But first he opened a book and placed it before him.

~

Before agreeing to go to Shimla, Chetan had, in a way, insisted that Kaviraj give him something or the other to do if he went with him. He was too proud to allow himself to be a burden on Kaviraj.

It would be hard to say whether the idea that he should be concerned for his pride had actually occurred to him of its own accord, or whether he had got the idea from listening to Kaviraj talk about events from his own life. But on hearing Kaviraj's proposal that he go with him to Shimla, and on learning that he would not have to do much work there, he had expressed his gratitude. In the course of that conversation, Kaviraj had told him an episode from the initial struggles of his own life: 'A friend of mine gave me some financial support,' he said, 'but at that time I could not pay him back, so for an entire year I tutored his children without taking any fees.' As he warmed to his topic, he told several stories of this type—how, whenever he had received something from various well-wishers, he had given them so much more in return. Chetan had insisted right in the beginning that he be given some work to do, but when he heard all this, he refused to go along without being given some task.

Then Kaviraj, with apparent reluctance, told him he was thinking of writing a book about the birth and death, loving and raising of children. He had also shown him a journal from America which touched on the subject and suggested he go to the Punjab Public Library as well and take a look there. If he found any books on the topic he should immediately become a member of the library. Chetan had understood what he was saying, and in order to repay him for his kindness he decided that he would write a very good book for him.

In conversation, Kaviraj explained to him that this book would be published under his—Kaviraj's—name. It would be a collection of introductory information about all the illnesses of children, and readers would be advised to immediately seek the advice of some famous vaidya or doctor if there were any complications.

Chetan had taken five books out of the library. He had even mentally created an outline for the book. Right now he had one of these books open before him.

~

Yadram's wife glanced at him from the corner of her eye a few times as well. It seemed to Chetan there was also a slight smile playing about her lips—the kind of smile about which it is difficult to tell whether it is on the lips, or in the eyes. She had a wheat-coloured complexion, with light smallpox scars on her face, a skinny body and dark lines on her teeth. She was not beautiful, but there was something attractive about her eyes and smile that made Chetan stop reading his book and look at her and then begin to talk with her.

There were not many travellers in the compartment. Those who were there were lying sound asleep, unconscious, their mouths agape, heads hanging, striking very strange poses. The leg of a sleeping man was swaying quite a bit from the luggage rack above the opposite berth and Chetan feared that if the man changed position slightly, he would fall off. Yadram was sound asleep right below the hanging leg. His light snoring punctuated the silence of the compartment. It was Manni who first started the conversation.

'You don't feel sleepy, Babuji?' she asked, smiling familiarly. Chetan liked her smile. There was sympathy in it; it was friendly and enthusiastic.

With his gaze fixed only on his book, he again looked at Manni from the corner of his eye. 'I can never sleep on trains,' he replied, with a chuckle.

Manni was half-sitting, half-lying down. She sat up and asked Chetan about his home, his parents and his brothers and sisters.

There was such affection in her questions, in her speech, in the yearning smile of her eyes, that Chetan began to feel warm inside. Manni started to seem very attractive to him in that nighttime silence, in that compartment lost in sleep. Chetan was growing stiff from sitting up, so he stretched his legs out a bit on to Manni's berth.

'Feel free to stretch out, Babuji,' said Manni affectionately, practically pulling his feet. At the same time, she stretched her own legs out on to Chetan's berth.

'One gets stiff from sitting,' she laughed.

For a few moments Chetan continued to quietly read his book. Then he glanced at Manni's feet from the corner of his eye—small, sweet feet; on her toes there were silver twists and rings and on her ankles heavy bracelets and hollow anklets. The soles of her feet were decorated with mehndi, the colour of which had mixed with dirt and mud and turned to black.

'You don't wash your feet, look, they're getting black,' he said, first touching them and then running his hand over them.

'I wash them all the time, Babuji, but I have to do housework all day long—scrubbing the pots, sweeping—how long can they stay clean?' She showed him her hand, where black streaks lined the red colour of the mehndi.

Chetan felt like kissing those red and black hands, but just then Yadram changed position. Chetan's hand returned to his book and they moved their feet away from one another a little.

But this time Yadram had his back to them. Then Manni touched Chetan's feet nervously and said, 'But your feet too are black, Babuji!'

'Mine?' Chetan laughed. 'When do I ever get the time to wash them? I walk around all the time! And the only shoes I have are these sandals, so if there's just a little bit of water or mud, they get sticky.'

Manni's skirt, which had slid up to a little above her ankles, hung between the two berths and the pale white skin above her ankles was showing—it was the colour of pale white almonds. Chetan wished he could stroke her foot all the way up to her pale white almondy calves. But at that moment, the train stopped at a station. Just as debris floating on the sea washes up on to the shore with the current, some travellers washed up into the compartment from the sea of people at the station.

The silence of the compartment was broken as the new passengers settled in, putting away their luggage, sitting down, lying down and talking on and on in their crude, unpolished mountain speech. Yadram continued to sleep deeply, as before. The person sleeping on the opposite upper berth pulled up his leg and wiped the sweat from his neck and face before turning over. Some dozing travellers sat up with a jerk of their heads; others sat up sleepily, cast a drowsy eye all around and then went back to sleep. One drank a *pav* and a half of warm milk; one ran off with a *lota* to get water.

Just then a man sleeping in the corner woke up with a start.

'What station is this?' he asked a new traveller in a heavy voice.

'Ambala!'

'Ambala!' His mouth dropped open. Then he shook the person with him. 'Arré, get up quick, it's Ambala, the train is about to leave.'

His companion got up as though he had been struck by lightning. He quickly gathered his luggage and they both left the compartment.

~

Chetan's gaze settled on the newcomers. After taking care of their luggage and so on, they had settled down on the opposite berth. There were three women among them. The two men were not dressed particularly well—they wore tight, dirty pajamas that came down to just above the ankles, and checked shirts under Pahari jackets. They both had wide sideburns, the tops of which were hidden in their round hats. Their braids hung down their backs from beneath their hats, like mouse tails. The women were quite neatly turned out, but they looked flashy. Two were young and one was middle-aged. Both the younger ones looked somewhat older than their age. A lack of self-control had etched lines in their faces which were clearly visible despite the application of cheap powder and rouge.

When the train set out and everyone had settled down, one Pahari youth took a pack of cigarettes from his jacket pocket and handed his companions a cigarette each. In just a moment everyone had begun to smoke cigarettes with great relish. Chetan gazed at the women, astonished. They were smoking cigarettes quite casually, as though they were quite skilled in the art. They were having a wonderful time blowing smoke rings as they puffed away contentedly.

Chetan himself did not smoke cigarettes. Cigarette smoke was unbearable to him. If someone sitting near him in a room were smoking, he would start to feel dizzy. Nonetheless, he had many friends who were addicted to cigarettes. But the idea that women might also smoke was completely new to him.

Now that more people had entered the compartment, the air had become stifling. The train was going at full speed. Puffs of warm air came through the open windows along with the dust of the road and the smoke from the engine. The mixture of dust and smoke with the stench of the passengers' sweat was already more than a little suffocating, and on top of this, these five people had begun to smoke cigarettes. Chetan started to feel claustrophobic. He was getting slightly dizzy. But the Pahari women, reclining with their legs outstretched and crossed, had altered the atmosphere of the entire compartment; they were smoking with such self-assurance that Chetan felt like stretching his legs out too, slouching back, getting a cigarette from somewhere and blowing tiny smoke rings from his nose and mouth just like them. But in the midst of this, he really began to feel quite ill; he stuck his face out the window and took several deep breaths.

Although the moon was shining up above and there was no sign of clouds at all, a curtain of dust hung suspended between the earth and the sky. It seemed as though the moonlight were having trouble reaching the earth. It spread its light hesitantly: as though its arms had stretched out just a short distance and stopped; they were incapable of penetrating the darkness. All around, the dry earth lay spread out in the dusty light. The rains had not yet started. The shrunken withered greenery had become a part of the dust-filled moonlight. The trees and plants, like fleeing shadows, emerged up ahead. From the front of the train, the engine again began to puff out smoke. The black cloud of smoke grew in the pale moonlight. Like a python it leapt right over the train towards the rear. The sparks of its eyes burned in the darkness. Chetan quickly drew his face inside.

Everything was exactly the same. Only Manni had placed her hand on her husband's thigh and gone to sleep. She had covered her face with her veil and wrapped her legs well with her skirt. The rings and twists on her toes gleamed as before.

Lifting his gaze up from those gleaming rings and twists, Chetan again glanced at the Pahari women. They were smoking as before. Chetan observed a lack of reservation in their eyes the like of which he had never seen before, except in the eyes of the prostitutes of Kotwali Bazaar in Jalandhar. A number of times, instead of coming home from school through Mohalla Mahendruan, he had crossed the police line and gone through Kotwali Bazaar across from Sabzi Mandi and stood motionless, watching those women for ages. They were dark and ugly, and smeared with powder, and they sat boldly in front of their rooms, joking coarsely with the Jaats who came into town from the villages. The boldness in the eyes of these Pahari women was exactly like that in the eyes of those prostitutes.

Just then his gaze moved to another person who was staring hungrily at the mountain women. Following the man's greedy eyes, Chetan saw that the centre of his attention was the woman who was the youngest and comparatively most attractive of the three. She wore a pink silk churidar-pajama and a shiny kameez under a beautiful chartreuse jacket; her head was covered with a silk dupatta and she reclined on her bedding supported by one elbow, her head resting in her palm, like a picture of a Mangal Dweep empress. The silver pendants hanging from the centre of her ears and her nose ring complemented her sharp attractive features. She was also wearing less powder on her face than the others—perhaps because her face had fewer lines. The man staring at her was middle-aged with a pointed salt-and-pepper beard and a shara'i moustache cut from beneath the nose; he was bare-headed, with rough salt-and-pepper hair, and his eyes betrayed keen hunger and a glimmer of lust.

When the women had finished their cigarettes and thrown the butts out of the windows, the man got up and went over to sit next to them. He took a pack of cigarettes out of his pocket, took one for himself and then held the pack out to the two Pahari youths. They each took one cigarette. Then he held out the pack to the two women. They also took one cigarette each. Finally, with a grin that revealed his yellow teeth, he shyly held the pack out to the Mangal Dweep Empress. After all, she was the Mangal Dweep Empress! In her regal fashion, she shook her head, 'I don't smoke those!'

He pulled back his hand with a mortified laugh, and clenching his teeth, he asked in a hopeless tone, 'So . . .?'

'I smoke only Cavenders.'

'I have only Lal Badshah!' he laughed sadly.

The woman then regally ordered her companion to take out the packet of Cavenders.

The Pahari man took out the packet of Cavenders and gave her a cigarette. Holding the cigarette between her lips, she continued to recline and did not so much as move her hand. When he lit the match, she moved her face forward slightly, still in the same position, puffed on the cigarette until it was lit and, then, fully the Empress of Mangal Dweep, she began blowing smoke rings.

Chetan tried to read his book, but he felt as though something were pressing down on his head. His eyes didn't feel at all sleepy but they stung. A line of pain ran above his eyebrows and his body was weary. He lay back with his legs stretched out on the berth across from him and closed his eyes.

But he didn't fall asleep. He could hear everything: the conversation of the Pahari women, the mortified laugh of the lusting man and the rattling of the train in the background.

The man was joking with the Mangal Dweep Empress in a vulgar manner and she continued to put him off with the same contemptuous smile. Just then, he heard another voice, 'Arré, go sit near her, why are you lying over there and giggling?'

Chetan opened his heavy tired eyelids and saw that another man had woken up and was sitting up and urging the first one on. But the first man didn't have the nerve to go and sit near the haughty woman.

Just then the train stopped at a station. The first man got up

and bought some sweets. He took the packet and went and sat
near her. He bared his dirty yellow teeth in a grin as he held
out the packet of sweets with one hand and with the other he
held her knees and squeezed them to his side, a lustful gleam
flickering in his eyes.

Chetan's half-closed eyes opened completely.

The Empress of Mangal Dweep raised an eyebrow and
looked towards the packet. Then, with contemptuous hatred,
she suddenly propped herself up on the bedding with her
elbow, freed her knees from his grip and pulled back, kicking
the packet so hard the sweets flew out the window leaving a
few reminders of his folly on his face.

'They're prostitutes!' the other man said. 'They've earned
their money and they're going on furlough.' He laughed.

The first man, rather chagrined, wiped his face and went
and sat in his seat. The sparking lust in his eyes had grown
dim, like extinguished coals.

Chetan closed his eyes.

Furlough!—that sweet-sounding English word! On his day
off from the office, he never even went as far as Ganpat Road,
forget about Bengali Gali. And if he had to go to Anarkali
Bazaar, no matter how far he had to walk, he wouldn't even
turn his face towards the road going to the office. He felt
strangely sympathetic towards the prostitutes. They had
gathered up their limbs, tired, broken, slack from a whole year
of selling their bodies, of leaving them to the mercy of violent
hungry beasts; and now these poor creatures, worn down by
fatigue, were going to get some rest. And that greedy man . . .
that low-life! An impotent rage began to burn in Chetan's
mind like a bonfire . . . But his eyelids were growing heavy, his
limbs relaxed, and the bonfire grew dimmer with each passing
moment. He leaned his head against the window, his arms fell
to his sides and he fell fast asleep.

In the Insane Asylum

The three of them—Chanda's mother, Chanda and her husband—walked quietly along Lawrence Road in the blazing May afternoon. They were very far outside the city, and across the mall.

Chanda's mother was thinking. *Why should our life always stay the same when no one else's does? Climbing up only to fall down—is this all that's planned for mankind? And then what does mankind have to do with all these ups and downs? It's all up to the All-Powerful Master—if He wants, He can make His toys climb to the highest peaks—or He can throw them to the very depths. What business do we have feeling sad about it?*

She walked along, trying to steady her mind as she considered this. It was usually like this—she would try as best she could to suppress the anxiety she felt in her sorrowful heart, but her heart never agreed to it. And even now, in the streaming sunlight—with sweat pouring from her head down to her toes and not a tree in sight on the street, and the hard part of the trip still to come—she kept coming up with all sorts of ideas: *Let the Master watch our games of joy and sorrow if He wants to; let Him enjoy watching them; He can watch these games even if He cheers people up when they've been sad. But when you get ground to a paste in the pestle of sorrow after having once felt joy, what a terrible punishment it is, what terrible torture. Why doesn't He raise man up instead?* But then she always arrived at the answer to her own question: *If He only*

167

raised man up, who would enjoy the fruits of their karma from
previous births? On several occasions, overwhelmed with
sorrow, she had invited death, but death doesn't come just like
that. No one could die until such time as only one hundredth
of the bad karma from the previous birth is left. So, how could
she expect death to come to her? She had given birth to five
children and, with her own hands, soothed them to eternal
sleep in the cold earth of the cremation ground; she had
watched a healthy business go to ruin before her eyes; she had
tolerated barbs from those relations she had raised with her
own blood, as well as this misfortune of her husband's after
they had lost their home. Chanda's mother sighed deeply: who
knew how much more sorrow was written in her fate that she
had still to endure? What was there left to see? What karmic
burdens remained?

~

Chanda's mother stopped in the shadow of a bungalow wall.
She sighed deeply as she wiped the sweat dripping down her
neck with the edge of her dirty dupatta. Chanda and her
husband went and stood near her. For a few moments the
three of them stood there silently, each absorbed in his own
thoughts and, then, just as silently, they set out again.

Chanda was angry with her mother, very angry. Her father
was suffering and his daughter had not even been informed!
The joyful days of childhood passed before her eyes, in which
only one thing, the boundless love of her father, shone in the
sky of her memory like a brilliant star. Her father had run a
brick oven in Bhogpur. It did quite well. He was well-respected
in the village. She was very small then, she had been born to
her parents after they had suffered the loss of many children;
she was their only surviving offspring! Her father used to carry
her around. At that time in Bhogpur, the bridge for the railway
line had not yet been constructed over the rain drain, which

they called the 'cho'. During the rainy season, when it rained in the mountains, this cho would begin to flow with a charming drunken gait, as though it had found its lost youth; it usually washed out the railway line. Chanda found it enchanting to watch the crazy dance of the cho and, whenever the line washed out, she would insist that her father walk with her along the water's edge. She especially enjoyed watching the transshipment, when travellers would get down from a train stopping on one side of the water and cross the cho to board the trains waiting on the other side; as they lifted their packages on their heads, held up their pajamas and dhotis, and kept their groups together.

In the afternoon, sitting in the shadow of a dense banyan tree, her father would look over his accounting books. She would come along and playfully pick up his register and throw it to one side, then climb into his lap and demand that he play with her in the cool breeze under the dense shisham trees. Her father would get up quietly and begin to play with her in the shade of the trees along the long road. At such moments, a thoughtful smile always danced about his lips and he would laugh and say again and again, 'You really are a pest, Chanda!'

After this, although his financial situation slowly grew worse—several times he was forced to close down his oven and go elsewhere because of the selfishness and ingratitude of his older brother and his maternal uncle—he never let his troubles affect Chanda. She remembered when she used to go to school, she wore more ornaments than even a newly wed bride. She also remembered that day when her father had sold his operational oven to his older brother because he did not have enough money to pay for her marriage, and thus, in his old age, he had chosen to present himself as a tasty morsel to that terrifying python, unemployment.

And no one had even informed her when this same father of hers had become so ill that he had taken leave of his senses. She had been enjoying the attractions of Lahore with her husband, while her father . . . Just thinking about it, her eyes filled with tears. She looked at her mother—her broken-down body, her lustreless eyes and dirty clothing—dragging herself along in her shoes with the worn heels, wrapped up in her woes and overwhelmed by the flood of misfortunes that surrounded her.

'Mother, is he in his right mind now?' Chanda asked.

Her mother started, as though she had been sleeping, 'Yes, the last time I went there, he recognized people.'

'And Mother, they don't make him work, do they?' Chanda asked again.

'No, dear, he doesn't work at all, the chowkidar was saying that day that everyone else works, but Panditji doesn't work, he spends the whole day in prayer.'

'And Mother, how is his health?'

'He seems better than before, Daughter!'

A dense vine with red flowers blooming on it clung to a tree next to the gate of a bungalow. As though by some silent consensus, the three of them went and stood in its shade to rest a little.

Since Chanda's husband was wearing a suit and hat and Chanda herself was attired in a lovely sari, they didn't have the courage to sit down though they were tired. But Chanda's mother had no such hesitation; she was exhausted—she put the vessel she was holding on the ground and sat down right where she was in the warm dust.

Chetan, Chanda's husband, glanced at his mother-in-law surreptitiously: she had dusty, dry, brittle hair, drooping eyelids, loose wrinkles, rough hands and feet, and a face grown black from too much sorrow and work. He forced himself to suppress a deep sigh as the past several years flashed before his eyes in moments.

Before the wedding, he had built castles in the air about what life would be like with his in-laws, inspired by the way they had treated him—his mother-in-law's love, deeper, more affectionate, more open than that of even his own mother; her face blooming with pride when she praised her son-in-law; the entreaties, sweet scoldings and chiding as she fed him. What happy fantasies those had been. But how quickly the castles had collapsed! Even during the days of the wedding, he had felt that the atmosphere was a bit strained. The members of the wedding procession were given a good meal. The appropriate dowry was given as well and there were no flaws in anyone's behaviour; but nonetheless, it was evident that someone was bearing a heavy burden and there seemed to be too large a measure of etiquette and formalities. He saw that his mother-in-law was depressed, ground down, fearful; and he found his father-in-law silent, serious, rather lost. Only once, when it came time to bid his daughter farewell and Chanda wept loudly and threw arms around her father's neck, did he see a sorrowful smile on the face of that mild-mannered and serious man, and he heard him say, 'Now, now, don't be a child—there, there, go on, now go and sit in the tonga.'

Remembering those moments, Chetan sighed. His mother-in-law stood up and they set out again. Lawrence Road had ended and they had reached Jail Road. The three of them quietly turned on to Jail Road. Chetan again became lost in the pages of the past.

After the wedding, when he had gone once or twice to his in-laws, although he had received a warm welcome, he had felt a lack of friendliness and finally, one day, he had learnt the reason for this. Chanda had pressed her hands together and, choking back her tears, she had told him everything and begged him to forgive her parents. She told him how successful her father used to be, but that he had put down everything he had into the wedding and now neither his house was his own, nor his shop. He didn't even have his own oven and felt ashamed to speak with Chetan.

Chetan had always felt sympathy toward his father-in-law for some reason—there was such tenderness in his face. When he found out about all this, about how his father-in-law felt troubled by Chetan's visits, he started to visit his in-laws less often and kept Chanda in Lahore more. At first he had gone with her to their house sometimes, but it had been a year since he had last gone. And then, one day, all of a sudden, he had heard from Chanda that her father had gone crazy and was locked up in an insane asylum in Lahore, and that her mother was spending her days working in the kitchen of a wealthy Seth's house.

He recalled how he had stood there speechless. The castle of his hopes had already collapsed, but that even its ruins should be razed—he had never considered such a thing possible.

A childhood girlfriend of Chanda's also lived in Lahore. She had just come back from her parents' home so Chanda went to see her to get news of her own mother and father. It was only then that she had found out. Her girlfriend had said, scowling, 'You're a fine one, aren't you? There your father is, rotting away in an insane asylum, and you haven't even gone over there to find see him! There's been a lot of talk in the neighbourhood.'

That day Chanda had said to Chetan, weeping, 'Let me see my mother, I want to ask her everything.' And that very evening, as soon as it had fallen dark, Chetan had taken her to the Seth's house. When the two of them had seen Chanda's mother they had begged her to leave her work at the Seth's and come live with them. After all, what real difference is there between a son-in-law and one's own son? But she would not agree; and she told them that her husband had started to babble incoherently because he had been insulted by his brother; perhaps he had also tried to hit his brother; and then that cruel man had had him committed to the insane asylum. But no, he wasn't really so very crazy—which had made the two of them feel a little better.

They leaned against the wall, standing in the semi-darkness of the dim light of the lane. Chetan pitied his mother-in-law, his wife and, most of all, himself. It was decided that if his father-in-law came to his senses, they would meet with the doctor and get him discharged from the insane asylum. Then they would get a separate house and keep him there, and Chanda's mother would also live there—even she agreed to this. That was why they were going to the insane asylum on this blazing afternoon.

Chetan sighed deeply. His heart had filled with a sharp hatred for his mother-in-law—or not really towards his mother-in-law, but towards the old ways and customs. Chanda's mother would not agree to go in a tonga. Perhaps she didn't have the money, or maybe she did, but it was all spent in getting shelled almonds, sugar lumps and milk for her husband and, since it was a sin to take money from one's daughter, they had come walking three miles in this doomsday sunlight.

~

Outside the insane asylum the three of them sat down in a small garden.

The gate was not yet open and the doctor whom Chetan planned to meet had not yet come, so they had to wait for a while.

It was a little cooler here beneath the dense trees. The day was also drawing to a close and the breeze began to blow sweetly. Chanda's mother put the packet of almond nutmeats on one side and the vessel of milk on the other and lay down on the grass. Looking quietly at the blossoms on the mango tree, her imagination had taken wing and flown off to beautiful gardens: *If you get sorrow after pleasure and pleasure after sorrow, then, after experiencing so much sorrow, days of happiness must certainly be coming.* Twice a week she had permission to see her husband. On those days, she would take whatever money she had managed to save from work and buy almonds, remove the nutmeats from the shells, put sugar lumps in some milk and come here, crossing these long, flat, sizzling streets on foot in the harsh sunlight. She would feed him the almonds and the milk with great love and devotion. *It was just because of the lack of good food and the cruel behaviour of his relatives that his mind had gone a little bad; that was the real reason. Imagine someone who has always had milk, cream, yoghurt and buttermilk, having to live for so long deprived of good food. The humiliation!* She would feed him an entire pav of almond nutmeats, then mix the sugar lumps into the milk and feed it to him, and she would imagine that when he got well and came home, she would save up some money and have him open a small grocery shop, and the few days that were left in their lives would pass in comfort.

As she lay on the grass, Chanda was staring at the huge, tall iron fence across from them, where a Sikh sentry stood guard. Inside, there were countless rooms and, in some room, her father was locked up because he had gone crazy. As he lay in his room in this heat, did he remember the bygone days? He must certainly think about his daughter! He must definitely think her cruel. For her part, she had had no idea of all this. Chanda's eyes filled with tears and she covered her face with the edge of her sari and began to cry.

Chetan leaned back, resting both his hands on the grass, and mentally rehearsed the conversation he would have with the doctor after seeing his father-in-law. He did have a recommendation letter but, all the same, he knew that he would have to tell the doctor why it was necessary to take his wife's father out of the insane asylum and bring him home, and he was turning over in his mind a few strategies and clever sentences he could use in English.

At four o'clock, the large gate opened and a band of lunatics emerged, wearing long, loose shirts made of thick, rough cloth and tight pajamas that did not reach their ankles. Some were speaking to themselves, others gesticulated murderously, others just laughed for no reason. The sentry who was with them told them to pick up some flower pots—so they all picked them up—and then he went off with them perhaps to have them put the pots down somewhere else. Another group emerged in a similar fashion and began to water the flower pots. They were all crazy; they made strange gestures; but all the same, they did all the work like trained animals. Watching all this made Chanda agitated; her heart was in her throat. Her father too must have to work, and this merciless sentry—how he must beat the lunatics to make them work! Just the way they do with wild animals—those who can't use their minds can still learn many tasks for fear of punishment. She would not let her father stay here for even one instant longer. With this thought in mind, she shook the shoulder of her husband, who was staring up at the sky, absorbed in some deep thought, and said, 'Tell the sentry to arrange for us to see him.'

～

Chetan started and got up. He smoothed down his collar and tie and went to the gate. He introduced himself to the sentry and said that they were here to see Pandit Dinbandhu and, as he spoke, he took him to one side and put a rupee note in his hand.

There were four Dinbandhus in the insane asylum at that time. The sentry looked at the register and told the chowkidar to call for the Pandit Dinbandhu from Jalandhar and bring him out. In the midst of this, the relatives of some other lunatics had also come and the sentry was having their relations called according to the names they gave him. They were ordered to look at their relations from outside the large gate, but the sentry brought Chanda and her family inside the gate. Chanda and her husband sat down on a bench. Her mother sat right down on the ground. Just then, they saw Pandit Dinbandhu coming with the chowkidar.

Chanda's heart began to pound.

As he drew near, Chanda saw that her father was wearing that same thick coarse shirt and tight pajamas the other lunatics were wearing. She felt choked up and her eyes brimmed with tears.

'Sit down!' the chowkidar ordered and, like a trained beast, Pandit Dinbandhu rested his back against the wall and sat down. Then he looked at the chowkidar and at the three of them and burst out laughing.

Chetan saw that his father-in-law was not half the size he had been. His teeth were coated with yellow filth, his face was shadowed with jaundice and when Chanda's mother opened the packet of almonds and handed it to him, he saw that his hand was trembling.

Pandit Dinbandhu took all the almonds and chewed them up in one or two mouthfuls. Then Chanda's mother began to dissolve the sugar lumps in the milk.

Chanda was impatient.

'Mother, doesn't he recognize us?' she asked.

Gazing at her husband through her half-blind eyes, Chanda's mother responded, 'Why wouldn't he?' And then, pulling her sari back from her forehead a little, she motioned towards Chanda, and asked, 'What, don't you recognize this one?'

'Why wouldn't I recognize her?' replied Pandit Dinbandhu, laughing.

'So then, who is she?'

'She's my wife, who else?'

Chanda covered her face with the edge of her sari and Chetan heard her sob.

Then Chanda's mother asked, signalling towards her son-in-law, 'And who is this?'

'Why, it's my brother!' he said, and looked at all of them as though to say, 'Do you people think I'm crazy?'

Tearfully, Chanda's mother asked, 'Don't you recognize me?'

'Oh my!' Chanda's father chuckled, 'Wouldn't I recognize my own mother then?' The thought made him chuckle even more loudly and he grabbed the container of milk from Chanda's mother's hand and gulped it down.

A Listless Evening

'Oh, hello!'

Professor Kanetkar's heart nearly stopped for a fraction of a second, then started pounding rapidly; his face reddened slightly. She had come.

She had called out 'Hello' to someone, who replied and then they started talking, but Professor Kanetkar had heard none of it. All his instincts were overwhelmed by her presence: the sound of her convent accent, the sweet laughter that rose and melted in her throat, the honey of her voice that pervaded his consciousness.

The pen had stopped its rapid course across the page and lay in his slack, half-turned hand, resting on the middle finger with the support of the index finger, a little above the page.

Kanetkar sat for a moment, listening intently to her voice, then slowly raised his eyes. Her voice was coming from just outside, but the concrete porch with the railing outside his window—which his friend called 'the terrace'—was empty. The beach beyond the terrace, the people walking along it, the lighthearted youths preparing themselves to do gymnastics near the small bridge over the large open drain, the ocean coming in with the tide, the sun dropping gradually below the horizon—none of these arrested Professor Kanetkar's gaze. He set the pen down on the table and got up. He stood and looked out the window: she was sitting on the terrace. Not in front of the window, but to one side, a little to the left. The shutter had been blown half-closed by the breeze from the sea. If it were completely open and he leaned a little to the right, he would be able to see her from his chair.

Professor Kanetkar was about to open the window fully when she cast an oblique glance in his direction. He felt the blood rush to his face; his heart began beating quickly. He did not have the courage to open the window. He sat down on the chair and fixed his gaze to the right, beyond the terrace, and watched the boys gathering near the small bridge over the drain. They had taken off their clothes and put them near the terrace, and now, loincloths tied, shorts pulled up tightly around their waists, they were ready to begin their tumbling.

Maybe some circus had come to town, or there was a scouts' jamboree going on: these boys gathered here on the beach, every evening, perhaps after the mills or the factories closed, and formed pyramids, set up jumps for themselves and leapt over them. They played all kinds of games with incredibly awkward amateurishness. In his youth, Professor Kanetkar had been the champion of his college gymnastic team. His feats on the parallel and horizontal bars seemed so natural, it was hard to believe they were the result of years of practice. He had turned somersaults on the roman rings; he was skilled at vaulting; he held a record in the long jump.

For a few days after he had first come to stay in this room, he had stood in the open doorway for a while every evening watching the boys do gymnastics. But today his gaze did not rest there long. He imagined her sitting in silhouette on the terrace, directly above the boys on the beach. He averted his eyes, picked up his pen and, clearing his mind of all distractions, began to write intently as before.

But he had no idea what it was that he had been writing so intently. His ears remained alert to the conversation that was taking place on the terrace—not really to the conversation, just to that honeyed voice and laughter that rose again and again and melted in her throat. That laugh, like a fine mist rising slowly in a delicate fountain, drenched his whole being each time he heard it. In that fraction of a second, when she had glanced at him indirectly, he had seen that today she was not wearing a skirt, but had dressed instead in a deep blue silk kameez and a white cambric shalwar, and that her trimmed hair, which was usually loose and wavy, down to her shoulders, was today done up in a bouffant style, like a small two-sided drum. It was gathered high, off her shoulders, accentuating the length of her fair neck. To Professor Kanetkar, at that moment, she was an Egyptian princess who had emerged from the drawings of ancient times and had come to sit right there on the terrace. Continuing to write with his right hand, he opened the shutter all the way with his left. He took a square glass paperweight from the table and put it between the shutter and the window sill. All the while, he never lifted his eyes, but continued to write with complete concentration.

He kept writing, but he was sensible of the fact that she was sitting in front of him, outside on the terrace. Though he did not lift his gaze from his work, her silhouette lingered in his mind like the flash of a light bulb after one has closed one's eyes.

He shook his head hard and read the lines he had just written, then crossed them out, and, concentrating determinedly, again began to write.

But, despite all his concentration, he was entirely unconscious of what he was writing. His ears were fixed to that voice and that laugh, and the awareness of her presence continued to envelop him.

Finally he surrendered and lifted his gaze. The window sill cut off his view of her right across the middle, so that he could see only the top half of her body. Then she moved just a little to the left, again casting an oblique glance in his direction. Professor Kanetkar gave a starts and looked down. He got up busily from the table.

At first he wanted to go open the door and stand in the

doorway for a few moments. His friend had forbidden him to sit in the open doorway, as the damp, salty, sea air hit the left wall and was wearing away at the distemper. But the evenings were so beautiful and colourful, and one could not get a full view of the sea from the windows; so, even if he had kept the door closed all day, he usually opened it in the evenings, and while he was working he would go and stand in the doorway for a few moments now and then. But the awareness that she was sitting out on the terrace stopped him. He felt uncomfortable at the thought of going and standing before her without having anything to say. For a few minutes he paced back and forth in the room, from the front door to the inside door. He desperately wanted to open the door. But instead, he went back inside again.

Finally, he gave in and opened the door. A gust of cold air made him shiver with exhilaration. But he turned back again without even looking out and went and dropped on to the couch. He stretched, extending his legs and reaching his arms above his head; he locked his fingers together, cracking his knuckles.

But he couldn't stay seated. The next moment he leapt up again.

He was pleased that even at this age he could leap up at his first try. It was this energy that had recently prompted him to do a DPhil, even though he was past fifty. His college was about to become a university, and the principal had suggested that if he could manage to get his doctorate before the changeover, he would be made head of the department; otherwise, he could be passed over for a junior colleague. Years ago, Professor Kanetkar had decided to do a DPhil. His thesis topic had even been approved; but his job, his wife, his children, exam books, the textbook board and meetings had made him forget all that. Now, suddenly, he had taken the outline of his thesis from his old papers and thrown himself back into it with youthful devotion.

In Kolhapur, books and other necessary materials were scarce. His friend had solved the problem. Professor Kanetkar had shared his predicament with him the last time his friend had visited Kolhapur. He had mentioned this peaceful place of his on Dadar Beach in Bombay, where, far from the din of his own flat, Kanetkar could work, enjoying the cool sea breezes and also have access to the books he needed. His friend's film company was going to Kashmir for two months for some shooting and he suggested that Professor Kanetkar go and live in Bombay at his place during that time. He would leave the car and driver for him. His driver would take him to whichever libraries he wanted to visit. Why didn't he just gather his books together and write in the peace and quiet of the room? The driver would bring him food and in the evenings make him tea. He would have absolutely no interruptions and be able to concentrate and work peacefully.

And so, Professor Kanetkar had come to Dadar.

≈

He went behind the curtain and glanced in the mirror on the top of the small cabinet. Fatigue lined his face from working since morning. He put his pen down on top of the cabinet and picked up the little soap dish and the towel. Then he opened the back door and went into the bathroom. The faces of his colleagues passed before his eyes as he washed his face at the sink and he smiled slightly. So many of his colleagues had grown fat and awkward, soft and flabby, by the time they reached fifty, but he had maintained his slimness pretty well. He too was a little heavier than he had been before, his stomach protruded slightly more than it had and his cheeks had filled out, but he was by no means fat, he was still quite slender. This was because he had continued to exercise regularly over the years. Although he had given up that habit a few years ago and by now his body had grown a little slack, his energy was the same and he still edged out the younger men with the amount of work he did.

He came back into the room and dried his face off with the towel. Taking a little vanishing cream from the glass jar on top of the cabinet, he rubbed it into his skin and smoothed his curly salt-and-pepper hair down in front of the mirror. He had a round face, with large sensitive eyes and full manly lips. There was still a good deal of attractiveness left there.

~

Professor Kanetkar had hardly been working in this room more than fifteen days when this girl had unexpectedly attracted his attention. He hadn't analysed whether it was the sweetness of her smile or her honeyed laughter that first captivated him. All he knew was that one evening he had been sitting and working with great concentration, when two girls had come and stood beneath his window and started talking. One of them had irresistibly drawn his attention. It had become difficult for him to work. The two girls walked round and round the building, stopping again and again near his window, and each time his attention had been drawn away from his work.

This building, in which his friend had taken a small room, was known as 'The Sea Foam'. It was a five-storey building, right in front of the hospital on Cadell Road. When one entered from the street it looked exactly like thousands of other buildings in Bombay: neither the road nor the ground in the compound in front of the building was paved, but around the building and behind it, there was an area, about twenty feet wide, which was paved with cement slabs. All along the back of the building there was a cement terrace facing the beach, the upper portion of which was wide and shiny. Though the terrace was four or five feet high on the side next to the building, it was ten or twelve feet high on the side nearest the ocean. In the middle, on that side, there was a small gate leading to the beach. Professor Kanetkar's friend occupied the corner room in the flat on the left side of the building, which had windows facing out in two directions.

Since cars didn't come to the rear of the building, in the evenings the boys and girls and, sometimes, the women who lived in the building took walks along the cement railing; sometimes they went down on the beach; and at other times they came out to the cement terrace to sit. Whenever the girl came walking by from the left, Professor Kanetkar's ears grew alert and he couldn't do a thing as long as he could hear her voice and her laughter. Her laughter was very low, very sweet, very soft and very attractive. Once it had captured his attention he couldn't get it back. As long as she stood talking near his window, his powers of thinking and understanding were all collapsed into hearing. Each time she went away, it took him a few moments to regain control of his consciousness. Collecting his senses, focusing his instincts, deliberately gathering up his concentration, he would begin to move his pen, when again, from the left, he would hear her honeyed laughter and his pen would stop in its tracks. Whenever she came and stopped by his window, he wished he could open the outside door and take just one look. But he did not have the courage.

When it had grown fairly late in the evening, he finally got up. He opened the door softly and pushed it very carefully to the left, so that the strength of the wind would not make it smack against the wall. Then he glanced towards the two girls who were standing talking against the wall near his window: all he could tell in the semi-darkness was that both of them were wearing skirts. One looked as though she were seventeen or eighteen, the other twelve or thirteen. He could not figure out anything more than that. He could neither make out their faces, nor discover what colour blouses and skirts they were wearing. He looked quickly in their direction; then he went down the steps leading from his room and stood by the terrace. As soon as he came outside, the girls slipped away. For a moment he pretended to breathe deeply as he gazed out at the darkness of the sea. Then he took a deep breath and slowly began to walk along the edge of the terrace. There were still two or three dim rays of light spread out on the horizon before him and, beneath them, far away in the ocean, flickered the light of some ship or boat.

As he walked along the terrace, Professor Kanetkar glanced now and then at Worli Point's shining crescent of lights far off to the south, or he turned to observe the glittering lights of the Bandra railway overbridge to the north. But his gaze returned again and again to scrutinize the windows on the left side of The Sea Foam as he wondered if that voice or that laughter could be heard from one of them.

He walked around on the terrace for a long time. Once he saw a girl in a skirt in the next-door flat, whose dining room door opened out to the back, and it had seemed to him that that was her. He had walked by the flat several times and they had even made eye contact, but although that girl too was beautiful, he did not think she was the one, because she did not laugh that way even once. Despite his disappointment, he continued to walk around on the terrace for a long time.

$\sim$

In those ten or fifteen days he had come to identify her, although their eyes hadn't actually met. She was the daughter of the Sindhi tenants in the same flat in which his friend had taken a room. His friend had the only room in that flat that opened out towards the sea and the Sindhis lived in the rooms on the other side. Once or twice, when he was going to or from the bathroom, he had heard her talking to her mother or her father. He also heard that laugh and, a couple of times, he had heard her singing lines of a song from the film that was on at the Metro in those days. He had just come out of the bathroom after washing his hands and face, the door had been a little open, and then he heard the melody *I won't call to you*; a tender and lamenting, ringing melody! The silly girl had replaced the masculine verb ending in the song with the feminine. She kept singing that same line over and over again as she went into the hallway or some other room, '*I won't call to you, I won't call to you . . .*' It seemed to Professor Kanetkar as if she were singing those lines over and over again to him. Sometimes she stood directly outside his window on the terrace talking to someone or the other and disturbing him with her sideways glances.

And today, wearing a shalwar kameez, she appeared like an Egyptian princess—with her long fair neck, her sharp tapering face and that bun like a small two-sided drum—and sat down on the terrace right there in front of him.

As he scrutinized the attractiveness of his face in the mirror, he thought of that sweet melody and said to himself in Gujarati, 'But I'll call out to you, my love, I'll call out to you.'

Although he scolded himself for this flirtatiousness of his, he kept humming that same line over and over to himself as he combed his hair and smoothed it down with his hand. The days of his youth passed before him: how attractive his personality had been, how young ladies had constantly been drawn to him. One after another, their faces passed before him and then one particular face became delineated on his mental canvas—the face of the woman who had come and settled in his home as his wife; the one who had skilfully stopped all the other faces from coming near him forever more. But the next instant, that face moved away and the princess sitting on the terrace arrived and took form in his mind.

This girl, her honey-filled voice, her laughter, had made him suddenly young again. Her sideways glances had somehow stirred such vigour and energy into his veins that for the last few days he had started feeling like a completely changed man.

Smoothing his hand over his head, he could feel how his hair had not stayed quite so thick, but it would still take many years for baldness to establish its dominion over his skull. Smiling with satisfaction, he tightened the loose knot of his necktie, picked up his pen and began to walk about the room.

~

'But I'll call out to you, my love, I'll call out to you!'

He held his hands behind his back; his left hand grasped the wrist of the right hand, in which he still held the pen; leaning forward slightly, he walked about the room, filled with an odd enthusiasm.

'But I'll call out to you, my love, I'll call out to you . . .!' he hummed to himself.

The realization that even after crossing his fiftieth year, he could attract the attention of a completely unknown beauty had filled him with excitement. Whenever his female students in the college grew close to him, he would lovingly hold them on his knee, but they always thought of him as a big brother or a father. If they grew even closer, they would start calling him 'Daddy', the way his own daughters did, and he had pretty much become reconciled to his old age by then. Sometimes, when he was short of breath, or when his back, his finger joints, or his knees would start to ache—he would laugh and even mention his age . . . But this girl, and her glances, had made him believe that he was still attractive. In the mirror he had noticed that there was not one wrinkle on his face. Certainly the flesh on his throat had grown a little loose and one or two wrinkles were forming there, but they looked as though they had been caused by the tight knot of his tie. And then, there was a sort of glow to his face that he had never seen in the suffocating atmosphere of Kolhapur . . .

He continued to walk about the room, his hands on his hips. He would get as far as the door, then turn back without lifting his eyes, as though absorbed in deep thought. Each time he wanted to look at her just once, but he did not lift his eyes. When he had already walked around in that manner three or four times and he felt sure that going and standing in the doorway now would look completely natural, he went to the door and did not turn back again. There he stood against the door frame and began to scratch his temple with the end of his pen while gazing into space, as if he were working through some deep problem.

She was still sitting the same way, swinging her crossed legs at the edge of the terrace. The person talking to her had perhaps gone down to the beach. Professor Kanetkar's gaze wandered around in space and then came to rest on her feet. She was wearing white nylon sandals. He couldn't see the white netting from so far away, so it looked as though the soles of her sandals were bound invisibly to those fair slender feet.

He gazed steadily at her sandals for a few moments, so that it would seem as if he were not really looking at her feet, but was instead absorbed in his own thoughts, staring off into space. Then, shyly, his gaze slid up to her milky white cambric shalwar and her deep blue silk kameez, and moved up to her face. But it didn't stop there. She was staring right at him. His gaze moved from the bun in her hair and continued to rest on the western horizon.

The setting sun had gathered up its rays. A light haze shadowed the horizon, where the sea and the sky embraced, and the sun's huge vermilion platter seemed to rest upon it. But it was sinking imperceptibly with each moment. As Professor Kanetkar watched, it climbed down into the haze and began to shrink, becoming a huge orange. The lower part of the orange touched the surface of the ocean. Its reflection, a trembling golden minaret, reached from the ocean waves coming in with the tide, all the way to the shore. Professor Kanetkar's gaze slid once up that trembling golden minaret, from the horizon to the shore, and from the shore back to the horizon, and then returned. The gleam of the minaret was growing dim with the sinking of the sun, and the ink of the waves was deepening. Far off on the horizon, first the sails of one ship became visible, then those of a second, then of a third. In the light of the sinking sun those sails looked to Professor Kanetkar like comforting shapes suddenly illuminated in the sky of his memory. At a distance, where Bandra Hill reached far out into the sea, the water was quite shallow. In the first rushing stream of the tide, rivulets of foam again and again formed and then disappeared; and, in some places, the foam advanced towards the shore on the surface of the sea, up to the rows of herons, drawing white streaks along the beach, then disappeared. The tide was just beginning to come in. With every rushing stream, more sections of the beach became wet; Professor Kanetkar stood watching the approaching tide for a few moments. Then he glanced at the girl out the corner of his eyes.

She did not notice him. Her gaze was focused on the beach, her back towards him. At first it seemed to him that she might be searching for some acquaintance from among the people gathering on the seashore for their evening stroll. But there was not much of a crowd on the beach. A quarter of a mile ahead, on the Cadell Court beach, there was a large crowd. But in front of The Sea Foam there were very few people on the beach, and the ones who were there were just passing by. There was a bhel puri handcart, where four or five people were indulging themselves. Professor Kanetkar saw no face on the beach that could be the centre of her attention. Slowly he walked down the steps of his room and went and stood on the terrace behind the girl, at a little distance. She paid no attention to the sound of his footsteps. She continued to sit in that same position. Then he followed her gaze. He figured it out. She was watching with rapt attention the labourer boys doing gymnastics.

For a moment, he too watched the boys playing. They had started a new game. Two boys would lie on their backs in the wet sand on the beach. One, who was slightly taller, would come back towards the terrace and start running. As he approached the boys who were lying down, he leapt up in such a way that his hands barely touched the ground, did a somersault and went tumbling over on to the sand, landing with a thump on the other side of the boys. *Wrong,* Professor Kanetkar said to himself, *after landing on the sand, he should stand up completely straight; he shouldn't fall over with a thump like that.* And he wanted to go there and teach them how to perform a somersault in midair correctly. The second time the youth told three boys to lie down, the third time four . . .

Professor Kanetkar coughed slightly, but the girl, completely unaware of his existence, was watching the boys intently. Then something got into him: he walked past her swiftly, nearly running, and then, a little beyond her, he placed his left hand lightly on the terrace railing and jumped clean over it like some youthful gymnast, landing on his feet in the sand approximately twelve feet below. His knees bent from jumping from such a great height; he felt he might tremble and fall over, but in the next instant he regained control and stood up straight. He was breathing heavily from running and jumping from such a height. His blood pulsed toward his head and, for a minute, he felt he would get dizzy and fall over, but he held steady and stood still for a few moments. When his breathing returned to normal he wanted to cast a glance up above, but he controlled that desire and walked toward the boys with a completely natural air.

The boys had stopped their game and were looking at him. They were clearly impressed with the deftness of Professor Kanetkar's leap. So when he reached them and said he would teach them how to do somersaults correctly, they agreed enthusiastically.

The pen was still in Professor Kanetkar's hand. He handed it to the biggest boy and told the other four boys to lie down. He took off his shoes and socks, rolled the bottoms of his trousers and hiked them up a little, and walked towards the terrace, focusing his gaze on the ground very calmly. Then he turned from the terrace and came running; the next instant he leapt up and somersaulted in the air, clearing all four boys and landing on his feet on the relatively hard sand near the water. For a fraction of a second he felt he would fall over backwards, but the next moment he stood up straight.

When the labourer boy had somersaulted in the air, he'd fallen down on the sand and landed with a thump on his back, but Professor Kanetkar's knees had not even buckled. He was able to stand up completely straight. True, he had felt slightly dizzy, there had been a slight twisting sensation in his back as well, but at this age he felt no small pride at his success. At that same moment, he turned and looked towards the terrace. It seemed to him that the girl was staring directly at him. The extraordinary thrill he felt from the touch of that remote gaze was enough to make his heart pound and the blood rush to his head. Almost drunkenly, he walked back around the boys who were lying down and ordered the remaining two to go and lie down too.

The two boys, including the one who had been turning somersaults before, went and lay down with the rest of them.

Then, walking proudly, pressing his heels into the sand, practically giddy, Professor Kanetkar went up to the terrace. He turned with lightning speed and came running like a bullet. As he neared the boys lying down on the beach, he leapt . . . But then, for some reason, he didn't turn a complete somersault. He flew straight over the boys and fell on his head. His neck twisted and part of his lifeless body fell on top of the boys lying on their backs.

∾

The golden orange had sunk completely into the sea. On the surface of the sea, at the horizon, only a tiny golden sesame seed was visible.

A boy came running down from one of the upper storeys of The Sea Foam when he saw a crowd gathering on the beach. He came up behind the girl sitting on the terrace and asked in English, 'What happened?'

'That silly old man,' the girl said, motioning towards Kanetkar's room, 'has broken his neck over there.'

The boy went running down to the beach. The girl sitting on the terrace was swinging her feet with a supremely listless air. To the west, the deep vermilion bonfire had burst ablaze, its tongues of flame licking out across the horizon. Suddenly, the waves on the surface of the sea were silvery and the boats that had not been visible before now began to appear in silhouette. The girl shifted her gaze away from the crowd and began to watch the outlines of the fishermen standing on a boat in the middle of the ocean. They were silhouetted against the silvery waves of the sea, as though they had been drawn there, just the way she herself was a silhouette, seated on the terrace.

My First Letter of Resignation

By now my letters of resignation have become commonplace. My circle of friends is well acquainted with this aspect of my personality and, when I start a new job in a totally new profession, from the very first day, they start looking forward to my letter of resignation. But the memories of the stir created when I handed in my very first letter of resignation at my first job are still fresh in my mind today.

At that time I had recently joined the editorial section of a national daily as a translator, and, as was the custom, I proudly called myself a 'sub-editor'. My friends envied my good fortune. But actually there was nothing to envy in my fate. There were very few advertisements in our newspaper. The ads in newspapers in those days were usually for the kind of illnesses that afflict men, known as 'secret ailments'. Our paper was a national daily and it considered such ads harmful for the nation, so it didn't print them. The result was that it befell us three or three-and-a-half editors to fill eight large pages. I say 'three-and-a-half', because the head editor limited his activities to just supplying the headlines. We poor translators had to do all the work. We all had to work during the day from twelve-thirty to six o'clock, and then at night from nine-thirty to twelve or one o'clock in the morning; but from twelve to two o'clock in the morning the translators took turns staying with the editor.

But I kept my hardship to myself. To my friends I always

said that even if someone were to offer me command of Kashmir or Hyderabad I would never leave this editorship. (I never called it a 'translator-ship'.) 'Listen, an editor is an emperor of the pen,' I would say. 'If he wishes, he can shake the foundations of empires, turn ordinary people into emperors and overthrow the thrones of power, and so on and so forth . . .'

The result of my saying these things was that as soon as I handed in my letter of resignation from this 'sub-editorship' of mine, my friends and acquaintances were very critical of me. Whomever I ran into would stop me in the middle of the bazaar and ask why I had submitted a letter of resignation, as though I had been struck down by some horrifying illness and there was no hope of recovery, and he, kind gentleman, had come to nurse me back to health. Or as though this friend or acquaintance had come around looking for me to express his sorrow following the demise of someone or the other from among the enemies of my close relations (God forbid) and, when he met me, he had pinned me down and started in right then and there with, 'I was so sorry when I heard the news, my brother.'

I did recall that I was an 'emperor of the pen'; I was a public man and it was my highest duty to tell my friends and acquaintances the reason for my suddenly withdrawing my hand from this emperorship of the pen—otherwise I would have run screaming from these rude questions. And so, my friend, I just answered some questions somehow or the other, but when I saw that this 'somehow or the other' of mine wasn't working, I finally confessed to someone, 'Yaar, being an emperor of the pen just doesn't suit me. The work is so demanding it's beyond the capabilities of this delicate body of mine. Shakespeare also once said, "Uneasy lies the head that wears a crown," that is to say, being a ruler, whether it be of a pen or of a country, is the mother of all worries. And thus, yaar, I am fleeing from worry.' I told someone else, 'Sahib, it's starting to get very hot, so I've got a job in Shimla. I thought

I'd free myself from the daily grind.' (I had forgotten the part about being an emperor.) I told another person about my grandfather being on his deathbed and that he loved me so deeply he had demanded that I abandon the editorship immediately, no matter how admirable it might be, and come to him.

What I mean to say is that I managed through some ruse or another to satisfy those people whom I considered 'acquaintances' and those who were particularly interested in my letter of resignation, and who wanted to become heirs to my throne, to the point that they came to believe that in this era of economic depression, my submitting a letter of resignation from the editorship of that prestigious newspaper was, under the circumstances, not only necessary, but unavoidable.

But now, why was it that my real friends were not satisfied by these clarifications of mine? They totally refused to listen to any explanation I gave, such as, the sorrowful condition of my grandfather; the terrible ill health of my wife and children and me, myself, 'the emperor of the pen'; getting fed up with being ground to a pulp in the daily grind; sleeping during the day and then staying up most of the night like an owl or a flying fox and, at two in the morning, after getting off work, walking home while feeling one's way through the alleyways, and bumping into the charpoy of someone sleeping in the bazaar, and running off followed by cries of 'Thief! Thief!', and then walking along holding one's breath for fear of dogs. These were ordinary, or that is to say, two or three degrees centigrade less-than-ordinary types of reasons and, for those, how could a gentleman leave such a job in such times of unemployment? And they considered my submission of a resignation letter to actually mean that I had been forcibly removed from my job. Ever since I handed in that letter, I heard them often repeating the line from the ghazal, *I was thrown from your home entirely dishonoured.* No matter how many feeble faces I made, no matter how many times I said, 'Yaar, I've started to suffer from insomnia from all this staying awake night after night. I've developed bleeding haemorrhoids from sitting in a chair all the time and diabetes is eating away at my insides,' in response to my clarifications, I heard only side-splitting chuckles from my friends.

~

Years have gone by since that first resignation letter and, after so many years, there's no longer any reason to lie, because, to tell you the truth, for one thing, I wasn't fired. I handed in my letter of resignation, and if I then also happened to be fired, at least I wasn't humiliated first. And then, the real reason for my resignation letter, or 'escaping with my honour intact', was in fact having to stay awake night after night.

I can say nothing about those great souls who were born straight from their mother's wombs with golden spoons in their mouths and who have no other work save to eat, drink and sleep; nor can I speak about those gentlemen, who, fed up with the struggles of life, go into the forests, eat roots and berries and follow a schedule of sleep and only sleep—because I think of meditation as just sleeping, even while awake. I can also say nothing about those sparkless, desire-less people who sit in the sun and consider killing flies in a state of semi-consciousness the equivalent of climbing Mount Kangchenjunga. Also outside my discussion are those healthy people who get up in the evening if they go to sleep in the morning, and get up in the morning if they go to sleep in the evening—such demigods of sleep have always been my 'ideals', and I have always considered imitating them as my birthright on par with national independence. Go ahead and say it: I got a job in a profession where even mentioning sleep is considered impious. Unfortunately, with me, just loosen the reins a little and I'll fall asleep and stay asleep.

~

In those days I used to think occasionally that if, somehow, I could become the dictator of India, the first ordinance I'd enact would be one that decreed as mandatory that each night editor sleep the first two days and nights of every week. Each of them would have a sentinel posted at his bedside so that if any of them should make even the slightest attempt to get up, he would first be put to sleep with a pat or a lullaby; and if even that did no good, according to the sleeping ordinance, the police would have complete authority to make him go to sleep by any means necessary. After this, my next deed would be to demolish the daily newspaper offices of bygone days and establish offices in which every editorial section included a bedroom, so that if the translator or the editor got at all sleepy, he could go into the bedroom and rest on his bed and refresh his mind by closing his eyes for a few minutes instead of sleeping with his eyes open.

Far from becoming a dictator in charge of making proper arrangements for sleep, it was in fact because of lack of sleep that I was forced to resign from my job. What happened was that in those days it seemed that Mahatma Gandhi always made his plans in a manner somewhat like this: telegraphic wires regarding his activities never arrived in the newspaper offices before 1 a.m. Nobody had even heard of a teleprinter at that time and the chaprassi from A.P. or Free Press never came before one or one-thirty, and one or one-thirty in the morning was the time when we were all busy playing peekaboo between sleeping and waking. My nodding head would sometimes knock against the electric lamp and sometimes for a moment it would seem completely dark in the room. Sometimes, in this state, the table would become a mountain and I, as Farhad, would try to break it with my head instead of with an axe; and sometimes when I received some translation work to do in this state, after writing one or two lines, I would start to doze so soundly that the nib of my pen would double over and stop. On such occasions I would always pray that what they say about the transmigration of souls should be true, so that in my

next birth, the All Powerful One would make me Mahatma
Gandhi for a few days and make Mahatma Gandhi the junior
translator for some daily paper.

One night, a wire regarding Mahatma Gandhi's schedule
arrived under such circumstances. It was almost 2 a.m. and I
had already dozed off a couple of times; for this reason, I was
trying to sleep with my eyes wide open instead of sleeping with
them shut, out of fear of the editor-in-chief. Seeing my eyes
open, he believed I was somewhat alert and threw the wire in
front of me. I began to read it with little interest.

So there I was, trying to read the wire while my eyes kept
dropping shut. At one point the editor noticed my stupor and
my drowsy eyes met his, dull and sleep-deprived. I started
somewhat, cleaned off my glasses with my kurta a bit and sat
down. I put the hat I had been wearing back on the table, ran
my hand over my head, took off my Fleet shoes which had
become rather warm and, making myself neat and tidy, I sat
down and this time I glanced once at the wire and then wrote:

Poona, 18 April—

Now, when I ran my eye below this, I found that there were
two wires. One from Poona and one from Bombay. The one
from Poona was a bit longer and was related to the
Mahatma's statement on the subject of Harijan Day,
honouring untouchable sweepers; and the one from Bombay
was about a speech of Mrs Gandhi's. This was a little
shorter. Due to my drowsiness, I resolved to take care of
that one first and began to write something like this:

Mrs Gandhi . . .

At this point I began to feel sleepy and it occurred to me that
writing 'Mrs Gandhi' wouldn't be right; these Associated Press
types were linked to a quasi-official agency: they would never
write 'the Mahatma' for Gandhiji; they would just use 'Mr',
and similarly, they would just write 'Mrs Gandhi' for Mother
Kasturba. But I was the sub-editor for a national paper, so I
should never do such a thing.

This idea flashed in my mind for just a moment in my semi-conscious state, and I cut 'Mrs Gandhi' and wrote:

> Mahatma Gandhi's esteemed wife, whom we call Shrimati Kasturba, said, in giving a speech in an assembly, that independence could only be won through swadeshi clothing . . .

At this point I dozed off a bit, and a speech by the local Swadeshi League for self-rule—which I had heard in the afternoon in the capacity of reporter—came to my mind, and after napping a bit, I cast one glance at the word 'swadeshi', and continued to write:

> . . . leagues should be organized. The League secretary . . .

At this I again became drowsy.

'Have you finished the Mahatma's statement or not?'

'Oh, that's what I'm doing.'

'Well then, send that for composing. Look at the time! What's going on? The paper will be late.'

The press was only across the courtyard. I gave the written slip to the chaprassi and then, smoothing my hand over my head, I skipped three lines and began to translate Mahatma Gandhi's statement—and who knows what I wrote down. The editor saw me dozing, so someone snatched the wire from my hand. He himself gave it a four-column headline and, because the man from the press was kicking up a ruckus, he filed it with my translated slip and gave it to him, and ordered, 'Just look over the proof!' He put his Gandhi cap on his head and went away without looking at me.

The next day I had only just arrived in the office when the managing director sent the chaprassi to summon me. I was completely sure that my prayers of the last six months for a raise had been heard. Surely I was about to be promoted. I took off my hat and ran my hand over my hair. Then I stuck the hat back on my head so it was straight, smoothed out the wrinkles in my kurta and dhoti, and, adopting an air of enthusiasm, I went into the room of the managing director, where I lowered my head and greeted him with a smile.

The managing director responded to my greeting with a slight nod and indicated to me to sit down in a chair. My face blossomed and I also felt shy, because, before this, a managing director had never offered me a chair.

When I sat down, he slid a fresh issue of the paper in front of me and said, 'Please do me the kindness of reading this news item.'

It was the front page of our paper. The following news was printed below the four-column headline:

Householders Should Do the Work of Sweepers Themselves

Mahatma Gandhi's Announcement Regarding Harijan Day

Poona, 18 April—Mahatma Gandhi's esteemed wife, whom we call Shrimati Kasturba, said, when making a speech to an assembly, that independence could only be won through swadeshi leagues, which should be organized. The League secretary, Mahatma Gandhi, commands that the programme should begin at five o'clock in the morning. Food and clothing should be gathered, and everyone should give what they can. It would be better if, instead of food and clothing, the gifts are collected in the form of cash. In this way, needy Harijans can be cleaned with whatever money is collected.

A.P.

After reading this news item, I began to scratch my head and, even then, I was just wondering if all these errors were mine or the press's, when the managing director beseeched me respectfully and politely to have mercy on the paper and kindly submit a letter of resignation.

I looked at him rather pathetically, but he was staring at me in such a way that I felt compassion for him, and I didn't consider it proper to refuse his request—he, who was the managing director; he was the one supreme emperor of the paper, who had, according to custom, sent for me by chaprassi, respectfully offered me a chair and beseeched me piteously with his hands clasped together to have mercy on the paper. And so I presented him with my letter of resignation.

Now the truth is that I am not so heartless as my friends: if someone makes such a request of me I feel I must comply. In fact, I have again and again complied with such requests, and if the All Powerful One gives me the strength, I shall continue to observe this duty of mine in the future as well.

Dying and Dying

He had been sitting in the first-class compartment for the last half-hour playing cards with his wife.

He didn't like playing cards and, above all, he didn't like playing cards with his wife. For an hour, he had been looking through the window, enjoying nature's bounty as it was being bathed in the falling rain. But the moment the train pulled out of the last station, his wife, without any warning, had taken a pack of cards from her large black purse and started to deal. She didn't even ask her husband if he felt like playing or not, or if he wanted to play any other game besides rummy.

He especially didn't like playing rummy. For the past twenty-five years, he had considered himself an intellectual and rummy, in his opinion, was a game for which there was no need of a brain at all.

He started to feel jealous of the other passengers. A tall, fair young man, who looked like the owner or manager of some business firm, was reclining on the seat across from them, reading a newspaper. On the berth above the young businessman, fully stretched out, was a man with very dark skin from some other country; he looked like an important officer in an army. The husband and wife had taken the Secunderabad Express from Poona at ten o'clock in the morning. Now it was eleven or eleven-fifteen, but the army officer was still sleeping soundly.

There was a passenger sleeping on the berth above the man

and his wife. It was possible, the husband mused, that neither of these two men had slept well the night before, or perhaps sleeping was their favourite hobby; still, they both looked very comfortable to him. A little before the last station, the passenger lying above them had got up and gone to the bathroom a couple of times, but at that time the husband had been preoccupied with watching the view outside. He only had a vague sense of the passenger above him climbing down, going to the bathroom, spending quite a bit of time there, returning and climbing back up again to stretch out. He hadn't even noticed his face.

Everyone was enjoying the journey as they pleased, but for the last half-hour he had been playing cards. With his wife. Rummy.

Truthfully, only his hands were playing cards. Or maybe, it would be better to say that his hands were entirely in charge of his game. His eyes would rest a moment on the cards and then take off outside the windows and travel through the densely forested mountains and the pale green valleys. Sometimes the train would cut along the side of a mountain and the showers cascading from above seemed to fall right on top of him. His attention would drift from the game, but his wife would continue to play with total concentration. Over the last quarter-century, they had made this trip countless times during the rainy season and, for his wife, there was absolutely nothing new about the journey. But the husband continued to be captivated by these sights. Perhaps this was because they helped him arrive at the memory of a particular scene from his honeymoon journey a quarter-century ago, one that would always be inextricably linked in his mind with taking a journey in this kind of weather.

With the passage of years, the details of that honeymoon journey should have dimmed in his mind and perhaps they had, but every time he felt them growing indistinct, he would sweep all the dust from that one particular scene and make it brand new.

Even now, he was engaged in dusting and polishing that

scene in his mind. One of his eyes was listlessly engaged in arranging and discarding the cards, shuffling and making runs or rummy. The other eye, somewhat less listless, was involved in watching the scenes of nature outside; but his third eye, his true eye, was completely focused on that honeymoon scene.

He was fifty-five now. Just as he had kept his body fit even at this age—a symbol for him of the carefree days of his youth—he hadn't allowed that scene of his honeymoon trip to fade from his memory. Perhaps his body sagged a bit now. His muscles were no longer as taut as they had been. But in that scene, their tautness had not diminished in any way.

'Where has your mind gone?' his wife interrupted his thoughts suddenly. The train had stopped at some station. The dark-complexioned army officer from the upper berth across from them was getting off the train. It was the husband's turn to play but he was lost in his contemplation of that scene from the past, savouring its splendour.

He cast a cursory glance at the cards in his hand and discarded one. His wife picked up a card. It was of no use to her. She discarded it. He drew a card mechanically. He put it with another card in the hope of forming a run, and wearily discarded an ace. His wife's hand fell on the ace with the alacrity of a raptor. Then he realized that this ace was the one he had meant to put together with the three in the hope of drawing a two, so he could form a run. But he didn't care and picked up the next card off the stack.

After playing one or two hands a bit more attentively, his eyes again wandered out the window. A milky white waterfall cascaded down the mountain across from them. From where he was sitting, he could see the waterfall descend step by step—falling from high up on to a lower hill, and then plunging down into a deep valley.

The waterfall now behind them, his mind's eye again became lost in that scene from twenty-five years ago . . .

≈

This wife of his, with her puffy cheeks, buck teeth and wide waist—wide as a doorway, wider still than her chest—was then no bigger than a sprig. Sprightly, with fair plump cheeks, she was like a thali arrayed with all kinds of tasty delicacies set before a hungry man. Before Kalyan station, he had fastened the chain on the door of their two-passenger coupé and then dived into that thali as though he were starving.

Lying beside her up to Lonavala station, he had eased all her anxiety and shyness. When the train left Lonavala, he explained to her that it wouldn't stop anywhere now for an hour and, with that, he slowly took off her blouse and everything else but her sari and petticoat. She was not prepared to remove her sari under any circumstances in a train compartment with open windows.

Clouds had gathered outside. The light drops of rain were barely visible. He felt almost drunk. He took off all his clothing and stood up in the middle of the coupé. He wanted his wife to follow his example. This scene had become etched in his mind forever: in the light of the open windows, in a first-class coupé, his member erect, hard, straight like an arrow—he loved that shape. How splendid it was to behold when that small lifeless worm with no bones stretched itself out, ready to create! It wasn't for nothing that the first humans in creation had considered it a god, had seen it as exalted when joined with the vagina, and had set it up in a temple for worship . . .

This was the image of himself that he kept protected in his mind. His wife had not followed his example. But he was not interested in such details when he imagined the scene. Perhaps he had pulled at her sari angrily and had tried to get her to sit up on the seat, and his wife had sat up and lovingly put her arm around him and caressed him, pressing her flushed cheek against his thigh, and tried to make him sit or lie down on the seat. Or perhaps he hadn't been able to hold back and his wife had been the successful one. But he had no interest in those details. The scene he imagined was the one in which he unveiled his firm body and the splendour of his erection; he had never allowed that scene to grow hazy—that symbol of his youth, power, strength, masculinity. Whenever this image of himself began to grow dim, he dusted it off again in his imagination.

～

Suddenly his wife opened her mouth and laughed, showing all her teeth. She brushed daily with Forhan's toothpaste, but despite this there was still tartar caked on her teeth. He found that extremely repulsive. He had advised her many times to go to the dentist. But for some reason his crude wife, who, in conversation, was willing to show her teeth to all the world, was nervous to show them to a dentist.

She laughed because she was happy—not only had she not allowed her husband to win a single hand of cards, but she'd also made a diamond rummy and her lead had grown to a full one hundred points. She kept waving all the cards in her hand in front of his eyes, from the three up to the queen, to say, look, there's no card missing! I got a complete rummy!

His wife was happy with her undisputed victory while he was happy that now she would leave him alone and he could do what he wanted: either watch the view outside or lose himself in memories of that journey long ago.

But his wife had not had enough. She dealt the cards again.

'Arré, stop it with the rummy,' he said with disgust.

'Okay, let's play two hands of sweep,' his wife pleaded, and taking his silence as half approval, she put four cards under her leg and gave him four cards and then said, 'Bid!'

He had got the ten of spades in the first four cards. Bored, he said without thinking, 'Ten!'

His wife turned over the four cards from under her leg with great enthusiasm and first looked at them herself. Suddenly she smiled ruefully and said, 'There you go! You have won the whole game in the very first turn.'

She threw down all four cards in front of him. The nine of spades, the ace of diamonds, the king of clubs and the queen of hearts!

His face lit up when he saw the cards. He suddenly became very interested in the game. He picked up the nine and the ace lying beneath his ten of spades. Twenty points in the very first hand!

His wife dealt the next eight cards. He picked up his cards. He looked even more cheerful than before. He only had to win nine more points. He had all three kings and one was already on the table—he decided to himself he wouldn't let his wife get even one point.

Outside, the clouds had gathered in the valley and it had started to rain quite hard. He was now completely engrossed in the game when, from the reflection in the raised window across from him, he got the sense that someone's arm was hanging down. The arm was hanging on to the seat strap and trembling.

Engrossed in the game though he was, he turned slightly. It wasn't an arm, he saw, it was the leg of the passenger sleeping above. For an instant the leg trembled, then another leg dropped down and, instead of stopping on the arm of the seat, the two legs slid down and stopped for a moment on the trunk that was half-pushed under the seat across from them. The legs trembled and, before anyone could do anything about it, the entire passenger was sliding down from his berth like an avalanche of sand. He fell face down in the small space between their seat and the outside door. On one side was the trunk and on the other, the door of the compartment—his neck and legs were doubled over. His eyes, sunken in their sockets, rolled back, and he became completely unconscious.

The young man on the seat across from them put his newspaper on the trunk and approached the fallen passenger from one side; and from the other, the husband, holding his cards in one hand, leaned forward hanging on to the armrest of seat with the other. Then their eyes fell upon the puddle of liquid that had formed beneath the buttocks of the unconscious man on the rubber floor of the compartment—he had urinated.

The young man pulled the unconscious passenger's legs a bit on to the trunk, to straighten out his neck.

The husband threw his cards behind him and, reaching out over the armrest of the seat, he put his hand over the man's nose and saw that he was still breathing. He wasn't dead.

The wife had definitely been losing that hand. She gathered up all the cards and put them back in her purse.

The husband jumped up from his seat. Opening his thermos of water, he quickly removed the celluloid cup. He filled it up from the sink and handed it to the young man, so that he could pour water into the fallen passenger's mouth.

The man lying on the floor was of medium height with a skinny body and a gaunt face. The bones of his jaw were sticking out, his eyes were sunken and his body felt extremely cold. He was sweating. There were even drops of sweat shining on the white hairs peeping out from beneath the undershirt he wore under the open top of his nightsuit.

The young man splashed two drops of water on his face and then tried to pour water into his mouth.

The next moment, the fallen passenger opened his eyes. Screwing up his eyebrows, he looked about him in surprise. Then he put out his hand for help to stand up.

The young man held his hand and lifted him up. He sat down on top of the newspaper on the trunk.

The cool breeze coming from the open window hit him for a moment and then he became totally conscious. Just then his glance fell on the puddle of urine on the floor. His feet were going to get dirty. He pulled them up. Then he got up, pulled his dhoti off the upper berth and went to the bathroom.

∾

The young man looked at the large wet stain on his newspaper. An odd combination of emotions crossed his face: dejection, sadness, disgust, loathing.

The wife looked at the puddle of urine on the other side of the trunk and turned her face towards the window.

The husband washed out the thermos cup carefully and put it back on the jug. Then he came and sat in his seat. He had no idea what to do. He glanced towards the wet dirty newspaper. He considered getting up to see if the pages on the inside were also wet. If they weren't, he could take them out and read them. First he looked towards the young man sitting on the seat across—he had got up from one end of the seat and sat at the other end, so that his back was towards the dirty floor. Who knows what he was thinking! His back to the window, he was just staring into the void in the opposite direction. The husband cast a glance at his wife. Although she was looking out the window, she was taking stock of the inside of the compartment from the corner of her eye, and because of that, her eye met her husband's sidelong glance. He felt reproach in that half-glance from his wife and he turned away from the soiled newspaper and quietly sat down.

Then he thought he would again enjoy the beauty of the valleys and mountains outside the windows as before. Outside, the clouds had cleared and the hills, freshly bathed in the rains, looked lovely. But he wasn't enjoying the sights anymore. His wife was obstructing the whole view from their window and he was forced to make do with the windows next to the bathroom and in the middle. He could barely see the view because of his wife. He wanted to go and stand at the window. But he also didn't want to go over there.

He thought he might then refocus his thoughts on that honeymoon trip twenty-five years ago, but not a single scene from the journey would surface in his mind. Although he was seated with his back turned to the large, wet, round circle on the newspaper and the puddle of urine on the floor, those images kept intruding on his cherished memory. Suddenly, a saying of his grandfather's began to echo in his ears: 'When a man dies, his doors open up down below.' His grandfather had once told him this to explain why someone had soiled his bed while dying. *So, is the passenger on the upper berth going to die?* he thought. *What's wrong with him? He's travelling in a first-class compartment—he must be an important officer or businessman. He must have some terrible illness. What if he's fallen unconscious sitting in the bathroom? What if he's died in there?*

All at once, he felt a great pressure below his navel and he felt like he needed to urinate. He got up agitatedly and went and stood in front of the window. But he didn't care about the view outside. The pressure beneath his navel had increased unpleasantly. He wanted to go and tap on the door of the bathroom. But he didn't want his fellow passengers to consider him impolite, he decided, so he stopped himself and went and stood in front of the other window.

Just then the train entered a tunnel, but he didn't move away from the window. He kept trying to look at the wall of the tunnel in the dark. He couldn't see anything. After quite a while—though it seemed to him as if just a few seconds had passed by—a thin gleam of light appeared. Then the wall became visible and in the next moment the train emerged from the tunnel. He put his head out the window and looked towards the rear of the train. The train was turning. One could clearly make out the mouth of the tunnel from quite some distance. When another mountain came into view he pulled his head inside. He took his handkerchief from his pocket and wiped his eyes. The passenger from the upper berth had emerged and was lying on the opposite seat, his legs hanging down. He had left his dirty nightsuit in the bathroom and had put on an undershirt with the dhoti folded over and tied like a *tahmad* around his waist.

Suddenly the husband forgot that he had to go to the

bathroom. He sat down on the seat directly across from the
ailing passenger and stared at him intently. The darkness
around the man's eyes had become deeper and heavier. His
cheeks looked more sunken. His jawbones were protruding
even more than before and his face was downright ashen. He
looked strangely cold, as though a deathly pall had suffused
his being.

The ailing passenger opened his eyes and ran his tongue over
his lips. Perhaps he had opened his eyes because he sensed the
husband's sharp gaze, or maybe there was no particular reason.
The husband leaned forward abruptly and asked in English
what the problem was. In a voice that was fainter than a
whisper, the ailing passenger told him that he had loose motions.

Loose motions . . . diarrhoea . . . cholera . . . The husband
looked around the compartment, aghast. He again felt some
pressure below his navel. But how could he go into that
bathroom? He walked once around the compartment with
some agitation. Long ago, before he had built his bungalow,
when he lived in two rooms next to his landlord, the landlord
had come down with cholera. Immediately after eating lunch,
his landlord's health had deteriorated and, by evening, by the
time the lamps were lit, he had become totally incapacitated. It
was as though all his blood had turned to water and was
draining out of him on to the road below; even his hands and
feet had begun to cramp . . . The husband took the soap and
hand towel from the basket next to his wife and went into the
bathroom.

The bathroom was not dirty. But to one side, that dirty, wet
nightsuit hung from a hook. He turned his back to it and
unbuttoned his pants to urinate, but he couldn't make it
happen. Because of the immense pressure he felt below his
navel and his fear, he just stood there, waiting, for a long time.
The train jerked along violently. Much as he wanted to relieve
himself, he just couldn't. It was a very long time before he
finally managed to do so. Buttoning his trousers, he then

washed out the washbasin faucet with soap. He was in the habit of washing his hands and gargling after going to the latrine. So, after washing his hands, he filled his cupped palms with water without thinking about it. But as he was about to fill his mouth with water, he suddenly stopped and pulled his hands away from his lips, letting the water fall from his hands. He then decided to gargle with the water from his jug. He came out of the bathroom. He gargled, using a little water from the jug, and then went and sat on his seat. The upper-berth passenger got up and went back into the bathroom.

～

His wife was now sitting straight up. He looked at his watch— it was already twelve-thirty.

'Let's eat whatever we're going to eat,' she said to her husband. And without waiting for his reply, she took the tiffin box out of her basket and the two of them began to eat.

Suddenly he turned and asked the young man sitting across from them how long the sick passenger had been having loose motions.

'He's gone several times since morning. He may have been having trouble since last night.'

'Why haven't you called a doctor?'

'He said not to.'

'Maybe he has cholera.'

'Maybe!'

'What does he do?'

'He's an officer in the railway.'

The husband broke off a piece of roti and thought to himself, *That's why he's all closed off and shrunken into himself!* If he had been in his place he would have kicked up a fuss and made everyone help him, not just the passengers in his compartment, but those in the next one as well.

His wife was eating happily, but he was having trouble

getting anything down. While they were eating, the passenger from the upper berth had gone twice to the bathroom and, the second time he had come out, he was wearing just his undershirt and a khadi turban cloth wound round his waist. After he came out he lay down weakly and his legs began to cramp. A couple of times, when the cramping made him twist his knees from side to side, the turban cloth, which already provided inadequate cover, flopped open. But he wasn't even conscious.

The wife, who was sitting across from the ailing passenger, looked disconcerted. Noticing this, the husband wanted to get up and fix the turban cloth, but he was eating. He told the young man to do it. The young man heard him, but he pretended not to. Perhaps the passenger from the upper berth heard him. In his state of semi-consciousness he tried to straighten out the turban cloth covering the lower half of his body. But the very next moment, when his legs twisted with cramping, the cloth again slipped. The husband asked his wife to switch places with him.

His wife got up and went and sat in his place and he sat in his wife's place across from the ailing passenger.

Even though he didn't want to, he looked over at him. The passenger was slumped over, apparently unconscious. His knees kept twisting from the cramping and, when they did, his lower body was exposed. He had a lot of hair down there. The husband could see some whitish foam stuck in the hair. He quickly averted his glance. Whether or not the man was an important officer, he was still filthy, the husband thought to himself. He clearly had no idea about hygiene. He didn't clean himself. So much hair! He felt happy that he himself was very tidy—he shaved eight times with one blade and then he cleaned himself off down there. This man looked like an officer, but he obviously didn't pay any attention to personal hygiene. It was a good thing that he and his wife had switched places. How could he have anticipated that such a situation would arise even in a first-class compartment? The man probably wasn't even that hygienic when it came to eating and drinking. That's why he had cholera—or some other illness . . . Whatever it was, it was the result of intemperance.

But the next moment he reproached himself. Anyone could get cholera; it could happen even in a first-class compartment . . .

Just then the ailing passenger smacked his hand hard on the trunk because of a cramp. The young man got up from his place and came to sit on the edge of their seat.

'He is getting cramps,' he told the young man in English. 'Just press his arm a little.'

But the young man again ignored him. The ailing passenger seemed to repulse him.

The man was cramping horribly. He was flailing his arms. The wife was ignoring him, eating with her back to him. *Something like this could happen to me too*, the husband thought suddenly, *the same thing could happen to me*. And he imagined himself writhing in the passenger's place.

He swallowed the last bit of his lunch quickly and, taking some water from the jug, he gargled in the window. After he had washed his hands and wiped them with his handkerchief, he got up and went to sit on the corner of the trunk that was not wet. The newspaper had dried long ago. He pushed it to one side and began to press the ailing passenger's arm. He had hardly pressed the man's arm for half a minute when it cramped terribly, causing the man to sit up. For the first time, a sound emerged from his lips that sounded like a long sigh.

But he wasn't able to sit up for long. He lay down facing the other direction, but his legs kept folding up to his chest from the cramping.

The husband held on to the ailing passenger's legs. With renewed zeal, he began to press his calves. As he pressed his calves lower and lower, he finally reached his feet. For a moment he felt embarrassed. The man's feet were dirty. The husband realized that perhaps he wasn't conscious enough to put on shoes. He wanted the young man to feel ashamed for refusing to touch the sick man. By performing this good deed, he wanted to elevate himself in the eyes of his wife, in the eyes of the young man, even in his own eyes. Then he imagined himself lying sick and helpless, and began pressing the man's feet with supreme devotion. The joints of the toes, the toenails, the mounts beneath the toes and the big toes, the soles of the feet, the heels—with each part he pressed, he felt as though he were pressing his own feet. He wanted to press the man's feet thoroughly and crack his toes, but the man's calves cramped again. The husband could clearly see the man's calf muscles jumping. The man sat up again and let out a low moan.

Just then, they reached Kalyan station. The husband took some soap from his wife and ran out and washed his hands under a faucet on the platform, then gargled two or three times. After this, he went running to the station master's room and told him there was a passenger in the first class—perhaps a railway officer—who was suffering from cholera. He had soiled the floor. They needed both a sweeper and a doctor.

The station master immediately sent the sweeper. As for a doctor, he apologized and said that the station doctor had gone on vacation. He added that an ordinary doctor would not be willing to take up a cholera case, but he would immediately send information about the situation to Dadar station by telegram. They would bring a doctor there, or the invalid would be taken to the hospital in an ambulance.

Just then, the train whistle blew. He thanked the station master and ran back to his compartment. He was breathing heavily when he took his seat. He saw that the ailing passenger's head was tilted back and his feet were hanging down. The man seemed to have no consciousness of his body. The train whistle blew again and they started to move. The man suddenly awoke and sat up. 'I want a doctor here,' he whispered irritably in English. Then he lay back down on the seat and fell unconscious again.

The husband glanced over at the area where the ailing passenger had soiled the floor in the morning. The sweeper had cleaned that area. He had also cleaned the trunk. His glance again went to the sick man. His seat was wet and the sticky liquid had formed a pool that shone in the sunlight coming through the window.

~

When the train set off again, the young man from their compartment, who had been enjoying a stroll about the station, jumped into the moving train. As he entered the compartment and glanced at his seat, his fresh enthusiasm vanished and that same revulsion and loathing returned in its place. He closed the door and stood for a moment with his back against it. The husband slid closer to his wife and made room for the young man on their seat. He motioned to him to sit down.

The youth cast a glance at the empty space and then looked at that unconscious, half-naked, filthy passenger. Then he suddenly pulled at the chain holding the upper berth and, stepping on to the armrest of the seat, jumped up and lay down. He didn't get down again until Dadar station.

The husband suddenly wished that he could play a game of cards with his wife. But his wife was sitting with her head leaning half out of the window, as if the cholera germs were contaminating the air inside the compartment. After Kalyan station, there was an increasing number of local stations. He wished that he could tell his wife to let him sit near the window for a little while. But then his attention was again drawn to the man lying exposed on the seat across from them. He tried as hard as he could to think about that honeymoon trip a quarter of a century ago. He thought of the relatives who had come to see them off at the station. He thought of the nicely decorated first-class coupé, of his wife, as delectable as a tray of delicacies, but somehow he had lost his memory of that scene which symbolized his youth and masculinity. Whenever he tried to imagine his powerful, erect member, it transformed itself into that three-inch lump of withered flesh hidden in the pubic hair of the cholera patient on the seat across from them.

He felt fearful and got up to stand at the window and watch the sights outside.

~

Before Dadar station the husband began to arrange the luggage. The train had already entered the station, when suddenly the ailing passenger sat up. 'I have to get off,' he said. His voice sounded dry and extremely weak, and he asked if someone could hand him his pants.

The husband immediately handed him his pants. Then he turned away and, on the pretext of closing the cap of his thermos properly, he washed his fingers that had touched the trousers.

The man quickly began pulling on his trousers, but he had scarcely got them above his knees when his energy ran out and he fell backwards on to the seat.

The husband was turning around with the thermos in his hand when he glanced again at the ailing passenger. His head was on the seat. His eyes were closed, both his hands had abandoned the task of pulling on the trousers. They hung down limply. His lower body was exposed and his legs, partially covered by the trousers, were hanging off the seat. That three-inch lump of shrunken, shrivelled flesh in a jungle of pubic hair—that symbol of vitality—was imprinted in his eyes with all its pathos.

The train stopped at the station. His wife got down with her purse, her back turned to the sick man. The husband got down behind her. Then the conductor stepped into the compartment with the railway doctor.

~

Whether or not the ailing passenger died he never knew. But though the husband lived another fifteen years after that trip, it was on that day that his true death occured.

Sources

'Who Can Trust a Man?' was first published in 1949 as 'Mard ka Etbar'.

'Brown Sahibs' was originally published in 1950 as 'Kale Sahib'. This was translated into English as 'Dark Sahibs' by Edith Irwin and published in the *Arizona Quarterly* in 1973. The version in this book is based on her translation.

'Hats and Doctors' was originally published in 1966 as 'Topiyan aur Doctor'.

'The Ambassador' was originally published in Hindi in 1961 as 'Ambassador'.

'The Bed' was originally published in 1961 as 'Palang'.

'The Dal Eaters' was originally published in 1955 as 'Daliye'.

'The Cartoon Hero' was originally published in 1966 as 'Kartoonon ka Nayak'.

'Mr Ghatpande' was originally published in Hindi in 1948 as 'Mr Ghatpande'.

'Formalities' was originally published in 1948 as 'Takalluf'.

'Some Suds and a Smile' was originally published in 1961 as 'Jhaag aur Muskaan'.

'The Aubergine Plant' was originally published in 1940 as 'Baingan ka Paudha'.

'Furlough' was originally published in Hindi in 1940 as 'Furlough'.

'In the Insane Asylum' was originally published in 1936 as 'Pagalkhane Mein'.

'A Listless Evening' was originally published in 1966 as 'Ek Udasin Shyam'.

'My First Letter of Resignation' was originally published in 1931 as 'Hamara Pehela Tyag-Patra'.

'Dying and Dying' was originally published in 1966 as 'Marna aur Marna'.

Acknowledgements

After fruitlessly sending this manuscript around to publishers for a number of years following its completion in 2002, I finally decided to put it aside. Perhaps Ashk had been right and there was a vast conspiracy ranged against him. I had in fact given up on it entirely until recently, when Bilal Hashmi, a graduate student at New York University, put me in touch with R. Sivapriya, an editor at Penguin India, who proved to be favourably impressed with the collection and seemed to harbour no feelings of ill will towards Ashk. Although Ashk would not like to hear that his notoriety had lasted scarcely more than fifteen or so years after his death, I am sure he would also be delighted to see this work come out from Penguin, an outcome that he had dearly hoped for.

I must thank Ashk first and foremost, of course, for entrusting me with this project. After Ashk's death, his son, Neelabh, has been a great help to me as I have grappled with these translations. If it weren't for Bilal Hashmi and R. Sivapriya, the project would probably never have seen the light of day. Ambar Sahil Chatterjee, who has edited the volume, has been wonderful to work with. I have many people to thank for reading versions of these translations over the years, chief among them, my husband, Aaron York, and my mother, Susan Merrill. Other helpful readers have included Colin P. Masica, Amitava Kumar, Rupert Snell, Yigal Bronner and David Clingingsmith. Adamya Ashk, Aftab Ahmad, Manan Ahmed,

Salman Hussain, Sean Chauhan and Megan MacDonald have been on call for help with a wide variety of queries. Recently, a host of friends on Twitter have helped out with numerous details and knotty problems in the final versions of the stories. A big thanks to Musharraf Ali Farooqi, Sunny Singh, Siddharth Singh, Sabbah Haji, Prashansa Taneja, Awais Athar, Saurabh Gupta, Avni Majithia-Sejpal, Tula Goenka and Shashwati Tendulkar. Many thanks as well to Edith Irwin, who graciously granted permission to use her translation of 'Brown Sahibs' in this edition.